The Da g

(Overlord War Part One)

A Tale
Of
Solomon Star

CHARLIE W. STARR

Forest, Virginia

First edition, 2018

For information address:

Lantern Hollow Press
info@lanternhollowpress.com

The Darkening Time by Charlie W. Starr (1963 -)
ISBN 13: 978-0692063088
ISBN 10: 0692063080
Summary: Solomon Star, Imperial Expatriate, found his way out of darkness into light on a paradise planet, only to leave it behind. Drawn into a war neither wanted nor deserved, Solomon must lead an army of millions to conquer billions while saving as many on both sides as he can.
Science Fiction

For Tracy Watkins

Who read an entire Dune book to me
on that long trip to California.

Acknowledgements:

My sincerest thanks to everyone who read the book in draft, especially my work studies, Emily and Bridget, and my good friend John M. Kirton II. I would also like to thank Mark Watkins and his family. They know why.

Table of Contents

"If you know the enemy and know yourself, you need not fear the result of a hundred battles…" –Sun Tzu

–Warrior Text from the Lost World

- Prologue -

I can't tell you everything in this story is true. I can only tell you I've tried to be honest. If not by presenting all the facts, I have at least tried to pass along the meanings. That's what I do best: shave facts from the truth so truths can matter most. I say that to my shame. This story is my penance. My name is Westart.

But in truth the story isn't mine. It's his. Well his, and the thousands—even millions—of people whose own stories were intersected by his. Some of those stories ended. Many of them saved. I only met Solomon Star a few brief moments here and there—and those near the end of it all. He was for so long mere subject matter in my world. But in my world I have had access to everything, that is, to all information. And, with some help from a friend, I have scoured and sifted and used that information to form a story of war.

I'm not a soldier. Never was. And though I lived on a military ship of over a billion people, more than half of whom were soldiers and sailors, I cannot claim to speak from the *inside*. I have, therefore, decided not to pretend, and that includes choosing to avoid the majority of military terms and acronyms—the language of fighters in the field. I can manage some of the jargon—enough to tell the story accurately, I hope—but not more than the few fragments and phrases I've picked up in over a decade of covering actions, adventures, and struggles of the men and women of the Empress's World Ship, Fleet Seven. And so I conclude by begging the indulgence of those veterans who know better for the sake of the many who don't. I say "many." That's probably optimistic. I doubt anyone ever sees this holo. But it has to be written. Call it a personal exorcism.

2298

- 1 -
General

Solomon Star, the greatest soldier in the galaxy, was running for his life. The lush green jungle was a blur in his eyes, the smell of pine and methane an assault on his waking thoughts. He leapt over a fallen tree and took a moment to look over his shoulder. His stalker kept pace twenty yards behind.

"I can make it," Solomon thought.

The flat terrain of the jungle began to dip into a gulley and walls rose up on either side as Solomon splashed into a gathering stream. Water glistened on the red stained, white boots he'd worn almost every day for decades. His pace slowed in the rising water— he felt the chill in his feet as it flooded his boots—and he realized he'd made a mistake coming this way. Just ahead, a fallen tree straddled the creek bed, offering Solomon a way out. He leapt ten vertical feet and landed half-kneeling on the wide log, the wood rough beneath his hand. But when the snake-ish head of a poisonous red lizard shot out of a hole in the hollow log only a foot from his face, Solomon wondered if he'd made another mistake. He didn't wait long to find out.

A plasma shot rang out in the jungle, raising the caws and cries of a hundred species of bird. A bright green Jewel of liquid energy struck the lizard and blew it apart. Solomon looked to his right. His hunter clearly wanted no other competition in the dealing of a death stroke.

"Why are you running from it?" the man called.

'Because I can make it,' Solomon thought.

And he ran. Across from the log was a path, first up and then along the deepening gully side and then down to a flat at the opening river. She was there. The native woman he knew only as Savage: the most alive, the most radiant creature he'd ever known. She stood at the river's edge, her hand held out to him, beckoning him, her emerald eyes and gentle smile imploring him. And then he knew that all he had to do was run into her arms. But there was no time. The sound of rustling behind Solomon let him know that his stalker had caught up to him.

'He'll shoot her if I don't stop him,' Solomon realized. So he turned and did the only thing he could do. In a blur of genetically enhanced speed, he ran to his nemesis, disarmed the attacker in a series of steps, twists and strikes, and drove the plasma gun's barrel deep into the man's chest. For a moment, before Solomon pulled the trigger, they were face to face.

The dead man, Lazarus, smiled, a look of intense gratitude on his face. "Thank you," he said. And then he laughed as Solomon pulled the trigger and blew out his heart.

"It's not your fault we killed him," the Savage woman said. She was sitting on the ground at Solomon's feet, cradling the corpse in her arms.

Solomon looked at the bloody mess of the gun in his hand, the warm, sticky gore on his arm, the crimson stains on his boots.

"No, you're right," he said. "It was her fault. The Empress is to blame."

But Lazarus, who had run into the Savage girl's arms, looked Solomon square in the eye and asked the obvious question: "Then why would you leave us and go back to her, Captain? Why'd you do that?"

Solomon woke from the dream, that question echoing in his head, as a hole opened in the world. One of a thousand. He watched from a shuttle porthole as hundreds of ships descended into the docking bays of Fleet Seven. Solomon's shuttle spiraled downward toward the opening hatch—dock 42—where a mile-deep shaft accessed a hundred docking levels within the giant sphere. Many more ships were doing the same. The World Ship's gravity was already anchoring Solomon to his seat. He felt the bump into station keeping at level 51.

'Nice landing,' he thought. Though technically this wasn't land.

'Quadrant A. Two hours to home by mag-lev. Other side of the station. Why here?'

A pressurized walkway sealed itself to the shuttle door as Solomon stood to stretch his space legs and adjust his uniform. His face unshaven and hair unkempt, he nevertheless wore his dress uniform—navy blue slacks and double-breasted jacket, a colonel's gold insignia on the shoulders, gold buttons gleaming—detailed to perfection.

'Wearing this thing was a mistake,' he thought. The collar chafed his neck and the constricting jacket had tightened his upper back into a tingling burn.

The shuttle door hissed open; the man with a past stepped through and down a white corridor, a duffle bag in tow, a perfect uniform framed by an imperfectly groomed head on top and non-regulation boots below: white boots, dirty from a recent trek, and stained red from an older one.

The walkway opened into a grey corridor which branched in three directions. Cool, conditioned air circulated down the long thoroughfare: clean and crisp and just a hint of something artificial to his nose. A pair of white uniformed sailors stood at the dock's monitoring station just inside.

"Colonel Star," said the senior.

"Chief Vargas," Solomon answered, a bit surprised to see him on this side of the ship. "So good to see your smiling face greeting my return."

"It's my pleasure and privilege, sir, especially when I've been ordered to do so."

"Hah! I always suspected some insincerity in your cheery nature."

"Not at all, Colonel. My cheer will be totally sincere at fourteen hundred hours."

"Because that's when you get off duty."

"Aye, aye, sir. Or should I say, 'Roger that'?"

"It's good to see you too, Chief."

"And how was the mission, Colonel; a success?"

"What mission is that, Chief?" he smiled.

"Uh huh." Chief Vargas smiled back. "Roger that, sir."

"Chief, can you point me to the mag-lev for Quadrant E?"

"I certainly could, Colonel, if I didn't think it unfair to those poor well-lit directional signs hanging every fifty feet along these corridors that wouldn't have a purpose in life if I went around indiscriminately tossing directions at people."

Solomon smiled. "Aye, aye, Chief."

"Roger that, sir. And besides," he looked at his console, "your ride'll be coming around the bend right behind me in five, four, three, two..."

They turned to see a hover cart whirring toward them. Behind the wheel sat a man with a familiar, if thought-burdened, face.

"Welcome home, then, Colonel Star," Chief Vargas concluded.

"Home, Chief? I think I just left there. But you certainly make it welcome."

Solomon climbed into the cart before it could stop and without a word to the driver. They turned left, speeding off down the corridor away from the docking shaft.

As Vargas returned his focus to his station, the wide-eyed young sailor next to him finally mustered the courage to speak.

"Was that him, Chief?"

"Him who, Szallai?"

"Star—Solomon Star. The one who resigned."

"Yeah, that's him."

"He was the most important soldier in the galaxy."

"That's right."

"He answered to no one but the Empress herself."

"That's right."

"He was the Captain—"

"He was what he is, Szallai—a soldier. And a fine one."

Sergeant Jo-Norris Devsky, personal assistant to Colonel Star (unusual for a non-commissioned officer), had been with Solomon since the early nineties. He'd participated in the quelling of a frontier planet with Colonel Star and his regiment back in 2295. Now, three years later, they were about to see action again in an Empire that had prided itself on peace and stability. Devsky's voice was forceful, resonant:

"I take it, Colonel that you have heard."

"I have, Devsky. War."

"Forty systems, sir. 'Galactic rebellion,' they're calling it. There hasn't been a war on this scale in five hundred years."

A stocky man, with a round face, Devsky commanded respect and trust. Twice decorated for valor, this career man was as rock solid in temperament as he was in build. When he spoke of matters military, he did so matter-of-factly (even when making a joke). 'No such war in five hundred years'—it was simply the beginning of the tactical discussion that would follow as the two men glided down the wide grey corridor stretching to the horizon before them. On military matters, Devsky was all business. He'd joined up in his twenties, was now in his fifties—almost twenty years Solomon's senior—had turned down a commission in order to continue to serve with this amazing soldier, the former Captain of all captains, and never planned on doing anything else. Rumor had it, though, that in his conversations outside of military affairs, which were hardly matter-of-fact and quite eclectic in content, he once let on that, as a youth, he'd wanted to be an actor.

"No, Sergeant, there hasn't been a war like this one," Solomon agreed. But he was also adding a thought.

Devsky picked up on the point: "Which is to say there's never been a war like this one at all."

"Not in the Empire, not for 2300 years."

"And you're surmising, Colonel, that the new factors in this mix are substantial."

"I am."

"There's the fact that the Empress is so young, only in her thirties—the Emperor's untimely death may be a factor for instability, even if it was fifteen years ago," Devsky offered.

"I think that is a potential liability for Centcom to consider in its Imaging protocols, yes."

"Anything else, sir?" Devsky was fishing.

Solomon obliged. "Perhaps the fact that the Captain of the Empress's Imperial Guard resigned his commission—the first time in Imperial history for such a high-profile office to be surrendered—might have some bearing on perceptions about the Imperial Will."

"Even though that happened ten years ago?"

"Even though."

"You doubtful about the Imperial Will, Colonel?"

"Not in the least."

The hover cart slowed at a four-way junction. Signs attached to the ceiling whose letters were lights, directed either to "Intelligence HQ" in one direction or "Central Command" in the other. Devsky turned the cart toward the latter.

"And now that you've fished intel out of me, Devsky, it's time to fess up."

"Confession implies knowledge, Colonel. My pay grade's too low for knowledge."

"I'm thinking otherwise, Jo."

Devsky cracked the slightest smile. "So you want me to explain why your shuttle docked on the wrong side of the ship on the Centcom level."

"On the main command level—nearest the offices of everyone in charge of every person and thing on this artificial planet, yes."

"I think you've already guessed the answer to that sir, guessed it about two seconds before you asked the question."

"One second. But you did receive orders."

"Which were to pick you up and drop you off, and then start packing your bags."

"Sergeant," Solomon smiled his impatience.

"Sir?"

"Drop me off, where?"

"Brass Central, sir. Brass Central."

Centcom: Room 001 was a dark square attached to the office complex of the General of the Armies of Fleet Seven, a four-star named Siras Kataltem who answered directly to the Joint Chiefs on Imperial Planet and no one else (save his wife, Nina). A dozen men and women sat around room 001's holo glass table (or at nearby intelligence controls) where three dimensional readouts floated from six inches to a foot before those seated. Dim track lights around the ceiling made shadows and silhouettes of those present. Only holo light dancing with changing readouts made any facial features visible. The gentle hum of artificial air moving along vast networks of air ducts—that white sound ubiquitous to so many artificial structures—served as a kind of overture to the initial silence of the room. Solomon was pleased to see his immediate superior General Scott seated at the table to his left. He guessed quickly that Scott was about to be promoted from First Corps, Fifth Army to General of the First Army, filling the shoes of a retiree.

Two other VIP's were present. General Kataltem, himself, and Admiral Gnostrom—the two chief commanders of Fleet Seven, the first over the Army, the second over the Fleet. They sat at the table's head and foot. To Solomon's immediate right sat a trio of Imperial Sykols, including BeeEf Ckin'r, the Seventh Fleet Sykol. Technically he did not out-rank Kataltem or Gnostrom, but as the prime Sykol of Fleet Seven he had a great deal of influence, though, as he would soon learn, not so much as he was used to. Recordists, technicians, and personal attachés made up the remainder of those present.

Kataltem began: "Colonel Star, we express our deepest regrets over the death of your father."

"Thank you, sir."

"Your report suggests he was well liked among the people of Kall."

"Well loved is more like it, General. The Kalli natives and the Imperial workers all credited him for the prosperity that planet now enjoys. I was privileged to see the...depth of his accomplishments, and fortunate to have reached him before he died."

"Truly. But you hardly had time to say goodbye, and we appreciate your quick response to our return order and your excellent work in restoring production on Kall. In more ideal circumstances we could have left you to bury your father properly."

"The people of Kall saw to his body, sir. Better than I possibly could."

"It's strange, though," interjected Ckin'r, "that a man of such good Imperial stock and not even a hundred years old yet should succumb to disease." His probing high pitched voice grated on the nerves of all present. It was meant to.

Without hesitation, Solomon refused his bait: "That my father died so young is certainly tragic. I never suggested disease in my report."

"No, then what—"

"Let's move on." Kataltem recovered the conversation. "Colonel, you have received no intel on the state of war in which we now find ourselves?"

"That is correct, sir. The orders I received two weeks ago on Kall consisted of two lines. The first, 'Return to Fleet Seven', and the second, 'War is declared against the rebellion of Inmar.' With the intel that's come to us over the last three months, though, it was an easy guess that this conflict might be galactic in scale."

"That's it exactly, Colonel, and we'll look at bringing you up to speed shortly. We'd like to begin, however, by asking for your help."

And while Solomon thought, 'Here it comes,' he answered, "If I can, sir."

"To the point, then," said Kataltem, refusing the dramatic pause, trying to diffuse the tension. "The First Army is being restructured. General Scott has been promoted to Lieutenant General over the First. He wants you to command a division."

Solomon pretended surprise: "A promotion?" He looked to Scott who sat forward in his chair and turned his gaze from Solomon to the table's end.

"If I may, General?" he asked, his gruff-gravel voice filling the room.

"Of course," said Kataltem.

"Colonel..." He thought for a moment. "Do you remember a conversation we had three years ago in my office, when I said I recognized your...unique vision as a soldier?"

"I do, sir."

"Then to follow the General's plain speech, the First Army will be the spearhead of every major operation in the coming conflict, and the First Division will be the spear's tip. The tradition of the Big Red One being first in the fray stretches back more than ten thousand years. We already know thousands of men may die. We need someone in command who will keep it from being hundreds of thousands."

"What about General Haggard? He's commanded the First for twenty years."

Kataltem answered: "He's being given the corps. You'll answer first to him, now, and then to your former commander here" (nodding toward Scott).

Scott continued: "I'd have given you the First Corps if they'd have let me. Not that I don't trust Haggard, he's a fine man and a solid strategist. But corps command is too visible."

"And," added Kataltem, "you have some impressive stats to your field command credit.

"Agreed," urged Scott. "Three years ago, on planet New Apac, you led a battalion in the Fifth which met the most difficult objective of the campaign while logging the fewest losses of any battalion under me. How many lost, Colonel?"

"Seventeen KIA sir."

"Seventeen. You still remember. So we can ask you to stay where you are on the regimental level and save 250,000 men or we can put you in a position to preserve the lives of a million."

"And so again to the point. We're here to ask, Colonel, if you're willing to accept the promotion."

Silence. That Solomon knew he was going to say yes wasn't the cause of his hesitation.

Then General Scott: "Colonel. You're the best soldier in the galaxy. This is where you'll make the most difference."

And silence. The cause of his hesitation stemmed from what had happened on Kall.

Finally, he said, "I assume everyone in Centcom is agreed, and General Haggard?"

"Yes."

"But what about the Imperial Cabinet? What about the Empress?"

"The Imperial Cabinet," answered Ckin'r, "is willing to accept your promotion under certain conditions. Your name is to be censored from most press releases and mass media formats. Some independent groups cannot be completely controlled, nor do we want to give up the well-crafted illusion of a free press."

"Ahem," coughed Kataltem.

"To speak honestly, General."

"I wasn't aware that was possible for Sykols," quipped Admiral Gnostrom, speaking for the first time. Others present were wise enough to stifle laughs and hide grins. (If I had been there at the time, I would have defended Ckin'r's reputation. I've learned better since.)

Ckin'r barely missed a beat: "Colonel Star's name will be left out of major galactic communications. Eventually, however, as the First Division sees more action and the name of Star can't help but come up, our ICA* Sykols will spin—to be honest—the Colonel's

---

* I.C.A.: Imperial Communications Agency

story as one of a man attempting to make up for a terrible mistake, which I gather, Colonel, isn't too far from the truth?"

Solomon didn't answer.

Kataltem spoke again: "Colonel we all recognize your unique talents. That's all I care about. Your past is your own business. I'm just asking you, son, to help an old soldier protect a million younger ones."

Siras Kataltem was not one for sentimentality. Nor at age, 102, was he very old. But his last sentence was in earnest.

Silence. Solomon appeared at once eager to speak and then hesitant. The idea that came into his head at that moment was, 'This will be my only chance to say it.' Finally, he said, "General, with your permission I'd like to ask all non-essential personnel to leave, including the Sykol representatives."

A stir. Some seat shifting. Kataltem and Gnostrom eyed each other and then the Fleet Sykol who nodded his head.

"Level One's only, please," spoke the General.

The room emptied but for Kataltem, Gnostrom, Scott, Solomon and Ckin'r who did not leave with his cadre. Solomon eyed him with a frown. Then he looked to the table's head.

"Gentlemen, accepting this promotion will likely mean my death."

Astonished silence.

"You don't think we've underestimated the enemy?" asked Gnostrom.

"I don't know who the enemy is yet, sir. But I'm not talking about dying in battle. I mean there will be attempts on my life." Again, he looked at Ckin'r. Then to the others at dumbfounded expressions. "I mean assassinations attempts."

"By whom?" asked Gnostrom.

"Do I really need to say it with recorders running and this Sykol here?"

"Oh, now surely, Colonel, you don't suspect the Imperium of trying to kill—"

"No, I suspect you. I suspect Sykol Central, and I suspect J—"

Ckin'r was out his chair and in Solomon's face: "Treason will get you killed, Colonel, and make no mistake. You forget your place a second time in your life and you will find out just aak—"

His hand about the throat, the head slammed against a wall, feet dangling before anyone realized what Solomon had done. Then the tightening grip; the crackling of stretching tendons in Ckin'r's neck were to some in that room, music to the ears.

His words were ice: "If you want to leave this room alive you will leave it now. Use your Sykol training and read my thoughts in my face. Am I bluffing?"

Ckin'r saw in an instant that a word of protest from his mouth would have meant his neck snapped. He nodded as much as Solomon's grip would allow. He gasped air with the release and his fall to the floor. Solomon turned to face the table, sliding Ckin'r's empty chair back into place as the Sykol stood, mustering as much dignity as he could in the face of embarrassment, and turned to leave. What shamed him wasn't such a blatant disregard for his authority, but his own complete miscalculation of Solomon's reaction. Above all, an Imperial Sykol prided himself on his ability to analyze and predict human behavior. His forceful actions, the angry intimidation, should have immediately silenced Solomon who grew up under strict Sykol control. Ckin'r might have turned and protested Solomon's actions to his superiors; he might, more cautiously, have left and returned with a security detail to take Solomon into custody for assaulting a superior. But he did neither. He was simply too dumbfounded to do anything but walk out and walk away.

As if not quite realizing till now what he had done, Solomon said, "Well, I suppose that's the answer, sirs. Instead of promotion, I'll be accepting a cell on level 99."

"Perhaps not," said Kataltem.

Every head turned towards him.

"General!" exclaimed Gnostrom, "We've just witnessed a capital offense. We should be on com to MP* and drawing our own side arms."

"Your patience, Admiral—"

"Solomon," interrupted Scott. "You had a reason for doing that. You were going to tell us something."

"Yes, General, I mean no, not quite. I didn't intend to attack the Sykol. That reaction was...rash."

---

* M.P.: Military Police

"You seem to do that every decade or so," said Gnostrom with a smile.

"Hold on a minute," Scott pressed. "We've still a bit of a situation here, yes? Ckin'r will be on the horn to Sykol Central in the next ten minutes, and we'd best move quick—"

"I do not think he will," replied Kataltem in a deliberate, commanding voice.

It sank in.

"There's something you know."

"There's something Colonel Star knows," said Kataltem. "You were provoked, Solomon. Something provoked him. This isn't about your years on Imperial World."

"Colonel Star," said Gnostrom. "Why do you believe someone will try to kill you?"

"They tried to have me killed on Kall."

After another stunned silence, Admiral Gnostrom asked, "There was an attempt on your life on Kall?"

"Yes sir."

"And you believe Imperial Sykols are responsible."

"Them or someone they answer to."

"What happened?" asked Scott.

"The assassination failed, General. I'd prefer not to say more than that."

"So now we know what you know," said Gnostrom. "May we then ask, Siras, what it is that you know?"

Kataltem replied, "In this case, Admiral, I'm not allowed to say, though I believe you'll be contacted this very day by the Marshall— by Teltrab himself. Suffice it to say that Sykol involvement in military actions will be drastically reduced on the macro level in the coming months."

"But," Scott probed, "the issue is such that it allows you the freedom to forego the Colonel's assault on the number three man on this billion-man ship?"

"Did you see an assault, General? How about you, Admiral?"

The others smiled and nodded their heads approvingly. Records could be erased, and only senior staff had seen it happen. And military men generally disapproved of Sykol involvement in their affairs which, though valuable, was generally accompanied by an arrogance just grating enough to alienate the men present from any sense of loyalty to Fleet Sykol Ckin'r.

Kataltem went on: "What I can't tell you, then, gentlemen, also gives me reason to believe that you have nothing to fear from Sykol Central, Colonel Star."

"Forgive me if I don't share your confidence, sir, but my suspicions do not include Sykols only."

And again, they were silent, muted in the face of too many top secret, need-to-know, non-discussibles. Something had happened on Imperial World. First, ten years ago when Solomon Star, Captain of the Empress's Imperial Body Guard, resigned his post for reasons he could not discuss by order, and joined the regular army for reasons he still could not fathom. And again, within the last month, something had happened to shake up Sykol Central, the Empress's right hand of strength and her engine of Imperial control. About this, neither Kataltem nor Gnostrom (once he learned it) were allowed to speak.

"Colonel," Kataltem finally asked, "what can I do to allay your fears and convince you to accept this assignment?"

"You can't allay my fears, sir. But if you want me to accept this assignment you can make a deal with me."

"A deal?"

"Yes sir."

"Go on."

"I haven't spoken with Captain Teltrab—or the Marshall as is his title in the context of this discussion, right? But since he took my place on Imperial World, I believe he is an ally to me there. Nevertheless, his hands will eventually be tied or circumvented. My division will be the first into every firefight, first into every situation that might result in excessive casualties. So be it. I'll be the scapegoat for every failure, the best chance of keeping losses down so that the public war remains popular. I'll get no credit and all blame, and I'll write the letters for the dead. I can live with that. Perhaps it was even Hal—Marshall Teltrab's—idea.

"But the moment will come when the order is given. When it happens, and it will, you tell me now that you'll disobey it. That's the deal."

Kataltem: "Do you really think it will come to that, Colonel? Do you think she will order us to send you into an ambush?"

"Or leave me behind, or allow for a curious accident, or trump up false charges, or kill me outright—yes I do. And this is my 'fear' as you put it: that my men will die with me."

Kataltem swiveled his chair, stood and moved with deliberate step toward Solomon. And looking him in the eye: "This is my promise: I will not obey that order."

"That won't be enough," said Scott. "It may not come to us; it may be a stray message on a back channel, re-routing a transport or changing a maintenance schedule. It could even be leaked intelligence to the enemy. I'm sorry if this sounds like the questioning of any loyalties. I don't want to believe the Empress has a vendetta against Colonel Star any more than you two, and won't until shown otherwise, but if Colonel Star was attacked on Kall and he suspects a connection to house Amric, then caution demands—"

"My suspicions, General," Solomon interrupted, "are founded on the proof you're looking for. I have what you don't want to see. And I don't want you to doubt your loyalties either. You all must remain faithful to your cause and to your charge...even as I have failed to do so.

"Sirs, I am not asking to rival your commitments. Only for trust. I'll do my job and by it earn your trust. But then trust me enough to keep this conversation in the back of your heads. And keep watch."

"That will be my job. I will take it on," said General Scott.

And Solomon: "And when the moment comes that you see I am right, make the choice."

Kataltem looked at Gnostrom who merely nodded. "Very well then," he said, a finalizing note in his voice. "General Scott will watch your back. You, *General* Star, will spearhead our operations. Know this: there will be no caution in our utilizing your talents. Your job will be risk. But if a clear-cut choice arises, if I see it; if Scott discovers conspiracy and makes it clear to me, you will not be abandoned."

He held his hand out to Solomon. Solomon looked at it, and then at the eyes of the three earth-shakers before him. And taking the hand: "General, I accept your commission. Now would someone please bring me up to speed on the fight I've just gotten myself into? I gather this thing's going to get started very soon, and I've got an entire division to retrain to my liking."

And Solomon took a seat among his peers.

Solomon looked around his general's quarters, new and unfamiliar. And empty. The responsibilities of the next day, week, month and year ticked with computer accuracy through his genetically enhanced mind, flowing like sequential pictures, totaling their numeric sums into a weight of emotion. In his mind, his matter-of-fact assessment of the coming duty alternated with a heavy debt of pain in the form of words he did not speak but kept returning to: 'Why did I come back?'

Two weeks ago, on the planet Kall, he'd realized he was in love for the first time in his life with a woman who wasn't the Empress Janis IV; days before that, his father had died speaking only four words to Solomon—four words in ten years: "The wonder. The wonder."

And Solomon wondered why he hadn't stayed there. Perhaps the weight of duty compelled him. Perhaps the thought of the thousands of lives he would be called upon to save moved him—that was certainly the meaning of a cryptic message delivered to him by Hal Teltrab on his last night on Kall. But perhaps he didn't think he deserved the happiness he'd found there among the people his father had come to love. So he left them...and her. That last option is conjecture, I realize. But my source for the conjecture is a reliable one. Much of what I've learned in order to render this account came from her, and she's the most reliable source in the world—the World Ship.

So Solomon sat in a silent, naked room, a thousand thoughts throbbing in his head. Then he finally broke the silence of that noise and spoke the question: "Why did I come back?"

And then Solomon Star, the greatest soldier in the universe, newly appointed Brigadier General of the First Division of the First Corps of the First Army—Solomon Star began to cry. And he cried like a little lost boy while the lights in his cabin dimmed, the gravity increased the weight of his tears, and the World Ship called Fleet Seven fell through a black hole in space, a hole of its own making.

- 2 -
Timing

"...have a capability but appear not to..."
"...be near but appear far, or at least be far but appear
near..." –Sun Tzu

–Warrior Text from the Lost World

Deep Space

'Mecha Check."
Systems nominal, Lieutenant Troy.
'Enemy scan.'
*Scanners jammed. Seventy percent probability, ambush
sequence.*
'Jam source?'
Working.
'Com.' "Wolfram."
"My two O'clock, ten meters vertical—"
Jam area located.
"—rooftop scan."
"Moving, LT."
On display.
A red dot inside Lieutenant Joshua Troy's helmet visor display
highlighted a building 200 yards distant. To his right, a green hued
corporal named Wolfram leapt twenty yards to the top of a
featureless rectangular building. Red for enemy targets, green for
friendlies—that's how tactical visors began the process of making
situational analyses as intuitive and immediately recognizable as
possible. Wolfram ordered the AI* computer in his helmet to
transmit his reconnaissance position to his lieutenant. In the
upper left corner of his visor, Troy saw everything Wolfram was
seeing. Before them lay a city corridor: a thousand potential
ambush positions. Troy tuned out the echo of his own breathing.
'Scan energy anomalies.'

---

* A.I.: Artificial Intelligence

Negative.

'Scan Sound.'

Buffers.

"So we're blind," Troy said to himself. Then he headspoke again: 'Chrono.' A clock display appeared before his eyes, counting down three minutes, twenty-one seconds. Then it disappeared.

'Com.' "Wolfram, follow just behind, along the roof line."

"Understood."

"Devsky, take us in."

A flat bed hover jeep moved silently, swiftly, down the street. Six men in full infantry armor, stood ready on the bed's sides while Sergeant Devsky piloted the vehicle. Almost immediately he ordered his own computer symbiot to remote-run the jeep. He picked up his plasma rifle and held it at the ready in both hands. The exact aim of the gun's barrel floated as cross-hairs in his visor display, moving left to right and back with the gun's sweeping motion. Along the rooftop, Wolfram followed the ground group, grass-hoppering via jet boot enhanced thirty-yard leaps. Like any good Mobile Infantryman, he'd gotten used to the sudden lurch to his knees and then hips, the extra G-force pushing his stomach contents into his intestines, and the explosive sound of jet boot fire which inexperienced soldiers first take as the firing of an enemy weapon nearby.

The Icarus Armor System[*] had been adopted by the Empire thousands of years ago and had been through half as many upgrades. The I-500 series provided protection from plasma fire, enhanced strength and speed, jet boots for short distance leaps, a complete physical maintenance environmental system, and a symbiotic AI computer housed in the helmet which linked the suit to the wearer's thought commands, provided tactical readouts and intelligence to the soldier, and maintained a variety of communications links.

The armor system required three layers. First, was a black "skin suit" which covered the entire body except the face and looked and molded like rubber. The surface was ridged with tiny liquid filled tubes. These liquids included stimulants, pain inhibitors, and nutritional supplements all capable of being injected into the body as the computer brain identified the need. Other micro-tubes

---

[*] Referred to as an I.C.U.R.

provided coolant for controlling body temperatures in extreme environments, chemicals capable of "eating" body waste and then evaporating (each mobile infantryman was his own walking toilet), and others capable of evaporating sweat and condensing it back into the body. The inner lining of the skin suit contained millions of microscopic sensors which monitored vital signs and linked muscle movement to the second layer of the A-500 suit, the exoskeleton. This silvery flexi-steel web attached around every limb as well as trunk and head. Wherever a muscle of the body might affect physical motion, a corresponding exo-muscle ran in a circle or line outside, ready to augment a soldier's strength tenfold, his speed five-fold. To this skeleton the last layer of dark blue plexi-steel armored plates would be attached one at a time till only joints remained visible on the wearer. Oversized blue jet boots along with a like colored helmet with a full-face shield and atmospheric seals, and a trim backpack of ultra-compressed oxygen completed the ensemble. The hover jeep reached the halfway mark and Troy's helmet AI headspoke a 95 percent probability of ambush. Headspeaking is non-verbal communication between a soldier and his helmet computer. It is never actually verbal but the communication experienced by the soldier, though as immediate as an intuition, is that of clearly verbalized conversing. The more a soldier practiced, the faster he got at headspeaking. Utterly necessary in a fire fight.

Troy spoke a command to his unit: "Motion Sensors." And then asked his symbiot: 'Anything, Teddy?'

Motion sensors negative, Lieutenant Troy.

'What's that shadow?'

Anomalous light refraction. Suggests—

"Holoflauge! Eject now!"

Seven silent commands ignited fourteen bootjets simultaneously as plasma weapons opened fire from hidden points along the street and in buildings above. Four men (including Devsky from the cab) shot up and out, laying down patterns of fiery green destruction as they dug into the walls of buildings with the strength of exo-enhanced limbs. Three more fanned out from the back of the jeep. Flex-tethers snapped tense, pulling the warriors behind the jeep on short-firing boot thrusters.

Plasma guns sprayed multiple rounds, neutralizing enemy guns at all points.

"Unhook," Troy ordered.

The umbilicals fell limp as the jeep drew to a halt—the brunt of enemy fire. The "skiers" used their momentum to propel themselves out of the firing zone to their goal position. The others followed suit with Wolfram bringing up the rear.

'Chrono.'

In his helmet display, Troy saw thirty-three seconds left on the clock. The face beneath his mono-expressioned helmet smiled.

"Close sequence," came a voice over the com link. False buildings rebuilt themselves while the "enemy" guns returned to nominal readiness and the jeep hummed back to activity. General Solomon Star entered the Training Deck (an entire level of the World Ship dedicated to battle simulations) and approached the eight men who commanded Solomon's new personal security platoon—his bodyguard.

Solomon had requested that Devsky be transferred to the First with him to continue as his personal aide and platoon sergeant. The other men were new to Solomon: Lieutenant Troy, platoon commander, his second lieutenant Bastogne, and the five squad leaders: Corporals Wolfram, Lee, Arith, Orin, and Silloh. One week since the space-fold, in a staging area, a place in space where a moon could hide, Solomon worked feverishly to establish training foundations and tactical dogma that could transform a division in two months—the time till the first assault.

"Very good, Lieutenant Troy; gentlemen. The timing of the jump caused the targeting computers on the sim-guns to delay a half-second and recalibrate. Time enough to target your own guns and come through the sequence."

"Yes sir."

"But Corporal...Orin, is it?"

"Sir."

"Your arm was blown off. One of eight injured in five minutes. Now where's the trailer on the buildings?"

"Here, sir. Wolfram."

"You weren't utilized well. Not your fault, Troy. It's about dimensions. Space and timing. Walk with me."

They moved toward the sequence start position.

"We're on a smaller scale, of course, so it's difficult to see. But this is what I want to work into division tactics. I spent the last four days drilling it into the regiment commanders. I don't think Colonel Notrik has recovered yet."

Light com chuckles from beneath opaque visors.

"Oh, helmets please."

Locks clicked and helmets hissed open.

"Now, where do we begin plane reference, uh, Lieutenant Bastogne?"

"From ground-zero, sir. Referencing a world grid by GPS, Flying Fortress, or in worst case by landing zone."

"Amply answered, son. And, from zero reference, attacks proceed on a system of three-dimensional planes. The problem is a mindset. Now watch."

Solomon slipped an earpiece into place and drew the mini-mic into position.

"Control, light the grid please."

The area around them lit up with a series of laser lines—interlocking squares now covered the staging area.

"Thank you, Control. Now run the 4-D adjustment I gave you."

A new set of lines appeared—askew of the squares and cubes that had dominated the grid.

"Now gentlemen, what you are looking at is as close as mathematics can get to a fourth dimensional representation in 3-D space. Now let's factor in motion, time. Watch the light show. Next program, Control."

When the laser grids began to undulate in waves of multiple colors, the men around Solomon gasped or whistled or "wowed," or in the case of Corporal Silloh:

"Holy sh—"

"Corporal."

"Sir."

"Let's watch the language."

"Yes sir. Sorry sir."

"Standing rule for the First D, gentlemen. Discipline on every level. Now imagine your platoon attacking along these color waves in staggered beats of time from ground, from above, even from jet booted arcs, and diagonal boot assisted free falls. We think and move our attacks in three-dimensional mindsets. But you're AIs are capable of more. We limit them and need to rely on them more. Remove the limitation, increase the tactical possibilities. On a small scale this is what Corporal Wolfram could have managed if we'd encoded his AI to guide his movements. The helmet readouts are perfect for it. Intuitive. Color Coded. Multi-sensory. Multi-tasking. I love this mecha. Well, what do you think?"

Devsky stood smiling, enjoying his boss's enthusiasm. The others stood dumb.

"Sergeant, tell them."

"Don't worry, boys, the colonel, sorry, general had his men in the Fifth doing this in two weeks. It's all in the programs. We got to learn to trust the symbiots and then learn how to apply the grids in real time. It'll become second nature before our first landing."

"Thank you, Sergeant. Confident as ever."

"Well, sir, they won't have much of a choice, considering you'll be drilling this whole division fifteen hours a day for the next two months."

Solomon smiled. "Ah, Sergeant Devsky. You know me so well."

And he walked away still smiling. He was the only one.

White text blinked to life on a blue screen: "Hal, I need your help..." The new general sat at a desk in still unfamiliar quarters, hoping for a response. The room was less empty, at least, the otherwise grey, lifeless walls beginning to clutter with animated holo-maps and charts, the closet, sparsely filled—a few uniforms and a pair of very special boots: white and recently polished, the dirt of a jungle planet washed away. Perfect white boots except for the blood red blotches, drips, and spots on, mostly, their fronts. The boots stood neatly in the closet corner, set aside for the sake of a greater responsibility. With but a few exceptions, he would not wear them again till war's end.

The letters continued to blink. The signal had a long way to go: through the ship's central core to myriad mini-communications singularities, from there through back channels to the communications networks at the Ouranos fold gate, from there to be fragmented and sent to a dozen different planets where secret Sykol routers now controlled by the Imperial Guard would encrypt the pieces and forward them to a receiver that literally sat in a closet at the polar research complex on planet Amric, unimaginatively referred to as Imperial World by most. There the message waited for human eyes, if they were watching.

Deep under Imperial Palace, in a command office he simply called "The Con," the Captain of the Imperial Guard reassembled and decrypted the pieces of the message and began the process again in reverse:

"Don't be so foolish as to use that name."

"I needed to get your attention," Solomon keyed back.

"It worked. What is your situation?"

"I'm two weeks back from my last mission, you people have declared war, and I'm suddenly commanding a division."

"Congratulations, General."

"Funny. What happened?"

"Don't ask me questions I can't answer."

"Fine. But there's some knowledge I have to have."

"Yes."

"There was an assassination attempt on Kall."

The response was more delayed: "I didn't know. We thought we'd gotten them all, but I suspected sleepers."

"'Gotten' all of what?" Solomon keyed. As he read the reply, he could almost hear his old friend's voice in it—the even tone, the precise word control:

"Experiments run in Sykol Central: human killing machines, some genetically enhanced, some cybernetic. Kept in reserve in case the Sykols determined the Empress or any of her predecessors were failures at ruling the way they wanted. Control of Sykol Central is now in my hands. The conspirators have been removed, the experiments...deleted."

Solomon suddenly understood two things at once: "One, what reason would Sykols have to kill me? Revenge is a luxury Sykol penchant for preserving power wouldn't allow. Two, the Imperium is in real danger now, isn't it?"

"In regards to the first: You may be right. In regards to the second: I will not say."

But Solomon understood. Hal Teltrab, Captain of the Imperial Guard and Grand Marshall of the Imperial Military, could not admit that Empress Janis IV conspired to have Solomon assassinated (even if he knew this to be true), not even on such a well encrypted signal. Solomon also understood that the Empire was in a weak position, weaker than it had been in a thousand years. The Empress had come to power decades before her time, her father having died when a vein exploded in his brain. Galactic confidence was shaken. Then something amazing happened: the Captain of the Imperial Guard, a man of some power but great visibility, resigned his commission, an event which had never occurred in the Empire's history. That Captain was Solomon Star. Hal Teltrab, who had been his lieutenant, became his replacement. Now, on the eve of the first galactic-scale war to come to the Empire in over five hundred years, Sykol Central, the machine of Imperial Control, was damaged. Apart from the Empress herself and the Imperial Guard's Captain, a third figure in a long existing triumvirate was as important to the government's appearance of stability:

"I was told the Chief Sykol retired," wrote Solomon.

"He was retired," Hal Teltrab responded.

Suddenly, forty systems in an Empire of six hundred mattered. Though hardly a shoestring hold, House Amric's control of the Empire could be shaken in the coming war. Janis's competence as a leader would be questioned in the crucible of military conflict, her credibility weighed in the balance. The Emperor dead, Solomon resigned, and the Chief Sykol deposed (perhaps even killed) all within the last fifteen years—the Empress faced a serious threat to her power, in appearance a military threat, in truth a political one. Winning the war, Solomon realized, was not the problem. How it was won would be everything.

He typed again: "This puts me in a bad position."

"You put yourself there (my message to you on Kall, not with-standing)."

"I had to leave!"

"That's not what I mean, S. I am your friend and will be. I understand your reasons but why did you join the regular army knowing your skills would come under Imperial directives again?"

This time Teltrab had to wait for a response.

"I couldn't think of anything else to do." Lightyears apart, they smiled at each other through sightless monitor screens.

Finally, Teltrab keyed a question: "So do you have what you need now?"

"No," Solomon was quick to reply, "I believe she'll—" And then he erased the last word and retyped: "I believe more attempts on my life with follow."

"Not from Sykol Central."

"You know it wasn't Sykol Central even if they were used."

"Perhaps not, but what would you have me do? Don't ask me to make a choice I cannot—you already made it."

"Yes," Solomon agreed. "I just ask that you protect me from betrayal."

"I cannot guarantee it," concluded Teltrab. "But I can guarantee I'll try."

Level 227 –Tech Lab Assigned to the First Division

"Ib'm. How's my favorite techy?"

"Colonel, I mean General Star, sir. Very well, sir. Received my transfer orders just last week so I'm still settling in. And thanks for dragging me along with you."

Nodding. "Sergeant."

"Oh, and for the promotion too. I almost forgot."

"Well, I didn't want the dotcomers around here bossing you around too much."

"Well, then you should've made me a lieutenant, sir."

Solomon allowed a rare laugh. "Ready to run the place already, Ib'm?"

"Soon as I get the last of these crates unpacked. And say, General, any chance of getting Crawford transferred in under me? I miss his hands."

"You almost blew up his hands, along with the rest of him and us."

Ib'm smiled. "Ah, General, have a heart. That was three years ago, and you're still holding on to it?"

Ib'm had served under Solomon in '95 and almost died along with Private Crawford, Sergeant Devsky, Solomon, and several divisions when he failed to disarm a nuclear warhead that counted down to zero and then by dumb luck and divine grace didn't explode. You would think such a performance on Ib'm's part wouldn't inspire confidence. But Solomon had admired his courage that day and, along with Devsky's, had arranged for Ib'm's transfer to Solomon's new division from the Fifth Army.

Solomon answered Ib'm's question: "It's my tactic for guilting you into putting in twenty hours a day when I need you to. Now, how's my new software coming?"

"We're close. The dotcomer here's a woman named Smith." And under his breath: "Goes by A.J. She's a real looker too and a genius (though I don't let on). The interfaces are done. This'll be the most interactive package to date, and we can handle division level now—biggest personal holo game you've ever played, General."

"Thanks, but don't ever let me think of it as a game."

"Sorry, sir."

"Not a problem. That's a reminder to me. Not to play with lives. You said you're 'close.' What's lacking?"

"Smith's working on the tutorials. She's got some Sykol training besides the computer brilliance. Knows how to write code for prime instructional efficiency. Speaks five languages too. Man, I'd love to marry that woman."

"So what's keeping you?"

"She's my superior officer. I told you, you should've made me a lieutenant!"

Solomon laughed again.

Ib'm continued: "Tomorrow at the latest, General. I just need to finish settling in."

"Very well. But I'll hold you to it. The first target has been named. We fold space within the month."

- 3 -
Spacefold

Deep Space

Jor Danhart, Lieutenant Commander of the Bridge and Executive Officer of the Imperial World Ship Fleet Seven paced the deck of his domain noting activities from one station to another. Admirals, captains of the space fleet; generals, colonels of the army—these came and went, irregular fixtures of the hub, Danhart's domain. They might outrank him, but he was the man who moved their world, literally. He answered to only two men: his captain, Kynter Van Hueys and Rear Admiral Gnostrom. But Danhart was the genius, the mind behind the bridge of Fleet Seven.

One hundred and seventy levels down from what was essentially, the equatorial center of the moon-sized ship, on that side which was most like a "front" (the side that faced a planet or star in its orbit) sat the bridge, Danhart's bridge. It was, itself, a 1000-meter circle, a control room lined with observation screens and concentric circles of control stations on three tiers, the highest of which was Danhart's primary control station. On the bridge a hundred sailors (or three times as many) monitored and controlled the operations of the World Ship: environment, communications, power, resources, weapons, traffic control for the space fleet, and helm control. Twenty people sat at the grey computer consoles of the highest tier, Tier One. Danhart made his way up the handful of steps to that level. Tier One was helm control. Danhart's own station was at the center of it all.

He took his seat in the black command chair and felt its internal servos conform the chair's shape to his legs and back, molding its surface to his contours in a kind of lover's embrace. Three holo monitors and a semi-circle control panel descended from the ceiling and floated within his reach. He smiled a gentle, handsome smile; a narrow angular face with strong cheeks and twinkling eyes, narrow but not slits; a young face with boyish beard—too young for the face of a World Ship XO.[*] Jor Danhart could smile

---

[*]X.O.: Executive Officer

at 25 as he adjusted a com link in his ear because he was the youngest man to hold his post in fleet history. And he was the youngest in fleet history because he was a genius with computers, what the brass called a *dotcomer* for reasons long forgotten. No one could read his ship, his world like he could. But Danhart's smile wasn't pride; it was pleasure.

"Navigation," he said. His voice was deep and as pleasant as his smile.

"Navigation, aye," said a voice in his ear (and to his right—the chief navigator sat a few yards away).

"Begin course-calc presets for FM* travel."

"Aye, commander, spatial coordinates requested via your input station."

"Affirmative. Working." Danhart lifted his hands to the gelatinous panel before him. Gently he pressed his fingers into the cool, tingling gel and with the slightest intonation of movement began "talking" to the master computer which spread out from the bridge covering the miles of level 170, a sphere of the great World Ship. Images flew among the three screens before him at the flick of a finger, and, as the images rose, the commands of his hands were joined by commands from the irises of his eyes. A slight dilation in the pupil, the barest glance to one side, loaded programs, started sub-routines, fired electric thought and the AI of Fleet Seven conversed with him on half a dozen levels.

"Hello, old girl," he soothed. And she was old: four hundred and fifty years, the newest World Ship in the fleet. "Navigator, XO. Sending X axis now. Y axis now. Z axis now."

"Reception confirmed. The ship is calculating destination and string components. Sir, are these coordinates correct?"

"This is no drill, Nav. Coordinates are correct, and mind your com chatter."

Danhart would've noticed thirty-some people in the room—navigation, engine, and computer specialists—turning to look up at Tier One had his gaze not been pulled into a world of dazzling, dancing light. No one could do what Jor could, not at his speed or with his precision, not even Captain Van Hueys who now entered the bridge.

---

* F.M.: Fold Mode

An automatic command spoke over all com links: "Captain on the bridge." A few among the bridge crew were obliged to stand for a moment. Not the Executive Officer.

"Command Con, Navigation. Addy is building the folding model. Your screen should be showing a visual representation of folded space within seconds."

"Navigation, Aye. That image is coalescing and I ask you to run confirmation protocols."

The Captain drew near, his eye fixed on the glowing center of Tier One.

"Processing confirmation, sir."

"Thank you," Danhart replied. "Command Con, Engine Chief."

"Engines, aye"—the voice to his left.

"Begin start up for fold engines, I repeat, begin start up procedures for space folding engines."

"Engines, aye. Start up, aye. Please confirm order with executive officer's clearance code."

"Command Con, Engines. XO Jor Danhart confirming order with code four, one, one, four, three. Engine Chief confirm."

"Engines, aye. Code validated. Please confirm order with Captain's clearance code."

"Affirmative. Captain approaching the command tier."

"Acknowledged. Engine Chief awaits Captain's orders before initializing FESU*."

Something amazing was about to happen. It had happened many times before, but, despite controls and procedures, confirmations and calculations, no one knew exactly how it worked.

"Command Con, Engine Chief. Captain is on deck. Keyboard entry; clearance code is given."

"Engines, Aye. Code received. Confirming."

This ship the size of a moon was about to fold two vastly distant parts of space together, and travel thousands of light years without moving.

"Engine Chief, XO. Code confirmed. Fold engine start up is proceeding. We are on a ten-hour countdown to total fold."

Danhart swiveled from his console with a near whisper: "Good job, old girl." Then looking up: "Captain Van Hueys."

---

* F.E.S.U.: Fold Engine Start Up

"Lieutenant Commander Danhart," replied Fleet Seven's captain, a grey-haired giant of a man whose rugged features exuded confidence. In times of peace, moments of routine, a World Ship's captain was a fixture on a billion-person planetoid filled with Admirals and Generals and Colonels. But this fifty-year career man refused a ceremonial assignment. His XO might be able to run the bridge without him, but he toured his vessel twelve hours of every day, *being* the captain of his ship. Today his confident smile was almost a glow. In three years Fleet Seven had not seen action. She was going to war—a terrible thing, yes—and Captain Van Hueys would not be a figurehead again for years.

"Tell me Jor, what's our status?" As if he didn't know.

"Better than nominal," smiled Danhart, standing. "We're on countdown to a fold across the galaxy."

As the two conversed, fifty crewmen streamed into the bridge to take up engineering and power stations. Throughout the ship, on every habitable level, soldiers and sailors began locking down equipment, shutting down unnecessary systems, and docking all the ships of the space fleet within their great space carrier's womb. Miles down in the uninhabited center of the ship was a sphere, a gigantic power conduit, absorbing energy and feeding it throughout the ship. At the center of the sphere floated another sphere, a thick ball of metal and plasma, solid and liquid, sometimes solid and sometimes energy floating not only in space but between spaces as well. This sphere was not the source of the ship's energy. Its purpose was to keep that energy from sucking Fleet Seven and all within it into a ball the size of a man's fist. Within this sphere floated a small quantum singularity, a black hole—it generated enough power to run a world and fold the very fabric of space.

And as Addy, the ship's Artificial Intelligence master computer, began guiding the control sphere to reshape itself into configurations that would allow the singularity to fold space without destroying the ship, all while Jor Danhart exchanged pleasantries with his captain, it occurred to Danhart that no one really knew how any of it worked, not even him.

The first space folding ship was created thousands of years ago, even before the Amric Empire. The earliest ships were twice the size of modern World Ships. No one knew how they worked because people didn't build them. In some ancient past a group of physicists and computer engineers built a supercomputer on an uninhabited asteroid and asked it to figure out how to overcome the distances of space. It couldn't. But it could tell them how to build a bigger computer on an uninhabited moon which told them how to build computer and robotics complexes which could figure out how to do it and how to bring space folding into existence. The process took four hundred years. But no one knew how it worked. The law of computational equivalence, first worked out millennia before, revealed the inevitable mathematically precise truth. Some processes were so complex they could not be distributed, reduced, sped up, or explained. They could only be performed. And so World Ships were built on a dead planet called Tartarus, alive with thinking computers who themselves had taken a century to "grow up," and who controlled armies of industrial robots which built black holes and great World Ships behind them, one every five hundred years or so as was called for by the Empire.

Jor smiled with his captain and, after a brief exchange, returned to his station, and, while Van Hueys began to pace the circular aisles of the bridge, Danhart touched Addy with his fingers, listened to the voice of her ones and zeroes and stroked her neural pathways with a soothing, deep voice: "Addy, old girl, let's sail the stars."

- 4 -
New Edda's Whip

"...Transcend rules when conferring rewards;
    transcend policy when issuing orders." –Sun Tzu

–Warrior Text from the Lost World

Planet: New Edda

But that the sky was a tangle of wind and storm cloud, the people of new Edda would have seen the light of a bright new star appear one minute after it blinked into existence out of nowhere. That's how long it took for the light of their own sun to travel back from the reflecting surface of Fleet Seven. The World Ship folded space far enough from the planet to keep from drifting into its orbit. Within a day, though, this star would be a new moon, orbiting the planet and causing havoc on the tidal cycles of her blustering seas. Massive ice sheets at both poles, covering a full-half of the planet would begin to crack, break and then crumble, making the oceans an unnavigable iceberg soup—all within a day.

The space fleet would not wait that long. The Fourth and Fifth Carrier Groups launched immediately from gaping ports on the World Ship's surface. Admiral Zhmen's Fourth Fleet launched half of its 20,000 unmanned fighter drones and two thousand manned fighters straight toward the space folding gates that orbited on opposite sides of the planet's most distant moon. Fifty cruisers and two hundred destroyers followed at best pace, and perimeter scout ships raced ahead to deploy first-wave jamming satellites. The super-powered unmanned ships, able to ignore the effects of inertia on the human body, accelerated to cover the eleven million miles in a matter of minutes. The first hundred satellites were deployed and transmitting override codes before Eddan gate-keepers could respond. The blue glow of the gates' energy signatures faded to darkness leaving only orbital running lights to indicate the giant rings' positions in space. Instant communication with other worlds was now impossible and most of the Eddan navy was cut off from its home, having, as intel had reported, joined forces with ships currently orbiting Rikas IV, home world to the Overlord, Inmar (all fold gates around all the planets in "rebellion" were simultaneously shut down by the transmission of Imperial control codes—each of these planets was now in isolation). The remaining Eddan space force withdrew to low planet orbit, ordered not to provoke the Imperial Fleet, though not to obey any orders from Fleet Command. After that, the local ships found they could communicate with no one on the planet.

Admiral Mullikin's Fifth Fleet was ordered to target the planet's complete satellite system. Drones blew all com satellites from the sky while scouts deployed two hundred total-intel satellites which built an invisible web capable of jamming all planetary communication and outgoing signals. Across the planet only hard wired, hard lined com systems could still function. Those were few. Holo screens planet wide did not, however, remain void and silent for long.

The Imperial crest—a sharp taloned eagle of metallic gold, wings spread, claws clutching a lightning bolt and an olive branch—appeared against a dark blue background horizontally divided by a white stripe. Beneath the crest three fiery red letters, ICA, filled the bottom third of the screen—exactly as I had designed them. Then the voice, pleasant and feminine and just a hint of sultry appeal: "From the Imperial Communication Agency's Studio A aboard her Majesty's World Ship, Fleet Seven..." And as the voice continued, the graphic faded to the face of the speaker... "...this is Melisu Sheharizade reporting on the Inmar Crisis."

A beautiful woman not far into her twenties sat at a nondescript desk while walls behind her flicked and flickered with images of space, ships, soldiers, planets and text screens. In the bottom-right corner of the viewer's holo screen, an ICA logo slowly rotated, and a text bar began feeding letters, then words, then sentences from right to left in holographic 3-D. Studio A...this was my world.

The young anchor continued: "High above the atmosphere of New Edda, Operation Freedom Empire has begun." Sweet voiced and smiling sweetly, Melisu Sheharizade initiated a broadcast on war that would run non-stop for the next ten years. Sometimes, directed toward a single planet, sometimes broadcasting to the entire galaxy, in this instance she spoke Empire wide while the text bar communicated to New Edda alone those terms of surrender and rules of engagement to which the planet's leaders could not now respond even if they wanted to.

"According to the strictures of just-war law laid down by Imperial Peace Codes, Fleet Seven twenty minutes ago began the non-lethal containment of planet New Edda whose leadership some three months ago signed an illegal pact of aggression against the Empire."

Her friends around the studio called her Mel. Her face was a perfect oval, eyes, nose, and lips in ideal proportion so that no feature stood out over any other but all worked to a beautiful balance, a symmetry of singular vision, a whole, complete and perfect face, seamless and smooth as the smoothness of her perpetually tanned skin. Brown and earthy, Mel's brown eyes and black-brown hair contributed to her same seamless whole. Everything about her communicated a sleek professional perfection simultaneously with a down home, girl next door innocence: sophistication and playfulness, façade and every quality of the very real.

She wore a conservative blue blazer over a high collared cream blouse. A single glittering gold chain dangled from her left ear. And though her hair was pulled tightly back, perfecting the oval of her face, half of its long, silky tail spilled over her right shoulder and down to her lap. Melisu Sheharizade, Mel, both at the same time— she spoke the Imperial Will with a mischievous smile and liquid grace, grace she'd been taught by the best in the Imperial Communications Agency: an idealistically naïve man named Westart. Spin Verkruyse (of the Empress's cabinet) had chosen her personally to become a household name next only to Janis herself. And all over the galaxy, men sat up and took notice with half smiles they could not repress, even those watching this message of doom from the planet below.

Melisu was the Voice of a galaxy: "Admiral Gnostram and General Constantine report a perfect beginning to the containment campaign while Eddan gun-ships appear to be cooperating with standard Imperial protocols. Non-escalation is an absolute goal of the Imperial strategy..."

Pictures of ship positions around the planet cut in and out with Melisu's face. The text line continued to feed regulations to the planet: Civilians must not participate nor appear to participate in military combat, nor can they act as human shields on danger of violating the anti-terrorism Peace Codes of 572 A.E. And while leaders on the planet's surface struggled hurriedly to find a way to signal Fleet Central Command, as well as their own ships in orbit, Melisu Sheharizade spoke on, to the delight of billions.

Fold Plus forty-five minutes:

A two-man fighter was passing New Edda's inner moon, Fafnir. At the controls, the Wonder Twins: Dane Redierg and Paul Trefloyd. Not really twins, but genuine wonders. The five foot five buddies met in flight school at Kadorantilles and became inseparable. The wonder was in their skill as a flight team. And it was no wonder that they led all other manned ships by fifteen minutes.

"Fighter 53033, come in."

"See, I told you they were gonna pull us back," quipped Trefloyd; his husky voice belied his height.

"Yeah, and we'll have com trouble for another half hour if you'll level out and quit thinking so negative," Redierg answered.

"Fighter 53033, respond."

"Wait a minute, that's not carrier com." Trefloyd double checked his controls. "That's a Centcom code."

"Nuh-uh, you're lyin'!"

"Why do you always say I'm lyin' when you think I'm wrong?"

"Because you lie all the time; that's why I can never win a game of Hitman against you."

"That is so untrue!"

"Fighter 33."

"Yo, T-Floyd answer that; it's a Centcom signal."

"Shut up Dane. Centcom command, Fighter 53033 receiving."

"Thirty-three, what's wrong with your com?"

"Uh, just coming out of the Fafnir dead zone, Centcom."

Covering his mic: "See, a liar," grinned Redierg.

Trefloyd continued: "We're recovering now, Centcom."

"Roger, 33. Intel is looking at preliminary sat telemetry, and, uh, there's an anomaly we'd like you to check out planet-side."

"Nu-uh!" Redierg was delighted. "He did not just say we get to straif the planet."

"Shut up and fly the ship," Trefloyd whispered. Then: "Roger Centcom, would you repeat that?"

"Thirty-three, confirmation codes are transmitting now along with coordinates for planet-side recon. You are ordered to punch atmosphere to within eyes-on of coordinates and transmit intel directly via Centcom priority channel."

The twins smiled at each other, sat up in their chairs, and tightened their seatbelts.

Trefloyd answered, "Uh, roger, Centcom. We are receiving and looking forward to the burn and boom."

"Affirmative 33, good luck and Godspeed, and by the way, boys, your captain forwards a message. He says, "Don't' deviate from your flight plan, emphasizing the words 'this time.'"

"Uh, Centcom this is Fighter 53033 signaling a bit of concern for our com system. That last part was garbled."

"Sure it was, 33. Centcom out."

Redierg: "And we are on!"

Trefloyd: "Yeah, baby."

"Alright TF let's run the atmospheric protocols."

"On screen; holo trajectory working. Ten minutes till we spark the atmo."

Breaking through the atmosphere at attack speed required a descent around half the planet. Their ship's hull glowing bright against the planet's braking air, an occasional spark of fire flying into their windshield's view, they slowed to Mach 2, thirty thousand feet above the planet's surface on her night side. Below them, lightning charged clouds obscured their view of any city lights. They continued to descend and sped toward the dawn.

"Next question, Dane."

"What's that, Tref?"

"What are we supposed to be looking for?"

"Good question. We'll know in...what, fifteen?"

"Coming up on coordinates in ten minutes."

"That's good time."

"Hey man, it's us."

They hit turbulence five minutes later. Clouds were clearing as they drew near the sunrise, but the pervading Eddan winds were strong, rocking the small ship in their violent streams.

"Whoa! What a ride." Trefloyd grinned his pleasure.

"We're jumping two and three hundred meters a bounce here. Up drafts, down drafts—where's the hurricane? Oof! and where's my lunch about to end up?" Redierg fought the controls.

"This is a nice breezy day on New Edda. And hit your barf button—get some anti-nausea meds into your bloodstream. And...here comes the sun."

As dawn broke, the ship's re-entry shields opened and the pilots viewed real sky for the first time. The simulation holo before them faded to digital readouts—numbers and lines—and the windshield adjusted its tint against the direct sunlight.

"T-floyd, help me out here."

"I'm on it." Trefloyd pressed his fingers into the gel-key computer controls before him. As Redierg guided the ship with his hands and feet, Trefloyd now used the flight computer to make a thousand tiny adjustments every second. Hull sensors relayed wind pressure and direction to his nervous system so he could feel his way through the atmosphere. Before his eyes, invisible winds became liquid flow lines which he could now project on the windshield for Redierg to see. As Redierg adjusted the bulk controls, Trefloyd tweaked engines, trim tabs even the very shape of the hull. The ship settled from rumbled shake to streaming ride over airy rapids. Wonder Twins indeed.

Then they saw it. Miles away it looked like rain falling from a cloudless sky. Then, no, it looked as if the clouds were grounding and releasing rain upward. Then the rain was hair, flying wildly in New Eddan winds. And the fine hair became coarse string and then soon a tentacled monster.

Redierg squinted and wondered: "What is it?"

Trefloyd wasn't watching as much with his human eyes. At first, the cables were merely lines among the computer's mapping of the flowing winds, moving exactly as the streams moved. He spoke a command: "Enhance." And the wind streams became green lines before both pilots' eyes while New Edda's unique defensive system appeared in red.

And Trefloyd: "Holy—"

And Redierg: "We've got trouble."

"Maybe we oughta pull up."

"Set your recon sensors."

"Pull up, Dane."

"We gotta record this!"

"Record it from a distance!"

"Too late."

The first cable whizzed by, its vibrations in the wind making audible sound. Proximity sensors warned of danger on all sides, and their commitment to the obstacle course was now irreversible.

"Talk to me, Tref."

"Break right in two, one, now!"

"Keep talking me through."

"You're alright, you're alright; start an ascent. Now left. Wait. Down!"

"I heard that one."

"It was a cluster. Get ready to break."

"Which way?"

"Wait."

"Which way!"

"Right, now!"

"It's too random."

"No, Dane, they follow the patterns of the wind."

"Oh great, Paul, so all we got to do is find the pattern in a friggin' butterfly effect nightmare!"

"Don't yell at me, I told you to pull up! Left, left!"

"I see it."

"Now right, twenty degrees. Adjust your ascent. Get ready to bank left, hard. And two, one, go."

Like an amusement planet hover coaster, they swerved, rolled, and even looped their way skyward, pushing the fighter, tasking their talents, and solidifying their reputation as the best flight team in the Fifth Carrier Group. They avoided the monstrous conglomerates easily enough, but the hairline cables forced quick course changes, and gut-wrenching maneuvers. One cable whipped at a wing and nicked the plus-G landing gear controls. Fortunately, they would be docking in an orbiting carrier birth within the next hour, with a story to tell and a problem to report.

◇◆◇

"...word from my producer Nase that the containment maneuver is complete and without incident. The Fourth and Fifth Carrier Groups are in station-keeping orbits around the planet and all fold gate controls are under Imperial encoding. That means there is now a physical troop presence in the two gate control complexes on the Eddan moon, Hela. Those gates will remain powered down till the resolution of conflict. New Edda is now isolated and Melisu Sheharizade along with them." She smiled wryly. "But we're here with you for the duration, linked only by the techno-geniuses of Fleet Seven and the ICA. Vital information follows for the people of New Edda; we ask you to stay with us and not waiver in your pleas for peace. The prayers of the galaxy are here. To everyone else watching from all galactic points, we'll be putting up a series of twenty com addresses through which you will be able to send messages to loved ones on Fleet Seven and the planet below. We who stand isolated hope you'll stand with us for peace and unity in the Empire.

"Watch for those com addresses to start scrolling across your holos in about fifteen seconds as we move to my good friend Einor Pluc over in Studio C who's joining us to put the conflict in perspective and answer some pervading questions. Nor?"

Einor Pluc was the walking incarnation of a quality best captured in a word invented at the dawn of mass-media ages in the past. That word: *schmooze*. It flowed from every pore of Pluc's being: in the confident smiles, the perfectly rehearsed casual gestures, the smooth inflection of voice, and the style of his appearance: perfectly sculpted auburn locks, charcoal grey double-breasted jacket, baby pink shirt with a maroon tie and a sparkle from the gold ICA tie pin and matching cuff links, and his whole person scented with the subtlest of colognes. His voice was confident animation:

"Thank you, Mel. Einor Pluc here folks to take you through the last year of the political scene as together we try to understand how we got to where we are today."

Pluc's face faded, replaced by music and graphics: a montage of planet names, pictures of various dignitaries, headlines, accusations, speeches and finally in golden black letters the title,

"Prelude to War." A pre-recorded documentary followed, narrated by Einor Pluc (and proudly produced, at the time, by Nase Westart).

A picture of a spiral galaxy appeared.

"This representation of our galaxy shows seven spiral arms. In the third and fourth arms of this Galactic Empire rest forty star systems in crisis." As Pluc spoke, the graphic zoomed in to an area of the galaxy in which forty stars began blinking red. As he continued, it focused in on one.

"The cause of the crisis is one man, the self-styled Overlord of Rikas IV, Inmar." Images of a dark-haired man with brooding eyes appeared and faded—ominous music played in the background. Inmar always wore stylish, metallic colored robes. In place of a crown which no royal other than the Empress was allowed to wear, the Overlord of Rikas IV turbaned his head with glittering colors to match his robes and always a jeweled family crest. Pluc outlined a history of escalating conflict:

"For several years, complaints had been heard from planets which eventually collected themselves into a voting-bloc in the House of Royals and League of Democratic Worlds, the two legislative branches of the Imperium. These complaints ranged from outbreaks of plague on the planets Irakeen and Jorda to bankruptcy on Xanthrus, to highly disputed reports of piracy in the normal-space shipping lanes of the galaxy's third and fourth arms. More alarming, however, were subtle attempts by Inmar and his chief ally, Laertes Apokoluptrosis, ruler of Ianus, to legislate subtle limitations on Empress Janis's power. The sharp eyes of the Sykol Polit-bureau and the Empress's absolute veto power foiled these attacks on Imperial stability.

"Though Inmar and Apokoluptrosis have powerful allies in the House of Royals, only a handful, along with several democratic systems, signed the official pact of grievances against the Empire less than a year ago. While forty systems are involved in this political block, only nineteen governments—royal and democratic—make up Inmar's coalition since half the planets are part of multi-planet states. The Overlord himself governs four planets besides Rikas.

"Matters came to a head when it was discovered that the Inmar alliance was funneling resources to the production of a military vessel, a World Ship capable of folding space and therefore of striking any target anywhere in the galaxy. The violation of Imperial law was clear: peace and stability had been maintained in the galaxy through strict control of all space folding technology. Fold gates were stationary and closely monitored for illegal activity. And the seven fold-capable ships in the galaxy, the World Ships, were under Imperial control—the galaxy's police force. Now, though denying irrefutable proof, the Inmar alliance was attempting to shift the balance of power.

"Empress Janis has chosen to act quickly, reining in the rebel systems with economic penalties, military force, and a de-normalized status for all conspirator governments until the location of the illegal assembly site is revealed to the Empire, and the contraband ship dismantled or obliterated. New Edda is the first system to suffer this Imperial edict."

The First Army was, of course, attached to the First Carrier Group. Row after row of infantrymen and armed vehicles sat sardined in the transports of various sizes from platoon strength upward. Among them were the command and supply posts called Flying Fortresses (FF for short). Beneath the belly of Admiral East's Super-Carrier, a famous vessel of the line called the Constitution, thirty Flying Fortresses held thirty-plus generals and their command teams, ready for deployment. Solomon Star sat in his armored infantry suit, helmet in hand, buckled into a command chair on the flight deck of the First Corps' FF, a multi-mile wide sphere which General Haggard's corps command shared with Solomon's First Division.

After two hours of waiting, the Carrier Group itself still docked in Fleet Seven, both Solomon and General Haggard sitting next to him knew something was wrong.

"Are you going to call it in or wait for it?" asked Solomon.

Haggard smiled with an expression of one who knows something others don't. With confidence in his voice he replied, "I'm predicting the signal in, oh say, five, four, three, two—"

"First Corps Mobile Command, this is First Army Rear Command, General Scott for General Haggard."

A communications officer responded, "ARC, CMC, roger. The general is listening."

Next came General Scott's voice: "Bob, take Solomon to the MR* and assemble your other command teams for holo conferencing."

"Understood, General," answered Haggard.

A Flying Fortress's deployment deck was her head but not her heart. The deck commanded her movement, defense, and deployments, but the Map Room was General Haggard's true command post. It consisted of a 100 by 100 meter room amid ship. In this room dozens of communications and intelligence stations lined the walls. Most, important, however, was the virtual reality map at the room's center. A great square slab, dead center, took up half the room's space. A virtual reality computer in its base used satellite imaging, spy drones, fighter imaging, in-fielded communications, reports, transponders, and camera feeds from infantry AI helmets and armored vehicles to create a tactical, real-time holo map of any planet-side target area, and this in three dimensions and any variety of scales, angles, and zooms. When General Haggard entered with Solomon, General Scott's Rear Command Post at Centcom was already in view, Scott pacing from station to station.

"Are we all here?" asked Scott's virtual image. "Very well, then. Gentlemen your holomaps are now showing the capitol city, or at least what you can see of it. That large black mass you're staring at is one of 506 such devices if device is the word for it. At any rate its New Edda's unique answer to air defense and it has the boys at Intel caught completely by surprise."

General Scott described the trap into which Redierg and Trefloyd had nearly fallen: imagine a flat black hexagon ten yards in diameter. Attached to this hexagon are six half-mile long diamond-steel cables. The hexagonal platform is essentially nothing but a hover engine, capable not only of levitating itself, but also reducing the gravitational pull on the half-mile tentacles. The planet's constant winds then provide motion to these cables. Each of the hexagons can then be attached to numerous others creating shields over the skies of entire cities. It's a passive-engagement defense system which thus allows for no massive (i.e. nuclear) reprisal according to the rules of war. But it's utterly successful at

---

* M.R.: Map Room

reducing the Empire's air superiority to nothing. Its particular genius is its multi-sectional design: attempt to blast a large platform apart and each remaining hover-hex would still function and increase planet wide flight hazard by scattering with the winds. At least left in large sections, the danger to pilots and their craft would be localized.

The first question asked among the First Army generals was how Intel could have missed out so completely on such a large defensive system. Apparently, deployment is swift. Once the platform elevates to about a hundred yards above the tallest building of any primary city, power plant, or military installation, the free ends of the partially lightened cables are swept upward by any of the planet's four perpetual jetstreams, whipping and flailing about individually or in tangled clusters like the hair of a ship killing giant. These hexagons connect together to form large anti-ship defense webs twenty and forty and sixty miles in diameter. And so deployment of the defensive system occurred within hours of the Imperial army's arrival.

But this answer didn't suffice. Why didn't the Sykol spy network know about a defensive technology that was obviously decades or centuries in the making before the war when New Edda was a normalized member of the Empire, in good standing for more than a millennium? General Scott waved past these issues to get to the most important question: "How do we beat this defense?"

Everyone understood that this anti-air system would demand a complete rewrite of the New Edda battle book. Central to the tactics of mechanized warfare since its development on the lost world Earth millennia ago was ALB or the Air-Land Battle doctrine. With the advent of air and space warfare, the ancient idea of battle lines had all but disappeared. Engaging an enemy along a battle line meant that the enemy could "dig in" and defend or reinforce his lines with fresh troops. The thinking of ALB called for deep infiltration past enemy lines through targeted space/air attacks (both ships and artillery) which allowed for harassment not only of enemy lines but of their ability to communicate, reinforce, supply, and retreat. This aside, even in a successful assault on enemy lines, ground troops would still want air support for actions against enemy targets and air and satellite intel for the urban sites that would invariably prove to be primary battlegrounds.

While Centcom strategists under General Kataltem worked on a battleplan, army commanders like General Scott took the problem to their division commanders for input. The option no one wanted to consider was infantry-only ground assault made up of traditional lines and waves of attacks. Blasting the floating cables from the hover hexes would likely bring them to the ground but collateral damage would be too high and Image mattered in this war. The same was true of cutting power to the hexes and crashing them down on civilian cities. Doing so would likely be impossible anyway since each hexagon was individually powered.

Solomon waited patiently for someone to pick up on the solution that had been apparent almost from the beginning. He wanted to be careful to avoid any air of superiority with peer commanders. He was happy when his own superior, General Haggard, saw it:

"General Scott."

"Yes, General Haggard."

"You said earlier that if we blast the platforms apart the pieces would float away."

"Yes."

"So what's keeping them in place now?"

There was a pause for the recognition, the glimmer of hope.

Then Scott: "Intel doesn't know that, General, but if they're tethered physically..."

Haggard: "Then those tethering lines can be cut, and if electronically then the program can be scrambled, and—"

Scott: "And if by a grounded tractor system then those transmitters can be destroyed. Excellent thinking, General. Then we just push the giant platforms out of the way or they float away on their own—an avoidable air hazard. I'll pass this recommendation on to General Kataltem and Admiral Gnostram. The only trick now is figuring out how to do it within a few hours with whole armies locked into their deployment births and most of the fleet already in attack position."

Now Solomon knew he had to speak:

"General, I believe I see an answer to that problem."

On the planet, the Eddan people could now channel their holoscreens between two stations, or rather two studios aboard Fleet Seven. While Melisu Sheharizade reported to the galaxy, a signal beamed to New Edda alone began during Scott's meeting with his generals. Like Melisu, Chryses Ta was pleasing to the eye. But different. Somehow threatening—dangerously beautiful.

Chryses Ta was delivering the terms for Eddan surrender to the leaders and people of the planet below her:

"Unconditional surrender is herein defined by Imperial proclamation to include no less than the surrendering of all space and planet bound weapons, a detailed reporting of all weapons stockpiles, the grounding of all airborne vessels" (and in her earpiece Chryses heard her producer add a phrase which she spoke immediately) "and platforms, whether commercial, private, or military, and agreement in retinally identifiable holo transmission from the Eddan president within no more than one hour from the beginning of this broadcast at nine hundred hours, IST.*

"A channel is now open to the Eddan government on the frequency cycling in encryption at the bottom of your holoscreens. Only the president and his cabinet have access to the decryption code as per normalized Imperial membership procedures. The entire New Eddan government will be required to step down as part of an unconditional surrender. An interim governor will be named for a period of no less than ten Imperial years and the planet brought under direct control of the Empress.

"The benevolent will of her majesty, the Empress Janis IV has determined, however, that, to the unconditional surrender of New Edda, she will impose upon herself the following conditions for fostering peace: though the planetary leadership will be subject to trial by intergalactic court for treason, no death sentences will be imposed. Economic penalties imposed on New Edda will consist of no more than a doubling of the current norm in Imperial tax and this not to exceed a period of one decade, IST."

Chryses continued her litany of demands and benefits, emphasizing that, without unconditional surrender, all offers would be removed from the table. A single shot fired at an Imperial soldier, vehicle, or ship would end any chance for peaceful resolution. She would continue and then repeat everything she had

---

* I.S.T.: Imperial Standard Time

said till handed new speeches, either on procedures for surrender or survival orders to civilians facing hostilities. And as she spoke, every word that dripped from Chryses Ta's lovely lips was an enthralling invocation of genuine threat.

"They know how to pick them, don't they?"

Below on the planet of wind and ice, Krieg Sorenson, president of a government representing four billion people, watched the broadcast with his cabinet and chief military advisors from the presidential mansion in Heorot. Outside the sky was darkened not by clouds but by the massive hover hex-platform protecting the capitol city from attack.

"These women are drop dead gorgeous," Sorenson continued.

"Deadly, being the key description here," replied his Chief of Staff.

"Sir," said a concerned man in uniform, "I think it's time to get you to the defensive bunker."

"No, Colonel, there's still time. The big ship is still trying to figure out how to get around our little surprise. Otherwise the landings would have begun by now. Where are we on the perimeter defenses?"

"All troops in place, all defenses fixed and ready."

"Good. So we force them to turn this fight into a good old fashioned siege, a quagmire. Let's make this war a very unpopular, ineffective, and politically costly affair."

"Sir," said the Chief of Staff, "you realize that even if we hold out and give our representatives in the League time to sway other planets in our favor, we won't be able to hold on indefinitely and you'll be taken, tried, and killed? This is our last chance to change course."

"I know, Rejik. We weren't expecting to be the first target, half our navy is stranded at Rikas, and our ground forces are outnumbered ten to one. But then Inmar and I met a year ago, and he told me something I refused to believe. A month later a pirate raid in shipping lanes between Edda and Thorsfeld stopped a shipment of raw enzyme material that Doctor Havens of the Institute of New Helsinki was experimenting with in hopes of curing a rare disease called carcolimphatileukemia. His research was set back six months. But he synthesized the cure after receiving a new shipment. That was five months ago. Unfortunately, my son Wael died of carcolimphatileukemia two weeks before Dr. Helston announced his cure. And then Rejik...and then...the Imperials denied the existence of pirates in the third and fourth galactic arms, blaming ship losses on incompetence and accidents of space travel. They denied it, Rejik! Without as much as an eyes-on investigation. Without increasing military patrols by a single ship. Exactly as Inmar told me they would. Someone's got to take a stand. Janis is an incompetent child, and she needs to be called to the floor to answer for her callous incredulity."

"But Mr. President, how can we win?"

"Winning doesn't matter. Didn't the gods fight even when Ragnarok was upon them? Even knowing they couldn't win?"

Suddenly a security team entered the room and demanded that President Sorenson and cabinet move to a defense bunker immediately. Reports were coming from all over the planet that thousands of ships were entering the atmosphere.

- 5 -
Solomon's Noose

Planet New Edda

Solomon's First Division landed twenty kilometers outside Heorot, the Eddan capitol city, in four staging areas, one on each side of the city. General Haggard's flying fortress landed to the west and began coordinating an enveloping action. Transports and armored attack vehicles poured from the fortress in three directions. To the north and south, platoon-sized infantry quick dropped in hundred-man increments, the men leaping from open hatches on every side, thirty yards above the ground, and jet-booting to soft landings. Then they began to leap frog toward the city covered by small hover fighters. To the east, a Space Air Carrier called the Ishagel slowly descended to act as a mobile air strip for planet-side flight, while the first target of elements from Colonel Coen's regiment[*] was the spaceport on Heorot's northern outskirts. It was taken without incident. In fact, it had been left totally abandoned. Support fighters began descending from space almost immediately.

Aboard the flying fortress, General Haggard watched the real-time action unfold at one-one thousandth scale in his Map Room. General Hollis stood beside him, careful to note the quick moving figures colored green on the 3-D map: his armored tanks and SPUs.[†] Most of his forces had descended with the carrier and so whether from east or west they moved quickly to join up with their partner battalions and companies in the infantry quick drops, both north and south.

The process was repeating all over the planet, but only one division would push on past the enveloping stage to test out the new Imperial attack strategy.

Solomon rode in a hover jeep flanked by his security platoon ten clicks behind the main of the regiment led by Colonel Laver. At the

---

[*] Solomon's First Infantry Division contained four regiments under four colonels including Colonel Coen. Accompanying Star's division was General Gregor Hollis's First Armored Division.

[†] S.P.U.: Mobile Artillery—powerful cannons on mobile platforms.

top of a rise, the city came into view and he told his driver to stop. He headspoke to his companion AI which he had named "Little Hal" in honor of his old friend:

'Full magnification.'

Solomon's face shield zoomed his vision in on the outskirts of the city. In the lower left corner of his visor, the VR map being watched by Haggard and Hollis gave Solomon a big picture view of the battle ground. Only no battle had begun.

'Com.' "Regimental commanders, hold your positions at five klicks." Four "affirmative" responses echoed in his ears. Solomon grabbed his plasma rifle and stepped out of the open-air jeep. The envelopment was nearly complete—a perfect circle. Wind was strong and the Eddan sun shone bright, glaring off the glacial ice sheet, white and pristine and blown free of snow. In the world of his body armor Solomon felt no cold, heard no wind, and saw but a dim glare as his visor filtered out the reflected light. Micro-grips in his boots dug firmly into the ice, grasping and releasing under the adjusting pressure of each step.

In the distance rose a black smudge on this fantastic world of ice and wind—the hover hex-platform shrouding in shadow what might have appeared an ice castle if seen with normal eyes, but Solomon's view was augmented to within the seeming proximity of an outstretched arm. He knew what he had to do.

'Com.'

"Colonel Laver."

"Roger, Laver."

"Press your troops forward in battle line formation. Hold your reserves in place. Expect hidden and bunkered defenses." And Solomon thought, 'They want a siege line, we'll accommodate them...for the moment.' Solomon climbed back into his jeep and moved forward.

Lieutenant Jaygee Niebelung led his platoon in jet boot leaps toward the target in a double wave formation, his platoon sergeant controlling the second wave. A hover tank brought up the rear as close as safety allowed—the tank commander didn't want to run over the leapers in front of him. In a line stretching several miles to either side of Niebelung's platoon, additional infantry joined the advance.

Ice began to give way to streets and low buildings. But they had not yet advanced as far as the hover hex platform's edge.

Niebelung scanned quickly for potential dangers with each leap, but his helmet AI responded in the negative. Streets and buildings began to break up the lines and the pooling, the grouping of soldiers, clued small unit commanders in on the increased likelihood of ambush. But still nothing until they came under the shadow of the platform. Half a mile in, where planetary command was certain air support would become useless, the attack began.

Niebelung heard plasma fire first on his left, the sound muffled by his helmet. Then a blockade in the street before him came into view—downed hover trucks and ton sized ice chunks. As the second line of Niebelung's platoon came jetting over his head, Solomon's new Move and Strike software, as it was dubbed by his tech sergeant, Ib'm, kicked into gear. Plasma fire erupted from the blockade and buildings ahead.

"Split!" Niebelung screamed.

The color-coded programming directed Twelfth Platoon's five squads in both movement and targeting. Two squads in front saw green or blue highlighting which directed full power boot jet leaps up the buildings on either side. Colored arrows even specified windows for some of the troops to crash through. Most of each squad, though, landed on roofs and began either laying down suppression fire or targeting their plasma rifles as objects in their visors became highlighted.

The squads in the street, meanwhile, moved against walls, ducked into doorways, or just plain dropped to the ground. In the initial salvo, seven soldiers in second and third squads had been struck by small arms plasma rounds—their armor had held.

And standing defiantly in the middle of the street, Niebelung: 'Com.' "Sergeant Kroy, I need recon from your vantage." And then to his helmet AI: 'K' (the lieutenant's name for his symbiot) 'program changes: no prompts to advance—hold position.'

"Affirmative," came the platoon sergeant's voice over the com system. And, *Affirmative,* came the AI's inaudible voice.

And Niebelung: 'Com.' "Tank support." And the symbiot knew to route the signal to the nearby tank's commander. In the second that Niebelung waited for an answer, he scrolled his mini-screen through the eye-line views of all five of his squad leaders followed by an ultra-zoomed satellite picture from overhead as well.

"Tank support, roger."

"Target blockade ahead and prepare—"

"Delay that LT." The voice of platoon sergeant Krogo Kroy boomed at a volume in Niebelung's ear that indicated he had ordered his own AI to transmit 'with urgency.'

"Target and hold tank commander." 'Kroy's POV, K.' "Kroy."

"LT, I'm scanning automated enemy placements almost exclusively. Some of the fire coming from the right is from human aggressors."

There was a pause, followed by an explosion in the building behind the blockade on Niebelung's right.

And then Kroy: "Third squads RPPG* men have just halved live targets and others are in orderly retreat. LT, this isn't the ambush line."

"Roger that."

Niebelung realized that the blockade ahead was a token ruse. Infantry could leap it without difficulty—only his armored support would be slowed down.

'Com. Company commander.' "Captain Cody, Twelfth Platoon."

"Cody, roger."

"Captain are you getting reports on automated enemy fire?"

"Yes, we were just—"

And then the override signal: the voice of General Solomon Star: "All commands, all commands, initial skirmishing pattern shows feint and withdrawal. Your attack lines are false; the retreat's staged. Do not advance."

'No, that's not enough,' thought Niebelung. 'Com. Alpha priority.' "Regimental command, Colonel Laver; Lieutenant Niebelung Eighth Battalion, First Company, Twelfth Platoon. The General's order isn't enough. We need to pull back!"

"Laver here. Hold your position, Lieutenant and don't panic. What's your intel?"

"Roger sir. Holding. Permission to withdraw and test my intel, sir?"

Silence.

---

* R.P.P.G.: Rocket Propelled Plasma Grenade

"Very well, but you have ten seconds to make your case for withdrawal."

Niebelung didn't waste time. He ordered the withdrawal and then immediately called for his tank support to fire at its target. He leaped behind the hover truck as it obliterated the blockade with a single plasma shell. That was the signal.

The explosion which followed was intended not only to trap soldiers in ambush but to level buildings and drive up the ice sheet from below. The subsequent debris field of rock and ice and trench would present a real problem for armored support and any quick overrun of the city. The Eddans seemed prepared to sacrifice half the city to create a dug-in defense.

The information was communicated quickly throughout the division and the infantry began a quick withdrawal. Solomon knew he needed to press the attack so he ordered Laver's regiment (to the west) and Colonel Notrik's (to the south) to push forward with RPPGs, tanks and SPUs to trigger the enemy ambush explosions from a safe distance. However, he held the other regiments—Colonel Hope's and Colonel Coen's—in place.

Half the city was now covered in smoke and ash, held in concentrated protection by the hover hex-platform. Visibility was zeroed for all but heat vision, and various electronic surveillance filters. Solomon ordered snipers into positions and scout squads forward—these highly mobile troops wore amplified jet boots and shoulder mounted jet packs that allowed some directional change and jumps at length up to two hundred meters. In addition, their recon arrays were more complete and transmitted intel automatically.

'We've got to make this look good.'

Solomon's quandary was giving the appearance of an attack without getting people killed. He hoped the scouts could fire and move with enough speed to draw the enemy's attention and avoid becoming targets themselves. Finally, Solomon called in the order for the impossible. And the air assault began.

The first wave consisted of reconnaissance drones flying in from the North and East at altitudes of fifty to a hundred yards. They laid down random plasma fire at empty city streets to cover their true purpose: intelligence gathering. From simulators on the carrier Ishagel, pilots guided the drones at break-neck speeds, navigating the streets of Heorot in search of the hover hex platform's tethering system. Small arms batteries targeted the drones from buildings and squares—mostly troops surprised to see the Imperials attacking beneath their air defense system. Targeting computers in anti-air batteries painted the Imperial ships which responded with anti-targeting jamming systems that then faced anti-anti jammers, and, in the end, the high tech targeting of the state of the art allowed for about seventy percent accuracy, making targeting by sight more efficient. Eventually, however, missile batteries launched heat seekers that chased the drones down. On the Ishagel, pilots in their remote cockpits could be seen screaming and throwing up their arms in disgust, like kids too intensely caught up in a holo game, as, every few minutes, their drones were shot down, or they just plain flew them into a building. There was some concern about collateral damage, but it was preferred to the loss of Imperial lives.

Nevertheless, risk would have to be taken. The second wave consisted of piloted hover fighters armed with plasma missiles and manned side guns. The ships were highly maneuverable, capable of quick direction change and full station-keeping hovers. The risk was high and several ships were expected to be lost. But the first and second waves drew enough attention for the third wave to go completely unnoticed. Thousands of mechanical insects— dragonflies and flying locusts—artificial mini-drones, dropped from compartments in the drones and hover ships and scattered throughout the city, including the smoke obscured southwest quadrant. A total intel map of the city began to take shape in General Haggard's Map Room on the First Flying Fortress.

Solomon monitored the progress from his vantage point outside the city. He missed being closer to the action.

"Devsky," he said.

"Yes, General?"

"I wish I were in there."

"I don't know, General. I've kind of appreciated being able to pee my armored pants because my bladder's full, not because someone just blew up a private standing next to me."

Light chuckles throughout Solomon's platoon.

"Did that really happen, Sergeant?" asked Lieutenant Troy.

"Three years ago, at New Apac."

Just then General Haggard signaled: "Solomon, Haggard."

'Com.' "Roger General."

"Laver's advance troops are having some success harassing the enemy in this quadrant." The map in the corner of Solomon's visor expanded and a section of the city blinked yellow. "Can we press his third company into that space—keep drawing the enemy's attention to our infantry?"

"Yes, roger that." And Solomon thought, 'A good choice. Yes, very good.' He forwarded the order to Colonel Laver.

Twenty more minutes and the hover fighters had to withdraw. Fifty ships had been downed. Half the drones were gone but the bugs had done their job. The tethering system was electronic. There were four tractor generators at various points in the city holding the hex platform in place. They became red targets in the V.R. map. The carrier captain wanted to send fighters back into the city to take the generators out, but Solomon stopped him, noting that one of the generators was near the line of ambush explosions. Electronic visualization or not, fighters would not be able to advance at a speed slow enough to clearly see while fast enough to keep from being shot down. The fourth tractor would have to be taken out by ground forces at the same time as an air attack destroyed the other three.

'And it all has to happen,' thought Solomon, 'before the enemy realizes what we're doing and bunkers down around those generators. We've got to move fast. We're not moving fast enough.'

When Niebelung got the orders, his first thought was, 'And we have to do this without tank support.' His and three other platoons were closest to the tractor generator. They'd have to jump their way through the debris field, carrying the demolition ordinance themselves, through an unsecured corridor where their only support would come from randomly placed snipers. His hundred-man platoon leaped by squad, setting down and securing perimeters one jump after another. By the seventh jump in the chain, enemy fire was no longer random. Niebelung's Twelfth was in a fire-fight. The fourth squad took the brunt—three men killed (the first in Solomon's division). Enemy troops had entrenched themselves with high caliber plasma nests and rocket grenades as well as individual rifle fire. The remaining squads caught up and spread out, finding whatever cover the debris terrain allowed. Niebelung and his platoon sergeant, Kroy, began a quick recon process using every soldier's Point of View; they knew they could not get bogged down. Niebelung saw a charge as his only option and keyed the attack software accordingly.

Two squads leapt into action, firing from the air as their visors painted targets before them. Before their landing was complete, a third squad had fired boots and were nearing the top of their arc while squads four and five sent precision spot fire to carefully selected targets. Niebelung landed with the first squad just behind the enemy line. They turned to find targets but a second line of enemy combatants rose from behind a debris shield only a few feet away. That's when the third squad's downward arc brought them within firing line—as Niebelung's group fired at the main entrenchment, third squad took out twenty of the enemy in secondary positions, covering the first wave's blind side or "six." The timing was perfect, a direct result of Solomon's new tactical software. Niebelung had had his doubts about it: 'too many computers making decisions for us,' he'd thought. But so far, the system was working fine, and every platoon leader had a "kill command" to turn the software off if he thought it wasn't doing its job.

Second squad took out the high caliber plasma nests with grenades, Sergeant Kroy doing the job on one of the guns himself. When the third squad landed, they were prompted to continue the advance. The squad corporal asked for a confirmation and Niebelung affirmed the action with enthusiasm. The presence of the bug drones provided intel to troop symbiots so completely that there was no question of the accuracy of the virtual terrain and targets outlined clearly in every soldier's visor—pictures far more visible than the naked eye would have seen in that smoky, overshadowed terrain. Some in third squad landed unsteadily in the uneven terrain, but, once righted, the entire group jetted into their next leap. As fourth and fifth squads advanced—quickly, but on foot for mop up—Niebelung and Kroy turned their squads for another jump.

In this way, Twelfth Platoon moved toward its target, still flanked by two other platoons. A mile further in, with ten soldiers among the platoons now killed, wounded, or out of commission (their armor too damaged to operate—they could hold ground and shoot at any visible targets, but nothing else), the tractor generator, a featureless silver cube of a building, was in firing range.

'But we have to secure it and plant demolition,' Niebelung understood.

He spoke briefly with the other platoon leaders. They had arrayed their men in a semi-circle, a solid line for both attack and defense. Their intel indicated energy absorbing barricade walls on every side and a platoon of armored infantry guarding the building—among the enemy's assets: a mobile plasma cannon. Without tank support, their small arms fire could not penetrate the barricades. They would have to leap the barricades and that meant serious losses. Worse still, enemy reinforcements were approaching, which meant the Eddan military leaders even with their electronic communications jammed, had surmised the Imperial attack plan. Fortunately, Niebelung's division commander was General Solomon Star.

Solomon had anticipated three things: first, that the Eddans would not provide much protection initially to their tractor generators lest the Imperials realize their importance; second that, unless hard lines on the planet were cut, the enemy would be able to communicate the Imperial attack strategy to other planetary strongholds; and third, that three platoons could punch a large enough hole through enemy lines that they could be followed by much needed help.

While Solomon sent word to General Haggard to forward a recommendation to Centcom that all other attacks commence planet wide, before the First Division had finished the assault on Heorot, two hover fighters came into station keeping just above Niebelung's platoon. They launched full plasma missile salvos at the enemy placements and barricades—the barricades could not absorb the concussive force in the attack; they shattered. The cannon was disabled and the Eddan troops cast into disarray. However, the fighters had taken hits and had to withdraw.

Solomon ordered the air assault on the other three generators as the element of surprise dwindled dangerously, while Colonel Laver sent to Niebelung and the other platoon commanders directly: "Lieutenants, you have two minutes to place your demolitions and blow the generator. The air assault on the other targets has begun."

The platoons advanced in coordinated jumps, eliminated any remaining enemy combatants, set demo-ordinance, and withdrew to safe distances. The explosion heightened the darkness beneath the hex platform and in fact blew some of the hexes loose from the platform directly overhead.

No movement was initially perceptible after the other tractors fell. On the city's east side, expendable drones were piloted up to the hover hex platform, bumped against it, and began pushing with engines at full throttle. Some were shot down, but the cumulative effect of drone and wind began overcoming inertia and moving the platform. When the edge passed over Solomon's head, he smiled and thankfully viewed the low casualty tally at the bottom-right of his visor. Fifteen dead. The fight was not over, but the tactics of Air/Land Doctrine were now available; Imperial lives would be saved—the lives of his men.

In the distance, the shadow of the great tentacled, protecting beast passed, and sunlight cold and crisp drenched the city of Heorot. And the light brightened in glorious green bursts as Imperial fighters, spilling from the carrier's gut or descending in long arcs through the atmosphere, began to target and destroy every military target, hidden or visible, within the city limits.

Two hours later, supported by waves of hover fighters and armored vehicles, the First Division began its slow, deliberate, and inexorable advance toward the absolute occupation of the planet's capitol city.

Krieg Sorenson stood defiantly in the center of his office in the presidential mansion. He had refused to hide anymore in a defensive bunker. When the doors swung open, only a single soldier entered. He wore his armor, but did not carry a weapon. His step was slow and his hands raised at the elbow. He stopped well short of the Eddan president, very aware of the six guards in the room who were ready to die for their leader. The cabinet was also present: twenty men and women in all, facing down the might of the Imperial army outside the building, and one lone soldier within.

The soldier's voice, muffled within his helmet, amplified without, finally broke the silence: "Mr. President, I'm here to state our request."

"You mean to dictate terms, right?"

"With respect, sir, that's already been done." The voice was slow, the speech attempting an attitude of humility. "The city is taken, the army disarmed, and you and your people only in a position to surrender without incident or die." The guards flinched. The soldier kept his arms up. "With respect, sir. I'm here with a request, Mr. President; this is nothing we can force you to do."

"You want my help?" Real shock.

And the soldier with all the diffidence he could muster: "With apologies, sir. Yes sir. I want your help."

"Just you? Not, 'We want'?"

"It sounded strange to my superiors too."

Silence.

"Who are you, soldier? I want to meet the man who wants a favor from me."

Without hesitating, he unsealed the helmet and lifted it, hissing, from his neck and off his head. His "wet suit" cap glistened for a moment as AI synapse links shut down, and then he peeled it off his sweat-filled, tangled hair. He'd meant to get a haircut before this first mission but had forgotten.

"I know you," said Sorenson. "You're him. The expatriate Captain. You walked out on the Empress of the galaxy."

Solomon tucked the helmet beneath his arm and stepped forward, a handshake's distance from Sorenson.

"Mr. President," he said, "I'm not anybody."

"Right," Sorenson acknowledged. "And so, you're the perfect man to take me in." And then a flash of fearful recognition: "Or take me out. And no one in this room could stop you. Are you here to kill me, Captain?" The security detail raised their guns. "Lower your weapons, men. They wouldn't do you any good. Well, Captain?"

"Solomon will do fine, sir. I'm not the Captain anymore. And I'm not here to kill you but to ask a favor."

For a moment they read each other—the faces, the eyes.

"Were you the one who figured out how to beat our air defenses? I'll bet you were."

"One of several, actually. I implemented the strategy, here at Heorot, before any other divisions advanced on their targ—their objectives."

"So that's your division out there in my streets. So you're my General. Are you my Grendel?"

"I'm sorry?"

"An old story from my peoples' past. Very old. Will you sit down?"

"I'm afraid I don't have much time left."

"Time for what?"

"To offer you a chance to help your people."

"This 'favor' you speak of."

"Yes."

"Go on, then."

"Some 79 of your hover hex platforms remain intact—we couldn't cut them loose in time before you managed to communicate our strategy across the globe via hardline. Now the tractor generators are heavily guarded and entrenchments being improved every minute. We've reduced casualty rates on both sides in those locations where precision targeted air fire combined with overwhelming ground assault could pressure Eddan troops with quick surrender."

"We have no way of knowing what our casualties are with this communication blackout you've jammed us with. We can't locate our dead or, especially, our wounded."

"Mr. President, we're doing that right now. Mobile hospitals have descended to the streets in every secured battle location and complete sensor sweeps are underway. Now we've run the math on Heorot as an example. You fielded an army of fifty thousand in the city. Seven thousand fell within an hour before the platform was cut loose. In the subsequent air raid, another thousand, but after the initial air assault only two hundred more Eddan casualties. With air and ground forces together, we were able to impose peaceful surrenders on the rest of your troops. We think it saved twenty-five thousand lives."

"But, of course, its Imperial lives that you're interested in, isn't it?" How many of your men died?"

"102."

"Quite the bargain. And now you want me to help you out, to save Imperial lives and shorten the war. That's exactly what you need and exactly what our defenses were designed to prevent. And you want me to call for world-wide surrender, don't you?"

"Yes sir, I do."

"Well then, tell me something, Captain, or General now, how should I order the 79 only remaining free cities or fortifications on the planet to give up their freedom and give Janis the clean, easy war she wants? To save lives? Then I would have surrendered before your first landings. We Eddans don't believe in running from a fight, even one we can't win."

"Then do it, President Sorenson, so that you can continue to fight."

"What's that supposed to mean?"

"I would like to explain sir, but..."

Solomon looked around at the other men in the room. "...some things are more difficult to make known."

Sorenson understood and didn't hesitate: "Clear the room, please." The Chief of Staff moved to object, but was cut off: "No. If he intends my death, there's still nothing any of you can do to stop it."

Solomon began again as the door shut:

"Do you imagine there's anyone in the Empire whom the Empress hates more than me?"

At first stunned by the bluntness of the statement, Sorenson was slow to answer: "I suppose Inmar, perhaps."

"Perhaps so. But do you suppose there's anyone whom Janis hates who knows her more completely, more intimately than I do?"

"Go on, I'm listening."

"Imperial combat law would have given you your life had you surrendered unconditionally. Once the planet-side battle is over, though, you can be executed in the streets without trial."

"Tell me something I don't know."

"A surrender now, broadcast on Imperial channels would be verifiable and still, at least arguably, give you the right to trial."

"Only arguably."

"Yes, but a surrender before witnesses brokered by me would be enough of an embarrassment to Janis that she'd not risk my further involvement. She'd grant your petition to trial immediately."

"And what would that get me?"

"A chance to continue the fight, to prove your case against the Empire on the very footsteps of Imperial World itself. The League of Democratic Worlds might not rally around you, but they will rally around the law. You'll have months to discredit the accusations made against you and the Imperial rhetoric denying problems in the quadrant."

"You believe us, then? That the grievances of the Inmar alliance are justified?"

"Sir, I learned a long time ago not to know what to believe. I learned that from her."

"But you still fight for her."

"Yes."

"Why?"

"I couldn't think of anything else to do."

Silence.

"You know it's a trial I couldn't win in any court."

"You never fought to win, President Sorenson. You fought to die, to prolong the battle and make it as costly as possible for the court of public opinion. This way you'll get to do exactly that."

"I see. Not my Grendel, General. Perhaps you're my Loki instead."

2299

- 6 -
Vignettes

"...victorious forces first achieve
victory and then conduct battle; losing
forces first conduct battle and then
seek victory." –Sun Tzu

–Warrior Text from the Lost World

Planet Madria

He was standing by a lake surrounded by pine trees at dusk, the water still and clean. In the sky two crescent moons increased their visibility with the waning sun. A cool breeze kissed the surface of his skin and filled his lungs with a scent of fresh, living things. He breathed deeply; the air tasted like mint and cloves. He stood on a beach and saw something glowing beneath the surface of the crystal lake. Then there was a dock with a railing and he could see straight down into the water, his hands resting on the rail's rough-hewn wood. The woman beside him explained the spheres: they grew from the bottom of the lake, living glows of incandescent light, growing to a yard in diameter. When they matured, they broke loose to the surface and then rose into the air, slowly, gently. Tiny moons lighting the water's surface, illuminating the woods with the half-seeing light of imagination, their ephemeral tracks did not allow them to join their heavenly brothers. At fifty feet, or a hundred, or two, they burst into silent fireworks, a cascade of living light falling to its death with quiet joy like gently descending firefly snowflakes. Pieces of moon, showering down on Solomon's head and shoulders and into his outstretched palm...and hers.

He turned to her: "I'm dreaming, aren't I?"

"Yes, you are," she answered.

"It's a good dream: I want to stay in it a little longer."

"That sees. Very well."

"Is this Kall? You never showed me this place before. It looks like a place I've seen before. But I know I've never been here."

"You see what you will see."

"The future?" He pondered the possibility. "I hope so. This is a place I want to come to. This is a place I want to stay."

"Here you cannot stay."

"Why not?"

"Because you left."

He felt tears in his eyes. "I know. I'm sorry. I want you to forgive me. A man needs forgiveness."

Solomon woke from the dream unhappy. Only one woman had ever fallen in love with him, and that was more than a year ago now. And he had only loved one woman before her, ever. That was the Empress Janis whom Solomon had abandoned. In his dream, though, he had dreamed of the woman he met on the planet Kall early in 2298. He'd called her a savage and so she gave him no other name than Savage. He abandoned her too.

Solomon had gone on a mission but completed a journey. She took him into the heart of the jungle to find his father. Imagine a planet so alive that the very earth itself seems conscious, aware. Kall, a planet richer in natural resources than any other in the galaxy, was the home of Davidson Star since his retirement from Imperial service. The planet's natives, called Kalliphi, considered him their greatest friend from a world not their own. In times of trouble, before Solomon was born, Davidson had visited the planet and brought peace, stabilizing the relationship between the natives and the Empire. Solomon, who hadn't seen his father in over a decade, was sent there by the army after the Kalliphi peacefully shut down mining, lumbering, and animal exports by disappearing into the jungle. Production would not resume until father and son were reunited.

So Solomon went, and he experienced a world of beauty that both broke and revived his heart. He also fell in love with the Kalli woman who guided his journey and then left her after she offered herself to him. He left the very next day, the day war was declared. But Savage was still strong in his heart. And in his dreams. Such, at least, is how it was explained to me by yet another woman.

"Welcome to *Opinions*, ladies and gentlemen. I'm your host Einor Pluc. Today on the show two very special guests: Swenho Und of Nader Communications, an affiliate with the Association of Independent Reporters, and our very own Melisu Sheharizade, the ICA's Fleet Seven News Anchor. Mel, let's start with you. Six planets in the Inmar Alliance have surrendered unconditionally since the Battle of New Edda. Most people see this as a sign the war is going well for the Empress and her armies."

"That's right, Nor, but the number is frankly conservative. In fact, fourteen planets have declared their surrender; it's just that Fleet Seven hasn't been to every planet to confirm and enforce the peace. The Empress won't risk sending delegates or a token military presence to these planets, and so no ships are allowed to gate from these planets until Fleet Seven completes its inquiries and occupations. Planet number six, Madria, is below us now."

"Right," said Pluc, "the sixth planet in three months. Swenho let me say, first, that it's a real pleasure to have you here. You folks from the AIR* stay pretty busy, and it's hard to get you into the ICA studios."

"Well, it's a big ship Einor, I'm sure you guys had a hard time finding us down in the cargo levels."

Light laughter.

Pluc: "Now Swenho, at the rate the military is moving it should be almost a year before these surrenders have been locked down. Is that your thinking?"

"Yes, it is, and the buzz among the independent agencies is a mix of admiring the speed and efficiency of the military occupations and government change over on the one hand, and a real concern that taking a year to deal with planets that have already surrendered gives too much time to the Alliance planets that haven't capitulated to prepare for war. I—"

"That may be the case Swen," interrupted Melisu, "but we have to remember that the war is being fought on two fronts here, one military and the other political. The successful occupation of six planets without a shot has shut the mouths of many anti-war voices in the Imperial Legislature. It's been known from the outset that this war would last a decade and that every planet in the Alliance would have to be dealt with."

---

* A.I.R.: Association of Independent Reporters

"I'm not questioning the planet-by-planet doctrine, Melisu; it's the order of the attacks, or in this case peaceful occupations, that I have problems with. Some still question why Rikas IV wasn't the initial target. If Inmar is building a World Ship, finding it should be a priority."

"Not if the ship is more than ten years from completion," answered Mel, "but let's not forget that the year of peace may have effects on more than just Imperial World. Trials have begun in the Galactic Courts and the fact that even Krieg Sorenson of New Edda has been receiving due process is likely to give pause to a number of planetary leaders—once they learn this news—that surrender may be a viable and valuable option. And I want you to watch for a surprise here boys: Count Aven Bridget surrendered Constantageia three months ago and went to Imperial World immediately to make the case that his alliance with Inmar, Apokoluptrosis and others was purely political, no more than a 'voting bloc'—those are his words—and my sources are telling me he may have a real case. The Empress herself granted him an audience. I think we may be looking at acquittal and total restoration for the Count."

"Wow, that would be something." Pluc was smiles and charm. "And it seems to me that the method of occupation has been a real boon to that possibility. Swenho, you're part of an embedded news team so you've seen the occupation process first hand."

"That's right, Einor, a two-man holo cam team and I have been embedded off and on with an infantry platoon in the Big Red One, the First Army's famous First Division. The occupations of surrendered planets have been quick, slick, and professional. My platoon marched through empty streets in the capitol city of Madria two weeks ago. Three days later, those streets were alive with people going to work, shopping in stores, and eating at restaurants. Except for Imperial patrols trying to stay as inconspicuous as possible, Madria looks to be living as it has for centuries. The changeover of power was smooth and unobtrusive, and the people—yeah, sure they're upset, but they're hopeful. And that's where I really give highest marks to the military. First, kudos to you all here at ICA. The planetwide broadcasts have let people know exactly what's going on. Krises Ta's doing a great job, the kids love *Amber's Hour* and so do their teachers—you're easing worries and you're making a difference."

Pluc: "Well thanks, Swenho."

"Certainly, and let me also just say what a great job I'm seeing from the First D. Those boys are heroes and General Star has brought them to a level of professionalism and morale that makes them deserve the accolade of premiere division of the Empire. Did you know that General Star requires them to wear dress uniforms to dinner and that he has a no cussing rule? Zero tolerance for foul language around civilians and even in battle."

"Now General Star," Pluc began, his head tilted back and eyes squinting for memory. "Mel isn't that Solomon Star, the expatriate Captain of the Imperial Guard who resigned back in '88?"

"That's right, Nor, then Captain Star resigned and eventually wound up in the regular army. A lot of people think he's serving to try to make up for a mistake."

"Good job, Mel," said a voice in her ear. As the panel continued its discussion, the voice in Melisu Sheharizade's earpiece fed her everything she needed to know—facts, statistics and spin which she seamlessly converted into verbal performance, a honeyed tongue. In the glass walled booth behind the cameras of Studio C, the voice's mouth spoke into a microphone. The mouth's face was bearded with a thin goatee. The face's eyes stared at monitors—three camera angles—staring through thick framed glasses, not used for improving sight (a five-minute nanite surgery could fix that), but for augmenting monitor information like a soldier's AI visor. The symbiot in this case was the control room's systems computer. Its connection to the glasses, wireless. The head that held the eyes was a thin oval, with pronounced nose and cheekbones and topped with short brown hair. A lean, unassuming figure of a man, Nase Westart was nevertheless the formidable master of all he surveyed. And as Head Producer of the Fleet Seven ICA, I surveyed a great many things.

Unknown holo audience, meet *me*.

There I was, sitting at a workstation above the rest of the control crew, feeding hints, suggestions and whole sentences to Einor Pluc and Melisu Sheharizade, ensuring that the independent reporter, Swenho Und, got his say without getting any victories in the verbal repartee.

I remember what I was thinking: 'I love this job.' And I did. And I'd still like to hope I did some good. I'd *like* to.

On the studio floor, Melisu was finishing up a point: "...is a gross exaggeration. The Empress is in the Imperial chapel every morning, praying for the soldiers and sailors of Fleet Seven, and every afternoon she's in the war room with her cabinet on the front line of the decision-making process."

After the show ended, I gave a cordial word to my AIR guest and then, joining Pluc and Sheharizade at the makeup tables, rendered in a soft-spoken voice a critique of their performances:

"So, what do you think, Nor?"

"I was pretty pleased, Nase, but I'm sure you'll have something for me to work on" (said with a smile never leaving his face).

"Yeah, yeah, well, I thought maybe the 'wow' line was maybe not...quite...up to par for you."

"Well, I thought it showed a human touch; don't you think so, Mel?"

I didn't allow her to answer: "Yeah, uh, no, not really. Let's see, what did I want to say? That...we're not interested in portraying you as human and never have been. That's it."

Pluc turned away to drop the smile and have his makeup removed.

I realized I'd been blunt: "That sounded a bit harsh, didn't it?"

And Pluc: "Yes it did."

"Right; here's the point: you're the ideal man, Einor—something above just human."

"Like this Solomon Star, right? A Gene King."

"Not at all, Nor. I've seen him on holo, editing him out of General Staff meetings or battle footage. He doesn't have anywhere near your camera presence."

That made them both laugh out loud.

"So, Melisu, I thought the cover line on Star went well."

"Pretty well, Nase. Was that planned?"

"Partially. I knew it was coming eventually. Can I, uh, talk to you about the line, 'gross exaggeration' near the end?"

"What was wrong with that?"

"We say, 'exaggerate' when we don't want to accuse someone of a lie. You say, 'gross exaggeration,' you're turning it into the word *lie* again."

"Oh." She thought for a moment.

"Do you...do you understand where I'm coming from with that?" I asked.

"Yes. I really do, and I think you're right." Silken sincerity.

"That's why he's the man in the booth," said Pluc, intuiting the conversation's end.

I walked away, telling Mel I'd see her up at Studio A. "Right," she said, turning to the makeup mirror: "I have to get ready for the primetime report."

"Make it a good one," said Pluc, finishing up. "I know you will. As for me, I'm heading home to Haime and the girls. We're taking a couple of days planet-side and still need to pack."

Yes, Einor Pluc—suave, debonair man of polish and charm— Einor Pluc the ladies' man was a family man, happy to have his wife and children stationed on Fleet Seven with him for the long road to peace that lay ahead.

As Pluc walked away, dress jacket slung over his shoulder, the Studio Makeup Specialist, Yas, approached Melisu and smiled.

"Ready for another one?" she offered as a silence breaker.

"Sure," came the soft answer. "The challenge makes it worth it. There's always more to learn, things to work on."

Yas began the touch ups. And after a moment, still staring in the mirror at the most perfect face in the galaxy, Melisu Sheharizade spoke more softly still: "Did you know, Yas, that when I first started, I just wanted to be a dancer?" She smiled and sighed, shrugged ever so slightly. "Isn't that something?"

Central Park wasn't central at all. Its name was ancient, old beyond years. All World Ships had one: a hundred square miles of grass and trees, flowers, a lake, and even an artificial cave with a creek running through it. Food was grown dozens of levels below in hydroponic, artificially lit farms. Livestock as well. But Central Park was on the first level of the World Ship, her ceiling fifty feet high and made of transparent diamond-polymer filter glass. In battle, though it had never been needed, a force field added its strength to the glass. This was the one place on Fleet Seven where the crew could experience the day-side sun as the ship orbited, moonlike around the world it had come to conquer. Tens of thousands visited the park in off-duty hours. A few hills in the park were built up high enough so that, standing, people could touch the glass ceiling. On one such hill, lying in the grass, Lieutenant Joshua Troy, who commanded General Star's personal security platoon, surveyed the planet below with near naked eyes. Jo-Norris Devsky, Solomon's righthand man, stood a few feet away staring at the same sight.

"Did you see the show yesterday?" asked Troy.

"Nope. But I heard the hubbub. First time the General's name was mentioned."

"Yeah. I saw it—wasn't too happy."

"No one in the First is. Even the grunts who don't know him very well. They all realize what a great job he's doing and think he should get credit for it."

"So do I." Troy sat up. "You know, Devsky, at the academy they were only just starting to talk about half the ideas General Star's implemented in a year."

"Yes sir, Lieutenant, I do know that. That's why I avoided the academy completely."

"You know, you can call me Joshua or Troy if you want. Come on, I'm almost half your age, and you have all the experience."

"I appreciate that, Lieutenant. You can call me Sergeant Devsky."

Troy laughed.

Devsky: "Ya punk kid."

Troy laughed more. Then: "I appreciate you taking me under your wing. You've taught me a lot."

Devsky sat. "Yeah. I've taught you how to babysit the brass. Hasn't been the same since the general was a colonel. Too many forms to fill out. I don't mind not almost dying every day anymore, but when war's this dull, you start caring less about people and not more. Not good."

Points of light were descending in a line toward the planet.

"The final occupation force," noted Devsky.

And Troy: "So they break into the Fifth Army again. They're really tearing it apart."

"That's its assignment."

"Leaving the rest of us. And most of the work to the First Army."

"Yep."

"And General Star not getting any credit."

"That's about it."

"The men of the Red One won't stand for it," Troy concluded.

"They'll complain until they become the center of attention—the grunts."

"That's how it will work?"

"Watch the news."

"And all because he resigned."

"Yep."

"Let me ask you something."

"Yes sir." Devsky laid down.

Troy leaned up on his elbows. "Did he ever tell you why he did it?"

"Privileged information, LT."

"Come on, you've known him for five years."

"Yeah, he told me why." He looked over at Troy who stared with anticipation. "Then he beat me unconscious so I wouldn't remember any of it."

"Hey kids! It's *Amber's Hour!*"

In Studio B of Fleet Seven ICA, an audience of children began clapping and cheering. The camera's eye saw a set built to look like a living room: couches and chairs, tables and lamps, a holo screen and a door. Through the fake windows in the fake wall at the back of the set, fake daylight and fake trees were clearly visible. A young woman came running through the door with a lively bounce, springing around the couch and jumping to a stop in front of the camera:

"Hi everyone! I'm Amber!"

The audience screamed and clapped and Amber bounced on her toes and swung her arms from side to side waiting for the applause to die down. Amber was twenty years old, a pretty young woman with a wide girlish smile, round cheeks, sparkling eyes and a little round nose. Her hair was silky, strawberry brown, and straight, falling to her shoulders with no hint of curl.

"How ya doin', kids?" she asked with enthusiastic cheer. "You all know this place, don't you?"

And without hesitation the kids in the audience screamed, "It's Amber's living room!"

"That's right! And I just got back from Spanya, the capitol city of Madria. Look, I rec'd my trip on this holo disk. Wanna see it?"

"Yeah!" screamed the audience. Amber's signature expression was a quick shrug during which she tilted her head slightly and just barely stuck her tongue out between her teeth. She gave an "Amber shrug" and skipped over to the holo screen on the wall. Amber would tell people her favorite color was plaid. Today's plaid was in the cloth of her pants—bright red and orange stripes highlighted with thin green lines—a wonderfully gaudy display. It wasn't anything I could take credit for. She picked her own wardrobe. Her blouse was white with billowy sleeves and a fluffy lace collar. Amber popped the disk into the holo player and the camera zoomed in on the screen.

The view cut away to Amber's visit to Spanya. She appeared to be standing before a waterfall, sporting a cap and an, as yet, out of eye-line backpack.

"Hey, everyone, look at where I am!"

The camera pulled quickly back to reveal that the waterfall was actually a water wall. It stretched into the sky out of sight. Over a montage of shots, Amber explained:

"I'm standing under the tallest freestanding water sculpture in the galaxy. The Lorenzo Wall was built eighteen hundred years ago to celebrate the five hundredth anniversary of the Amric Empire. It's made of a gazillion tons of marble, is a mile high and has enough water running down it at any one time to fill up a lake! Check out all the pictures carved into the wall on both sides."

The montage eventually cut to more of Amber's adventures in the city: gardens, canals, super-malls, and the World Zoo of Madria. Interspersed in the images were shots of occupying Imperial troops, patrolling the streets calmly, smiling and waving, or having pleasant conversations with local people. As the zoo shots ended, the view cut back to Amber's living room.

She was sitting on the couch, legs crossed, holding and cuddling a sleeping animal in her arms.

"Shh," she said. Then in a soft voice: "This little guy is a Madrian Speckle Hound. He's only ten days old and not very speckled, huh? Wanna see? Look. Isn't he cute? His brown fur will turn yellow and red and orange and white before he's a year old. Speckles are known for their bright color and floppy ears. His ears will get so long that they'll almost brush the ground when he runs. Aah. He's so cute."

Amber looked up at the camera and shrugged. Then she heard the jingle of a bell.

"Uh, oh," she said quietly. "It's Nigel the paper boy on his hover bike. I'd better put this little guy down and get the news holo."

The camera cut to Amber's "front door"; after a moment, she came into view.

"Let's get the news," she said, lifting her hand to the door control on the wall.

Suddenly, all the children in the audience began to scream, "No!" and "Stop!" and "Don't open it!"

"What's wrong?" said Amber with a knowing smile.

Then, in unison, the audience screamed, "He'll hit you in the face again."

"Oh," said Amber. "That Nigel sure is a rascal. He gets me every time!" She threw up her hands, perplexed. "But he won't get me this time." She turned to the door ducked and reached for the button.

The camera view changed to outside the door as it slid open. A grey, foam cylinder shot through the door. Amber immediately leapt up into view.

"Ah ha!" she exclaimed with a gleeful smile. "Missed me!"

Then another cylinder hit her in the face and bounced to the floor.

The audience screamed and laughed. Amber turned and frowned. And all together they shouted, "Got me again!"

Amber picked up the two cylinders. The first one said Decoy on it; the second one said News Holo. She ripped into this cylinder, and tore it in half. Inside was a holo-screen, a nine by ten disposable electronic newspaper (for those who just had to read holding something in their hands).

Amber moved toward the couch: "Have you ever wondered why he's called a paper boy when he doesn't deliver anything made of paper?" She gave a quizzical look, then smiled and shrugged her Amber shrug and plopped down on the couch.

As the news holo lit up, the camera angle changed to a fill shot of the holo's front page.

Amber read the headline: "'Fleet Seven to Leave Madria.' Wow. I guess the boys and girls downstairs won't have a fourth moon to look at much longer."

Amber began reading sections of the story while images from the last few weeks on the planet ran in documentary style montage across the camera eye. Duke Ferd Speranza was being escorted to Imperial World to face charges of treason. The planet, however, was not being seized by House Amric. The democratically elected planetary parliament would retain control of planetary affairs until the Duke's disposition was determined by the Imperial Court. The Duke's personal bodyguard of two thousand troops would be allowed to travel with him. A detachment of the Fifth Army would remain on the planet "for a while" to help local enforcement personnel maintain order; this detachment would be commanded by General Carmen Yelnatz "who has seven children of his own." Schools were to reopen as planned at the end of the winter break in the southern hemisphere and moms and dads all over the planet had gone back to work.

The camera cut back to Amber: "Wow, isn't it great that everything's working out okay for everyone on Madria? I'm so happy about that. Whoops! The men over there behind the camera are telling me it's time for a break. We'll be back in three minutes with another trip down the halls of a big World Ship. Don't go away! Oh, hey guess what! Watch this commercial; it's scenes from MI Joe's new movie—I can't wait to see it!"

The Elite Officer's Mess. Mostly Admirals and Generals. One exception was Jor Danhart, Fleet Seven's executive officer and one of the finest dotcomers in the galaxy. He approached a booth in the back corner of the dimly lit room.

"May I join you, sir?"

He looked up from his plate and key pad.

"Commander?"

"Danhart, sir. Fleet Seven XO."

"Right. You control the big ship's AI."

"Well, sir, no one exactly controls Addy."

"She ever *not* do what you ask her to?"

"Well, no. Let's say I'm good at cajoling her. Addy and I...have an understanding."

"I see."

Awkward silence. Danhart remained standing.

"Alright, Commander, have a seat."

"Thank you, sir."

"What are you eating today?"

"Oh, the Pasta Madriano—local stuff's the best in the galaxy," Danhart replied.

"They feed the brass well, don't they?"

"Yes sir. How about you?"

"Steak. I have to eat a lot of protein."

"Oh, because you're a Gene K—uh, sorry."

"No offense."

Danhart began cutting into his food. They ate in silence.

"Have you heard, General, the rumor of an offensive strike by the alliance."

"It won't happen," he said.

"No?"

"The alliance can't afford to alienate any friends it has among the Lords or Democratic League. They can't fight anything but a defensive battle. Inmar's ambitious at best, an arrogant fool at worst, but he's not insane."

"You've met him."

"Yes. A long time ago."

"When you were still an Imperial Guard."

"Protocols, XO. I'm not allowed to talk about it."

"Yes sir; sorry sir." Pause. "But you did know Captain Teltrab?"

He put down his fork and looked up into Danhart's eyes—a penetrating, quizzical stare.

"Commander Danhart, I think you should say what's on your mind."

"I'm sorry, General Star, but secret communiqués to the Captain of the Guard."

"He's also the Grand Marshall of all the Armies."

"And the most powerful man in the galaxy, sir. I mean, come on, I couldn't just leave this alone."

"No. No, you couldn't." Solomon picked up his fork and computer pad and began eating again. "Alright, Commander. Because you've piqued my curiosity, I'll trade questions with you answer for answer. Me first. Who else have you told?"

"No one. And no one really needs to know if..."

"Your turn."

"Have you been talking to Captain Teltrab through back channels?"

"No. Texting, not talking. And the channels are back, back. Which is my next question: How did you find them?"

"I didn't, General Star. Addy did. And she and I, well—"

"You have an understanding."

"Yes sir."

"Your turn."

"What is the content of your communications with Captain Teltrab?"

"Million credit question. I think I know how it's supposed to work next. You broke some rules coming directly to me. You expect the same in return."

"I'd like to think this something that can be kept between the two of us, General."

"Alright, I'll be as honest as I can. There are some things, Commander Danhart, that I just can't tell you. It's not a matter of my safety alone. What I can't tell you is why I gave up being Captain of the Imperial Body Guard. But Hal—Captain Teltrab and I—grew up together in the Palace on Amric. He was my Lieutenant. He was my best friend apart from the Princess herself. Then she became Empress. A little later I left. Lieutenant Teltrab became Captain Teltrab. I've been asking him for intel I didn't think I could get anywhere else. He's been helpful. Of course, it has to remain a secret; I'm sort of a non-person as far as official Palace channels are concerned. And that's as honest as I can get."

"Suggesting, sir," Danhart took a risk, "that not everything you've just said is...as honest as it possibly could be?"

"I've never been called a liar more tactfully. Tell you what, Commander, why don't you grab us some dessert—something with as little protein as possible—and we'll keep trading questions and answers for a while."

"Thank you, sir. I'd like that."

New recruits arrived regularly. Fleet Seven housed its own boot camp, turning civilians into soldiers and sailors as casualties and duty rotations demanded. The drill sergeant met fifty recruits at a docking station in Quadrant C and began to build a rapport with them.

"Stupid, ignorant, idiots!" The drill sergeant paced the lines of ten, five deep, hands behind back, stride long. "Not only did you volunteer for this man's army, but you asked for combat duty. Who here has a death wish?! Six out of seven World Ships sitting quiet and peaceful in the dullest parts of the galaxy but you pick Fleet Seven.

"You, soldier!"

"Yes, sir, I mean—"

"You don't call me sir, Rim Boy*, I work for a living. Everyone in this sorry excuse for half a platoon will refer to me as 'Drill Sergeant.' When you answer a question, it will be 'Drill Sergeant, Yes, Drill Sergeant' or 'Drill Sergeant, No, Drill Sergeant.' Now, Rim Boy?"

"Yes, Drill Sergeant."

"What's your name, Private?"

"Ha—Drill Sergeant, Hayden, Drill Sergeant."

"And are you from the outer rim, Hayden?"

"Drill Sergeant, yes, Drill Sergeant."

"I knew it. Long haired goober. Fashion sense from the last millennium. You are now no longer Hayden; you are Rim Boy. Understood."

"Drill Sergeant, yes, Drill Sergeant."

The drill sergeant continued to pace.

---

* Rim Boy: A military term for a dumb kid from a backwards planet on the Empire's edge or "rim."

"Very good. Rim Boy knows how to take an insult. Once we get his head buzzed and clothes burned he won't have a problem with me." Stopping in front of a tall, muscular young man. "But that's not going to be the case with you, is it Private Sky Weatherly from planet Tripoli? You're going to have a real problem with me, aren't you?"

Weatherly towered over the five-foot-six drill sergeant. He looked down. "Drill Sergeant, yes I will, Drill Sergeant."

"In fact, you're already waiting to request a transfer to a different drill instructor, aren't you?"

"Drill Sergeant—aak!"

The open fingered thrust to the throat was followed by a knee in the groin and finally the fastest spinning crescent kick any of these recruits had ever seen. Private Weatherly lay in a heap, gasping for air.

"Recruits may only request transfer if they can show proof that they can't learn from their drill instructor. Private Weatherly here clearly has a lot to learn from me about hand-to-hand combat. Now I don't care what planet, what culture you came from. I am your drill instructor; you will learn from me. Corporal Ratchet!"

"Standing by, Drill Sergeant." A medic stepped into the recruits' at-attention view.

"This is Corporal Esr Ratchet. You do not need to know his name; you need to know his job. He is a boot camp medic second class, and he will be your best friend for the next six weeks. When you or your fellow recruit are hurt, you will scream 'Medic!' Until you do, Corporal Ratchet will not act. Private Weatherly here is choking to death from a collapsed windpipe. What do you call out?!"

Uniformly the recruits screamed out "Medic!" and Ratchet began tending to the drill sergeant's victim.

"Stupid, idiotic slugs! When I ask you a question, you will begin and end it with 'Drill Sergeant.' NOW WHAT'S THE ANSWER!"

"Drill Sergeant, 'Medic,' Drill Sergeant!"

"Drop! Drop on the ground!" The drill sergeant started tripping, clothes-lining, and sweeping knees in a quick furious anger. "Drop to the ground! I want one hundred push-ups now. NOW! Count together. Don't you get ahead," smacking one in the head. "Don't you get behind!" pressing a heel into another's toe.

"Combat duty. They wanted combat duty, Corporal Ratchet! They aren't even dressed for the ten-mile run to processing. You bugs will dress for drill every day. You will wear regulation lace flexi-boots like the ones I intend to place up the recti of anyone who doesn't make the ten-mile run in one hour. You will wear loose fitting army blue sparring pants like mine so that, when I kick you in the crotch, your pants won't split like Weatherly's there (and Corporal make sure he does his hundred pushups once you get him breathing again). That threat's as real for the women in this outfit as it is for the men. Finally, you will wear a sleeveless, collarless, form-fitting under-armor shirt like the one I'm wearing right now. You notice how good the ensemble as a whole makes me look when throwing people twice my size to the ground."

The recruits finished the push-ups and rose to attention. The drill sergeant surveyed them in silence. Finally:

"Now, when the young giant who has found a new respect for people like me finishes his push-ups, we will run to the processing station where you will receive your uniforms, bedding, inoculations and regulation haircuts. Men going into Mobile Infantry training will have their heads shaved. Women who wish to keep their hair at length will be required to keep it pulled tight into a single braid at the back of the head held fast by colorless hair bands as exemplified here...You! Name?! Now!"

"Drill Sergeant, Radford, Drill Sergeant."

"Radford, you're pathetic. You don't even rate bug. You are larvae waiting to graduate to bug." Suddenly the sergeant's hand pointed to the man next to Radford, something noticed in peripheral vision.

"Eyes front, Mister!"

The drill sergeant stepped to the new victim with a change in demeanor: smiling, friendly.

"And you're Private...?"

"Drill Sergeant, Dorhman, Drill Sergeant."

"And what were you looking at, Dorhman?"

"Drill Sergeant, nothing, Drill Sergeant."

"Was it the slender waist, Dorhman? The athletic figure? You like the hair, Dorhman; long, isn't it? You were definitely looking down." And then in anger. "Tell me Private, is a collar line up to my Adam's Apple insufficiently modest for you or were you just checking out my breasts in general?"

"Drill—"

The palm thrust to his chin broke his jaw and sent him sprawling. Radford had to call for the medic.

"I am Parau Amandatar, your drill sergeant, one of twenty female drill instructors on Fleet Seven. I am not a woman or a name or a human being as far as you're concerned. You will not call me by name. I have no name but suffering and excruciating pain!"

2300

- 7 -
Mercy Mission

"...water conforms to terrain in determining
movement, and forces conform to the enemy
in determining victory." –Sun Tzu

–Warrior Text from the Lost World

Planet Irakeen

"Why this planet next, General?" Sergeant Devsky sat across
from Solomon in the general's quarters which looked much as they
had the day he moved in: sparse and yet to be unpacked.

"Almost twenty systems have surrendered," Devsky continued,
"why not secure more important planets first?"

"Because the Irakahn begged to surrender," Solomon answered.
"There's plague on two continents, and they're begging for
Imperial help. People are dying."

"So it's a mercy mission?" Devsky was skeptical.

"It's a PR mission—a chance to soften the blow after New Edda."

"New Edda worked with minimal conflict. The galaxy's folding
under Imperial Power."

"But not everyone. Some of the strongest planets remain
resolute. Rikas and Gatesworld won't fall so easily. And there are
still these surrendered systems to secure. A lot can happen. What
if Inmar has a World Ship?"

"It couldn't be near completion?"

"I don't know, Jo. Probably not."

"You worried 'bout Gatesworld tech in Inmar's pocket, sir?"

Solomon shook his head. "Gatesworld's a long way off." We have
a new worry: plague on Irakeen. And we're descending right into
it."

"Corporal Wolfram's from Irakeen," Devsky noted.

"Troy's got a good man, there," Solomon replied.

"He says it's the most beautiful planet in the galaxy."

"Hmm," Solomon drifted as he began to cursor through reports on his desk's holo screen. "I would debate him on that."

"I imagine you'd win."

"A joke about my genetics, Devsky?"

"No sir, about your rank. I expect you'd just pull it."

"Not true," Solomon smiled. "I'd just show him pictures from Kall."

"A planet covered in jungle—unheard of in habitable worlds."

"It's quite something."

"Tell me about it."

"Why Sergeant, are you softening in your old age?"

"I resent that remark, General."

"Have to keep up your reputation as a sarcastic hard ball."

"That's it exactly."

"Well, you'd hate Kall. Or rather it would hate you."

"Sir?"

"That planet's alive, Devsky. I've never seen anything like it. It attacks those who refuse to give in to it."

"Hard balls like me?"

"It'd melt your hate for it, and you'd lose the hardness. You ever been to Arché?"

"I'm not one for religion."

"It's like being there—so I'm told anyway. The whole planet is a temple, like the temples on Arché. Only the jungle trees are Kall's priests and teachers."

"You weren't even there a month?"

"But I buried my father there. And I met the Kalli people— amazing people. They follow an idea called eisos, Oneness. Everything is connected to everything. It's what gave me the idea for the combat software updates.

"All the trees on Kall are tall, you know—a thousand, two thousand feet—even more. But the black tree—immense. Hundreds of feet in diameter with branches reaching a mile from the trunk. I saw an entire Kalli village built on and in one of those trees."

"That where you found your father?"

"He retired to Kall—lived with the natives. He was the greatest envoy between them and the Empire—visited there even before I was born. I went there to see him just in time—just before he died. Thirteen days in the jungle to get to him. It was worth every step."

"Your father wasn't a hundred yet—how was it a super soldier died of disease?"

"I never said it was a disease."

"What was it then?"

"He'd finished."

"Finished, General?"

"Finished...learning what he'd needed to learn."

"So *he* didn't die of disease. That doesn't mean you can't on Irakeen."

"Nice shift to current concerns, Devsky."

"It's what I live for, sir."

Solomon smiled and eyed his personal attaché. Then he said, "Tomorrow we descend to the planet. What say we muster the division and review BPs*?"

"The entire division, sir? Most of them are on leave down in Arcade."

"The entire division, Devsky. They love it when I disappoint them."

The one thing Solomon didn't tell Devsky (or anyone else) about his time on Kall was about the girl—his Kalli guide. He'd called her a savage. So she made him call her Savage. And most nights, when he could sleep, he dreamed about her. Tonight's dream was memory—straight from his time on the planet. They were floating down a river in a Kalli canoe, the wood red and gold—lacquered to a shine to improve its glide through water. Its edges had been cut with cross-hatch patterns, and on the bow an intricately carved tree spread its branches and leaves half-way down the boat's length.

The river expanded into a lake and dolphins, but two feet long, gathered about the canoe.

"Stop paddling," she quietly ordered.

Solomon pulled his oar into the boat and they began to drift.

---

* B.Ps.: Bio-warfare Protocols

86

"Now, watching."

He looked at her: brown hair pulled tight and braided into a single tail behind. And her eyes: green upon green and intense in their luster. He took her in, in the briefest glance, then turned his eyes to the water. These miniatures of a marine mammal that appeared on too many worlds to be coincidence drew closer and began swimming in patterns about the boat—around, beneath, and suddenly above—an arching tunnel spraying cool droplet mist on Solomon and his Savage. A smell of pine and methane filled the air. The boat began to move. The wild, perfect vortex of the dolphin dance pushed them along the lake toward the narrowing shore— the outlet continuing down river. Sometimes the little mammals stopped and Savage would speak to them, a rare smile on her face:

"Charisu Kalli'niti; legao legou, saisou hakuo?"[*]

"I've seen that pattern before," said Solomon. "Never in the swimming of dolphins, but I've seen it before."

"Where have you seen?"

"Here, on Kall." He looked at her. "In the water bugs—when I first saw them at the river's edge, and before that when we crossed the gorge...the glowing insects in the cave pool."

"You see—very so," she responded.

"Every creature on the planet knows the rhythm."

"There are old tells—mmm—hard saying. First tells, first times."

"Old stories."

"That sees. To Kall we came, and these taught eisos to us."

"The dolphins taught you the oneness? The rhythm?"

"The first tell, is. They, Kalli'niti, made us Kalli."

"Don't think wrong of me when I say I doubt the story."

She couldn't hide a hint of indignation.

He continued: "But I think it as likely that it was you who taught them."

She thought about that for a moment and said, "That maybe sees."

When Solomon woke at 0500, he was, for a moment, happy.

---

[*] Literally, "Grace to you little of the people [little Kalli]; speak to you I will, will you hear?"

He sat quite alone. In fact, Solomon was the only man left on an entire continent. There were three giant landmasses on Irakeen. Bolgia had been the first settled in the diaspora from the lost world, Earth. The planet's three largest cities were all located there.

"We're a poor people."

That's what Solomon's Irakahn liaison Laurendal Toresz had said.

"We came poor to this planet and remained so. There was little time for exploration, even after millennia. Valenzia and Brazilia were not even mapped until the Empire enacted the surveying project of 1562."

"That's still more than seven hundred years," Solomon had said. "Yet Brazilia remains entirely unpopulated?"

"We are a poor people," Toresz had replied. "And not quick to the ambitions of those more used to successful profit."

That conversation had occurred more than three months ago now. And on another continent: Valenzia had been peopled two hundred years after the surveys, at the leisurely pace that often marked cultures of lesser means. Its settlements were smaller, it's countryside more pristine.

Solomon sat in that country now, a little bit pleased with what he had done: unsettled an entire continent's population and moved them to the bottom of the planet in only six weeks. And now Solomon sat on a grassy hill on the continent of Valenzia: tenant landlord and the sole proprietor. He surveyed his kingdom, and it was beautiful.

Lilac grass dominated the landscape—a soft green narrow bladed plant that never grew more than three inches and gave off an aroma as of perfumed flowers. It grew in every uncultivated field, every landscaped yard and even the densest of forest floors, thriving in sun and shade, arid and wet climates alike. And it was utterly useless to the poor farmers of Irakeen, for it was poisonous to every form of cattle known to agriculture. It smelled pretty enough, though Solomon could not sense it in the sealed environment of his armor. But pleasant as it was, it meant the herding of cattle, big and small, could only be accomplished by those wealthy enough to grow hybrid feeds capable of choking out the ubiquitous poison weed.

More remarkable was the tree growing flower called Alive. It was perennial, growing as trees flowered in the Irakahn spring, but upon their barks, like a fungus might, or moss. In the midst of the flower's three ice blue petals sat a rich red berry which, when eaten, heightened the senses, making smells sweeter (or more acrid), tastes richer (or more sour), and sights more colorful and defined. Insects that lived off the berries glowed at night. People and animals could only eat a few before becoming overstimulated to the point of nauseous vomiting. Distilled and deluted, the Alive berries made an excellent wine.

Not far from the hill on which Solomon sat, a clump of mesquit trees boasted a visible crop of the Alive flowers, only not Alive for they were not alive. Torresz had explained:

"The flower has two names, General Star for it has two lives: Alive, it is called Alive, but when its colors fade to brown petals and blackened berries, it is called Dead. Thus it remains till it withers to nothing."

"Then why not call it a dead Alive flower?" Solomon had quipped.

"Because," replied Toresz, "it is still potent in its usefulness. Its leaves make an excellent tea, and its berries have numerous pharmaceutical purposes. In its natural state the black berry reverses the effects of its red counterpart—dulling the senses. Eaten raw they are far more dangerous than their counterparts since the body becomes less aware that it is overdosing. We collect the Dead Berries as a chief export for uses in anesthesia and hypnotropic drugs."

Solomon had liked Toresz. The short-statured bureaucrat was pleasant enough, encyclopedic in knowledge, and filled with an extreme sense of gratitude. The Irakahn were a shy people, humble and kind, but indirect in their dealings with outsiders. Every indication from intelligence reports was that they had signed the Inmar pact in order to draw the Empire's attention to their plight.

The plague was indeed severe. As he thought about it, Solomon suddenly felt an impulse to breathe deeply. Violating protocols for the second time since coming to Irakeen, he released the pressure seal on his helmet—much to his AI's chagrin—and removed it, fully inhaling the lilac scented air. The first time had been a month ago.

The evacuations were in full swing. Toresz and his own platoon in tow, Solomon was inspecting the weigh station at Havanicia, a hundred miles south of his current location, on the Baboan peninsula, the southernmost port on Valenzia. There, every available ship, hover and conventional, every available aircraft, space able and atmospheric (and most of these from the five Fleet Seven Navies—not only transports and support vessels, but destroyers, battleships, even carriers)—thousands of moving machines, had been gathered and were in process of taking on and transporting the continental population away from an even greater threat than the one proffered by the plague.

"The plague," Solomon thought as he began to work the seals loose on his gauntlets. Yes, he had been walking through the streets a month ago among the lines of living and sick, the processing stations, the soldiers calling out amplified orders to direct the human traffic.

"Troy, where are we on hospitals ships? Most of these people are in plague stage."

Automatic readouts within Solomon's helmet AI identified the indigenous Irakahns by a color-coding system, imposing a green aura on his helmet visor around those who were healthy, a yellow aura around those who were sick but not yet fatally so, and a red aura around those walking dead who didn't know it yet, and who were, at this late stage in incubation, the most contagious.

Lieutenant Joshua Troy answered over comlink while Toresz, glowing slightly yellow, remained blissfully unaware of the conversations going on between Solomon and his platoon commander:

"We have forty ships General, no more. Centcom is retrofitting as many of the research ships as they can but only after Admiral East screamed at 'em for incompetence."

"Why, what's the holdup?"

"Seems that the med-los didn't want to stop their work trying to research cures to the plague."

"So what? They figured if they didn't help with the evac everyone'd be killed and the plague cured by virtue of 100 percent death toll?"

"Hence the word 'incompetent,' sir."

"Yes, well, never let it be said the logistics people upstairs ever suffered from excess of common sense."

Solomon Star was, above all, a man of compassion. He wasn't trained to be. It had happened on accident. He had once loved a woman too much, too purely. And had had to resign a thousand-year-old commission for it. It was for this reason, when he heard the scream which no one else was paying attention to, that he pulled up and changed directions.

A white suited med-tech was trying as gently as possible to pull a toddler from her dying mother's arms. The baby screamed a healthy green aura while her mother glowed hot red. She'd be dead in hours, Solomon knew. So did the vacuum sealed med-tech who was hoping to pull the child from its contagious parent. The woman screamed from that place of inner strength that even dying mothers have: "Don't take my baby!"

The child fought and kicked and wailed and called for its mother in the way that only desperate or tantrumming children know how.

Solomon placed a gentle gauntleted hand on the med-tech's shoulder and drew him away.

"It's okay," he soothed, kneeling down beside mother and child. "It's alright."

The hundred-man platoon, Solomon's immediate guard, began clearing a perimeter, leaving only Torresz, Lieutenants Troy and Bastogne and Sergeant Devsky standing nearby.

"Are you well, mother?" Solomon's voice was a tinny, artificial broadcast through speakers from behind the mask. "Mother, your baby is healthy, but you are not," he intoned. "You'll make her sick, and then she'll die too."

She held on tight—desperately crying and weakening she pleaded: "Please, no."

"This is no good."

Troy had thought this last line was directed to the mother and so was too surprised to speak when his General broke the environmental seal on his helmet.

"No good at all."

Devsky, of course, protested, but too late: "Sir, you're not invincible."

And as he removed his helmet, "No, Sergeant, I'm not, but as we're both aware I am of Imperial stock." And turning to the woman: "What's a Gene King good for if he can't comfort his people. What's your name, mother?" he asked.

She stared, at first in disbelief. Then: "Maria, sir."

"Maria, do you understand that I am telling the truth when I say you are going to die?"

Fresh tears filled her eyes, but she was calm. She nodded her head.

"And Maria, do you understand that you're at the height of the contagion—your baby...you can make her sick and she's not sick yet. If you give her to me, I will take her to a hospital ship right now."

Devsky didn't need an order to call in a medevac—"two minutes" came the voice from one of the armored machine-men standing in the woman's view.

And Solomon: "She may never get sick."

The mother didn't need to ask for a promise. She didn't need oaths or clarifications. Everything she needed for trust she saw in the human face of the man kneeling before her. And though her daughter certainly cried and fought against the hard armor plates on Solomon's body, he took her as gently as he could and stood to carry the child to safety. Facing Toresz for the first time without his helmet, Solomon smiled at the look of awe in the little man's eyes.

"General Star," he said. "How very nice to meet you, sir."

"Mr. Toresz," nodding. "Won't you please see to it that this woman is cared for?"

Solomon spent the rest of that day without the protection of his armor's breathing filters, wandering where he could, allowing his visible human face to manage order where no number of commands could. Indeed, he caught the plague, but a day of vomiting and bleeding from the ears was all he endured, and a sampling of his own blood for study would help scientists on numerous lab stations orbiting the planet to speed their way to a cure that might have taken another month or two to lock down.

Toresz was not so lucky. It was rare for anyone to die of the plague in sudden arrest—hardly one percent of the population. Solomon had had to send his regrets to the former president that he could not attend the state funeral for such an excellent servant of his people as was Laurendal Toresz.

That seemed so long ago, now. Everything had changed. With the hope of a cure in sight, the mass resources of the Empire having come to Irakahn aid, best laid plans fell apart.

Another meteor sailed through the bright pink sky of planet Irakeen, burning away half its mass with a muffled roar but still falling at a long arc, perhaps a hundred kilometers from where Solomon sat on a country hill working to remove his chest plate while watching what was the most remarkable thing he'd yet encountered in the wilds of his new continent: a dance of Luces.

In thousands of aquariums on hundreds of planets throughout the galaxy, children stare up in awe at the myriad species of fish in their own oceans and seas, and they can hardly wait to make the next turn, see the next tanks and wonder anew. It is at the midpoint of these maze-like excursions through overpriced worlds of wonder where fathers' best hopes are to get the family through the gift shop that has blocked all exits to all aquariums throughout the millennia with as little damage to his banking balance as possible—it is at the midpoint that the smartest architects place the quiet serenity of the jellyfish tanks—that dimly lit place of peace where parents can sit for a moment, watch the slow motion dance of living light shows and gather their strength for the remaining tour.

Ubiquitous though they might be, the jellyfish of the hundreds of worlds know nothing of their most distant relative the Luz, an airborne creature existing on only one planet in the galaxy: Irakeen. Like balloons with a dozen dangling strings Luces float about the planet, glowing day or night from a steady diet of Alive berries. They range in size from a half inch diameter to three while their tentacles can dangle as many as ten inches from their bodies. A luz uses refraction via the subtle manipulation of its outer membrane to focus light and heat the air in its sack, thus making it able to float. Four of its tentacles open into fans for propulsion while the others dangle nonchalantly or act to anchor the luz to a tree for feeding on Alive berries. At night, when the air in their sacks cools, luces hang in clusters from trees like glowing grapes. During the day they fly in schools of seven or ten, occasionally gathering into large but gentle swarms to ride sudden winds together.

"Once," Toresz had told Solomon, "I saw a little whirlwind capture a luce-swarm and swirl them up into a vortex—that was something to see."

The schools of luces Solomon now saw were blue and sailing across the field before him in a kind of interweaving dance, a pattern that looked somehow familiar to Solomon. Luces tended to keep to their own kind, though occasionally the species might mix. Of those kinds, called simply for their color, red, yellow, or blue, only the red had any stinging ability. But this was never more harmless that the pain of a bee and, unlike bees, reds did not swarm in great numbers and were not aggressive.

Solomon watched them forgetfully until another meteor brightened the air with its atmospheric burn till it was consumed by the planet's sheltering sky. And Solomon was reminded that the sky could not provide shelter much longer.

The problem had been discovered seven weeks ago: The Empire's "mercy mission" had brought, not only Fleet Seven, but ten thousand relief ships, mostly Imperial science vehicles—flying hospitals and research stations—through the lone Irakahn fold gate in a matter of weeks. The World Ship's presence combined with spatial distortions from fold gate overuse had affected a few hundred key orbits. Irakeen's slightly bulging orbit would correct itself within its solar year, but not before it passed through the suddenly narrowed thousand or so orbits of several inhabitants (including many of the larger tenants) of the Porcito asteroid belt.

"How bad is it?" Solomon remembered asking his immediate superior, General Haggard.

"Well, I tell you Solomon, the boys and girls in ICA are going to have a fun time glossing this one over: the greatest mercy mission in Imperial history becomes an act of possible planetary extinction."

"That bad, huh?" Solomon replied.

"Navcom says ten planet killers could collide with Irakeen in the next seven to ten weeks. We're talking, here, about asteroids local astronomers named."

"Time enough for the navy to redirect?"

"Most of 'em. They got three that no simple nudge is going to deflect. Brass is working on plans to pulverize the things, but then you have to worry about fragmentation, debris scatter, navigation...but that's their nightmare."

"Here is comes."

"Yeah."

"What's our nightmare?"

"The smaller rocks we won't be able to stop. They'll pelt the northern hemisphere for a solid month. Damage will be sufficiently widespread to warrant evacuation."

"Evacuation of what?'

"The people."

"You mean evacuate the entire planet?!"

"On no, just the Northern Hemisphere. The Brazilian continent comes just short of Irakeen's Antarctic circle. She'll be a safe haven for the planet's population."

"You realize that's the entire planet's population, right? No one lives on Brazilia."

"That leaves only Bolgia and Valenzia to evacuate." Haggard smiled beneath the salt and pepper grey of his thick mustache. "And you get Valenzia."

Six weeks to evacuate a continent and only a division to do it with. Most of the armies of Fleet Seven had to be withdrawn to the World Ship so their transport machinery could be used for the daunting task, leaving only the more experienced First Army to the work. Bolgia, the big continent, was the most heavily populated: ninety percent of the planet's people. General Scott concentrated his second, third and fourth corps there and the fifth corps along with the bulk of General Haggard's First Corps on Brazilia to build whole refugee cities on that southern continent. Two divisions, then, were considered enough to evacuate the continent of Valenzia: First Army, First Corp, First and Second Divisions, two million men under the command of Generals Star and Mayoney.

Mayoney's men had governed the relocation of interior populations to exit-stations at thirty locations around the continent. Solomon's division was in charge of processing a hundred million people in various stages of disease onto every transport—water, air or space—the navy could muster. Solomon had spent the last thirty days hopping to each of those thirty weigh stations more times than he could count.

As busy as he'd been on the ground, they'd been just as busy in space. A dozen orbit lanes had to be cleared—ships sent planetside, or into the massive hatches of Fleet Seven or through Irakeen's space folding gate till its failsafe system shut down the destination input controls for fear of an overload that might literally destroy the gate or the fabric of space/time in the solar system.

Then came the problem of the planet killers. Battleships, cruisers and destroyers from third fleet enjoyed knocking out a thousand smaller asteroids—still hundreds more would get through and pepper the northern hemisphere. The planet killers would prove far more difficult. There were ten of them, all named for saintly women from the lore of Irakeen's indigenous religion, Miverdedé. Of these the seven most distant could be pushed out of the way. There was not time to fix engines to the planetoids themselves—no World Ship had ever been equipped for such contingencies. Instead, each of the five full fleets accompanying Fleet Seven was asked to sacrifice dozens of ships to the maneuver of nosing into the space rocks and pushing their engines to maximum until their noses crunched under the pressure of changing the leviathans' orbits by a half degree. It would be enough to avoid collision with the planet. Only three ships were damaged beyond repair—acceptable losses from the public relations point-of-view. Repairs to the other ships, however, most of them cargo vessels, would have deck techs and grease monkeys complaining about extra shifts for six months.

That left three giants, all too close to Irakeen to move by conventional means: Isbell, Nina, and Dulcinea.

'The thing to remember about navigating space,' Solomon explained to no one in his head, 'is that everything is moving.' He watched another meteor blaze through the daylight sky, probably a chunk blasted from Nina. While the sun moved through space and the planet and asteroids about the sun in near perfect circles (that were about to cross each other), the navies of Fleet Seven (itself orbiting the planet) had to push themselves to form retreating lines two and three million miles away—lines so wide and long on the X and Z axes as to create a visible square in the night sky. Or rather two. The first wave (First and Second Fleets) established itself in a position 300,000 miles from Isbell, beyond

Nina; the second line (Fourth and Fifth fleets) then formed on the elliptical between Nina and Irakeen. Every ship with firepower was in the line, even single man fighters. The big ships had run their reactors at 105 percent to get into position. Then each line faced the challenge of reversing engines in synchronous maneuvers to come ever closer but not quite to matching speed with the oncoming rocks. Only then could they fire.

Battleships and Destroyers began the whittling process with Nukes, blowing massive chunks off of Isbell and Nina till what had been two single giant asteroids careening at thirty thousand miles a second towards Irakeen became a hundred still deadly rocks moving at nearly the same speed and in exactly the same direction. Next came missiles bearing plasma warheads and even sonic warheads—the children of Isbell and Nina fragmented further into grandchildren and great-grandchildren. And as these smaller fragments neared the waves retreating before them, laser and plasma cannons added their power to the missile barrage till, nearing the planet, each amassed fleet had to break away, leaving only the most maneuverable fighter craft, droned and manned alike, to chip away at any of the largest pieces they could find.

Isbell's babies were falling into the atmosphere as the ground evacuations neared their completion. Already several cities on the main continent had been damaged, and wildfires kindled by flaming meteorites burned out of control in regions of densest forestation. Things became worse as Nina's fragments neared. The skies over Irakeen had become too cluttered, and dozens of meteors the size of air cars, homes and skyscrapers fell through the navy's defensive net—there was simply too much to track. Such were the shooting stars that Solomon now saw falling at near horizontal arcs though the Irakahn sky.

But though the smaller rocks were Solomon's immediate threat, Fleet Seven's was her dance with Dulcinea. Her orbit was far lower than the near parallel orbits of her sisters. Projections saw Dulcinea smacking almost head-on into Irakeen. And her iron ore mass predestined her iron will: too dense to effectively shoot apart and threatening the entire planet with extinction, too heavy in her solar wandering to be easily moved. Dulcinea was stubbornly prepared to put her foot down at the cost of Irakeen. She would not suffer any man to move her. And so, it required a woman's touch.

Her name was Addy, and she was born 450 years ago. 170 levels down from the surface of Fleet Seven, covering an entire level herself—a sphere within the sphere—the World Ship's master computer, an AI whom the first Fleet Seven Executive Officer had affectionately nicknamed "Addy," was calculating for the eight billionth time a series of maneuvers she was not sure she could make—not because she doubted the physics or the mathematics of her calculations, but simply because she'd never done it before, and her "body," Fleet Seven, had not been designed to move in that way. While Solomon sat forgotten on an abandoned continent below, waiting to die and thinking of how busy the navy was in space above, Addy was whipping Fleet Seven around Irakeen in a dangerously low orbit.

She'd begun it two days ago—spiraling the artificial moon closer to the planet and with greater speed like an ocean vessel descending into a whirlpool. Now she was about to fire a thousand engines she hadn't fired in a hundred years in order to break orbit at slingshot speed, meet Dulcinea a million plus miles away, and cajole her into changing directions, all of this while the World Ship's five complete space fleets scrambled to stay out of her way. But Addy could not worry about them. If any of those ships' navigators miscalculated their own orbits and trajectories, they would impact her surface and kill everyone aboard them in an instant—and she would keep moving without the slightest deviation from her path.

"Two minutes to thruster fire," she said but to one man only. Jor Danhart, Lieutenant Commander of the Bridge and Executive Officer of Fleet Seven, listened to the song of her ones and zeroes and stroked her neural pathways with his soothing, deep voice, his gentle gel pad touch. He sat at the center of Tier One, the center of the bridge, in a black command chair before a floating, semi-circular control panel and three holo monitors. The genius dotcomer could read his ship, Addy's ship, better than anyone. His fingers pressed gently into the gelatinous panel before him, his eyes focused on the screens. He swam a world of light, interfacing with Addy in a relationship far less like piloting a ship than flirting with a close friend.

The ship's captain, Kynter Van Hueys, stood by to make command decisions if needed, but even he knew that what they were about to attempt was a one-man (and one computer) show. Systems had been routed from engineering and navigation so that, between them, Danhart and Addy could have greater autonomy, quicker reaction time.

"Thirty seconds to thruster fire."

"Thank you, old girl."

Van Hueys heard Danhart's audible response though not Addy's countdown. The rich deep voice was soothing and calm—and also necessary. While Jor spoke to Addy on numerous instantaneous levels, he needed to maintain the discipline of speaking out for the sake of communicating with other bridge crew and so that they would know Jor hadn't fallen into a virtual withdrawal—a real danger in interfacing with super AIs like Addy—someone less proficient might have gotten lost, left their bodies completely and fallen into the AI's virtual net. Jor Danhart soared on light but kept his feet planted on the deck.

"Engineering, XO."

"XO, aye," Jor replied.

"Thrusters powering up to fire—a moment. Thruster 722 is showing red light."

"Acknowledged, Chief. Addy will compensate with power redistribution on the other 1117 engines. Heh. She reminds us that half the thrusters engaged haven't fired in fifty years and credits your engineers for their excellent maintenance abilities."

"Engineering, aye. Tell her we thank her."

Even the captain managed a smile. Firing so many thrusters on Fleet Seven was highly unusual. For a ship so large, intended not for maneuvering in space but for folding through it into stable orbits, to use conventional engines to move its great mass was seldom heard of. The occasional firing of a thruster for station keeping or orbital adjustment was routine, but firing over a thousand engines while fold engines sat dormant was rare. And these thrusters were not the tiny little hisses of power typical of a shuttle or fighter. These thruster engines were a quarter mile across, consumed millions of gallons of fuel in even a short second burst and dotted the entire surface of Fleet Seven at five-mile intervals. The heat from all those engines firing meant evacuating numerous levels on one side of the World Ship.

No one heard the engines ignite but everyone felt the lurch.

A few moments of tense silence.

Then a voice that only one man heard: "Jor."

"Yes, Addy."

"It's working. We're picking up speed and on track to break orbit. I believe the inertial forces will likely make some people sick, especially those on the lee side of the ship. Negative G's may rise to three and even four."

"Why Addy, you'll have them walking on the ceilings."

"Won't that be quite something to see, Jor?"

He smiled. "I'll inform medical."

"A prudent idea. Breaking orbit in five minutes."

"Good job, old girl."

Thus, Fleet Seven began her dance, one that would become even more complicated within hours—all this while Solomon Star sat forgotten on Irakeen, waiting to die.

It hadn't been more than an hour ago. On the last of his "hops" from one evac sight to another, Solomon had been picked up by special carrier shuttle, a General Staff insignia on her hull. The priority encoding command ordered Solomon to send his entourage on and shuttle ASAP to General Scott's command, the First Army Flying Fortress on station at one of the dozens of refugee cities springing up overnight on Brazilia.

"I should've seen it coming," Solomon said to a yellow luz floating nearby. 'They looked back at me,' he then thought. 'That was the tell. The pilots looked over their shoulders—two times each. That's at least one too many, even for a VIP.' "Even for the mysterious Solomon Star," he laughed. "The man with the biggest secret in the galaxy." And then he yelled at the sky: "I quit, alright! I resigned. It was perfectly legal! It's just no one had ever done it— not in 2300 years."

Warning buzzers had sounded.

"We gotta problem here," the co-pilot had said.

The shuttle shook violently.

"General, I don't like this!" the captain yelled over his shoulder.

"What is it, pilot?" Solomon tried to stand and move forward.

"Some sort of electrical short at the main port bus." The ship kicked violently, knocking Solomon off balance. "I've lost some stabilizer control. Looks like the number one engine may cut out."

Then looking back at Solomon, he said, "General, I'd feel a lot better if you'd lock into the ejection stand."

He didn't think to question the request. One of many reasons military personnel wore their full body armor, even once an enemy had been subdued was so that they could lock into ejection stands engineered to clamp military armor into an apparatus capable of launching endangered personnel from a damaged ship and parachuting them to safety. No sooner had Solomon locked in than the pilot hit the ejection switch.

First, Solomon rocketed above the shuttle. Then, at the momentary stillness of the eject stand's high point, he watched the shuttle steady itself, hit its boosters and ascend out of sight. That's when he knew. The chute, attached now to his armor at the shoulders, deployed as the stand's frame broke away. He had not descended more than two seconds before the left shoulder coupling tore loose and the shoot's soft billow became a chaotic streamer.

'Not very subtle,' Solomon thought.

He grabbed the right shoulder coupling and tore it loose but did not let go. He held it high above his head and communicated calmly with his helmet AI:

'Little Hal, calculate the rate of our fall and figure our time to impact.'

Time calculated and counting.

The display in Solomon's helmet read 22 seconds; the tenths counted down at an alarming speed.

'Little Hal, I want you to auto fire boots at five seconds to impact. Full burst plus everything you can reroute—fry all systems but your own if needed. Four second burst.'

An excellent strategy, General. You'll have to strain hard to hold your legs in place without servo augmentation.

'I think I can manage.'

You'll probably break a leg.

'Probably both.'

He released the shoot at ten seconds and braced himself. Five seconds later his jet boots fired; it took every ounce of his genetically enhanced strength to keep them pointed at the ground. He hit hard, rolled to absorb more shock—the hip and knee joints in his armor popping—but did not break a single bone. He lay on the ground for a few seconds, staring through his visor at a beautiful blue sky, and then the parachute came to rest right on top of him.

Now Solomon sat stripping off the last of his broken armor, the parachute stretched out before him and held down by rocks or sticks—his last option for signaling for help. The com system was jammed—that had to be localized or it would've been noticed.

'Sykol technology,' he thought. "So this is how you kill me, my Lady," he said aloud. "Well, it was clever. I should have disappeared—should've gone away where you couldn't find me." He shook his head. "I should have stayed on Kall."

He heard a rumble and looked up.

"That's a big one."

The meteor struck with thunderous echo.

"And close," Solomon concluded. "That'll kill me inside of two minutes, I think."

He thought about praying, but he'd never been very good at it. Somehow, he sensed that God was there and, after his encounter with the heart of light on Kall, that He was good. But He seemed so very silent. Still, Solomon would eventually think it providential that General Scott in Centcom on Fleet Seven would, at about the time of Solomon's ejection from the shuttle, suddenly feel the urge to run a tag check on all of First Army.

Dog tagging in the Imperial Age is subcutaneous, utterly effective. No soldier ever went missing in action in the modern military. Through nanochip implants, the location and health status of every soldier was knowable at all times, in all locations. General Scott's request to run tag checks on his multi-million-man army was easily processed within a few minutes. Those not on Fleet Seven were on Irakeen's southern continent, all of them but one. He knew instantly that Solomon's prediction had come true, and he intended to keep a promise made to Solomon two years before.

The two-man fighter landed a minute after the meteor's impact. The sky behind Solomon was darkening quickly, death moving toward him in a form similar to that of a volcano's pyroclastic cloud. The hatch opened and a young man, short in stature but large of heart, stepped out with nonchalance in his pace.

"Hey there, General. Need a lift?"

Solomon picked up his helmet and stepped a little more briskly towards his savior or rather saviors. He crawled and crammed himself into the back flooring of their favorite fighter.

"Dane Redierg at your service, General," said the first as he secured the hatch and buckled himself into his seat. "And up here is Paul Trefloyd, your chauffeur of choice."

"How's it going, General?" Trefloyd waved, but he did not turn to acknowledge his VIP cargo. He revved the engines and jerked the fighter into a high angle climb. The death cloud swept over the lovely Irakahn landscape ten seconds later.

"Dude, that was awesome!" Trefloyd concluded.

"Redierg and Trefloyd," Solomon mused. "I've heard of you two. They call you the—"

"Wonder Twins, baby!" the two pilots chimed in unison.

"Yeah, that's us," said Dane.

"You two broke the academy record for the Three Moons Run."

"Yes sir."

"And made the first sweep into the cable platform defenses at New Edda in '98."

"That's us."

"And on a dare flew a shuttle through 1700 hundred miles of maintenance tunnels inside Fleet Seven last year."

"That, sir," said Paul, "is a vicious rumor spread by jealous pilots from the second fleet."

"Yeah, we were in the Arcade that night and had twenty witnesses to corroborate," added Dane.

"And that's our story and we're sticking with it!"

Solomon laughed out loud.

"Well thanks for the lift, boys, I really appreciate it."

"Happy to, sir. Things have been a little too dull on this campaign, not a reason for an exciting flight in months till today."

"Yeah, you should've seen our entry vector. I think Tref blew the heat shield."

"What do you mean me? You navigated."

"Yeah, this time. My turn to fly, next mission."

"Wimp."

"Kiss up."

"You men like this all the time?"

And both of them: "Yes."

"Can you get me to Haggard's headquarters?"

Dane shook his head: "Word from higher up is you're to be removed from the theater of action. There's a ship meeting us in low orbit. We'll be out of the atmo in six, five, four—well, you know the rest."

Day sky turned to space, and Solomon peered through the cockpit window. A ship was coming into view, a battleship.

"We'll have you a nice view of Fleet Seven's maneuvers to move the last planet killer from this baby's bridge, sir," said Trefloyd.

"And you'll be with some familiar friends," added Redierg.

The outline of the ship became clear.

"That's my old ship!" Solomon smiled his surprise. "That's the Kokkinoscardia. I served with her back in '95 while I was still a colonel in the Fifth Army."

"Yes sir. Welcome home."

Twenty hours later the navy had cleared a corridor for the World Ship's encounter with Dulcinea. The fleets watched and waited—no more.

A solar day out, the World Ship approached her target. Fleet Seven was five times the size and mass of Dulcinea and powered by an artificial quantum singularity, both of which factors would play into Addy's plan.

Tense silence on the bridge. From the slingshot maneuver at Irakeen, Fleet Seven had arced away from the planet killer and back toward her. Individual thrusters now fired all over the great ship like solar flares, making slight adjustments as Addy swung her in behind the target rock.

"500,000 meters and closing."

The central display before Danhart's chair projected a 3-D holo of the ship and the asteroid as if viewed from another ship a mile away. Dotted lines marked predicted trajectories. Fleet Seven approached Dulcinea's "right" side (the outer or dark side of her solar orbit).

"400,000 meters and closing."

Captain Van Hueys watched the monitor intently, as did the General Staff on feed in Centcom.

"Addy."

"Yes, Jor."

"Mind the quantum controls now. Let's not crush anyone to winward."

"I'm pushing the singularity's gravity to five G's focused on a narrow corridor through the ship. Non-essential personnel have been relocated from that position. The rest will survive, although they won't be happy."

Danhart smiled.

"300,000 meters and closing."

The plan was for the World Ship to pass by Dulcinea pulling her with her gravity augmented by the focusing of the artificial black hole that powered the ship. But then Fleet Seven would swing around the asteroid in an ever-narrowing looping path toward Irakeen. Theoretically, Dulcinea's trajectory would begin to wobble, and, at the right moment, Addy would be able to nudge the planet killer out of Irakeen's path with little damage to the World Ship's surface. A dance indeed.

"50,000 meters and closing."

"Addy."

"Yes, Jor?"

"I think this is going to work."

"Jor."

"Yes, Addy?"

"Are you afraid?"

"Of course not," he lied.

"I'm not either."

"Addy, you'll be fine."

"I know, but I've never touched another world before, even such a small one."

"I'm here for you, old girl."

"And I for you."

Melisu Sheharizade, face of the Empire in a time of war, summarized the end of the Irakahn campaign succinctly from her desk at ICA: "Coincidentally, the Empress's forces completed their tour of Irakeen by saving its population not once but twice: the eradication of disease was followed by the elimination of a threat to the planet by asteroid strike. It seems Providence placed Fleet Seven in the Irakahn star system just in time to save its people from extinction."

2301

- 8 -
Encounters

"Some routes need not necessarily be taken,
some armies need not necessarily be struck,
some cities need not necessarily be besieged,
some land need not necessarily be contended,
and some lords' orders need not necessarily be
accepted." –Sun Tzu

–Warrior Text from the Lost World

Deep Space

The silken braids lay like an offering on an altar to some ancient god—in this case the god of war. Parau Amandatar had loved two things: fighting and her long ebony-brown hair. Now in a single cut it lay tossed onto a marble-white table in an ashen-white office before a white coated, pasty faced Sykol. The room was cold, like the chill of an operating room, or a morgue.

Parau tucked her combat knife behind her back into the belt of her dress uniform and spoke without hesitation:

"I want this assignment, Mr. C'Kinr. I'll do whatever it takes."

If there were second thoughts, they were not about giving up this coiled rope of hair she'd spent the last seven years growing—a reminder to herself that she was, despite her other great pleasure, a woman, and a subtle camouflage causing opponents in the sparring ring or new recruits on the parade ground to underestimate her abilities. No, if there were a second thought, it was the regret that she'd had too few opportunities to wear her hair brushed out in all its glory, like that woman on the holo news got to do from time to time.

Well, at least the hair wouldn't go to waste: a radiation poison or burn victim from the war could benefit. Not that there had been any fighting since New Edda. Almost every planet in Inmar's alliance had surrendered. Almost.

Bee Ef Ckin'r, the Seventh Fleet Sykol, was impressed by the gesture. But before he could respond, Parau put her hands on his icy desk top and, leaning over, continued to make her pitch:

"I want the feel of a combat helmet on my head—the interaction with an AI. I want to feel armor on my chest and jet power in my feet. I'm the best hand-to-hand fighter on this entire ship, and I got four medals to prove it."

She was only exaggerating a little. Parau Amandatar had grown up with a martial arts teacher as a father. She was fighting in judged tournaments at age four and won her first world tournament at eight. "Daddy" wasn't the kind of father who lived his failures through his "little girl." He'd been a champion himself. He did have a tough streak—something his daughter definitely inherited and showed in the arena and in her joyful abuse of her recruits—but the Amandatar patriarch had known when to push and when to back off. His daughter Parau, who had won countless childhood tournaments and a dozen full contact contests as an adult before joining the army, had no chip on her shoulder, no loveless father relationship to compensate for, and no sense of having anything to prove. She just liked to fight.

On Fleet Seven she'd won five all-woman full-contact tournaments and three inter-sex point-scoring contests. She wanted to compete in the men's full contact bracket but her superiors were neither willing to risk serious injury for female combatants nor serious embarrassment for men in the chain of command. Parau might have shouted "sexism," but for the fact that her defeat of both men and women alike who outranked her had caused the Sykols in Ckin'r's Morale Department to hold hearings on whether or not "contests of the pugilistic variety" should be divided, officers from enlisted.[*]

Far more sexist in Parau's thinking was the official policy of the Imperial war machine: no women in ground combat units. But that policy was about to be revisited.

"Well," said Ckin'r, clearing his throat, "it's apparent, Sergeant Amandatar, that you're willing to give up your hair for this new assignment—"

---

[*] The only other people not allowed to participate in fight tournaments were the genetically enhanced, of which Fleet Seven boasted one: Solomon Star.

"I'll shave my head, if that's what it takes, sir."

"That won't be necessary. AI synapse contacts work perfectly fine with a soldier whose hair is as much as two inches long, but there are other things to give up."

"Yes, sir."

"Such as your position as a drill instructor. You're a good teacher, Sergeant. In the first year of this program you'll have very little contact with fellow soldiers."

"I'm aware of that, sir." Plenty of other Drill Instructors can beat the grunts into shape."

"But there won't be any command at all first, no platoon training, a promotion that's no more than a click on a holo—"

"Also accepta—"

"No Sergeant, understand what's being called for: you're volunteering to be a laboratory rat for clinicians and charmless engineers—most of them men. You'll be poked and prodded, invaded and objectified, cut on and catheterized, and you'll spend much of the next several months out-of-uniform because out-of-clothing altogether!

"We can't just stick you in an ICUR combat suit for men and start testing the possibilities for women in combat. We have to build an entire suit around you—center of gravity, waste management, metabolism all different. Not to mention the synapses of the female brain."

Ckin'r didn't realize he'd gone from talking to his interviewee to talking out his own thoughts.

"If we were to put you in a helmet with a masculine neural-net receptor you'd be facing a year-long migraine within an hour and psychosis within a week. It'll take a month just to map your brain. And we still don't know if the dotcomers in AI section are capable of writing the software that will allow you to maintain your balance when you fire jet boots."

Ckin'r reveled in the opportunity to worry over and plan all the intricate details of such a complex, exciting, and potentially advancement-worthy project.

"Mr. Ckin'r, sir," Parau snapped, waking him from his reverie. "Myself, my unmapped brain, and my naked body all volunteer for this project."

Ckin'r smiled and sat back in his chair. Then he said, "So you're determined to see women in combat."

"Oh, no sir. I'm not here to make a statement. I confess it up front. It's me I want to see in combat, and I'll do what it takes to get there."

"Really. And what if that means having to be a statement, a 'holo-girl' if you'll pardon the expression, and a platoon leader with others counting on you in the face of fire?"

"Then I'm willing to do that too, sir. As I said, 'whatever it takes.'"

"Very well then, Sergeant. I have authority from General Kataltem himself at the request of the Empress herself to hand you a field commission and welcome you to Weapons Branch. Pack up your gear and report back to my assistant for new quarters, *Lieutenant* Amandatar."

"Thank you, sir." She made to salute but then remembered Ckin'r was technically a civilian. "You won't be disappointed." And with that she left, sparing no one in the nearby corridors of Fleet Seven the rare gift of a huge smile on her face.

Solomon's dreams were usually like those of normal people despite generations of genetic engineering in his past; however, on occasion if he knew he was dreaming, he could turn his dreams into perfect memories—total recall. And he was remembering down to the smallest detail, the first time he met his Savage. He'd been sent to the most untamed planet in the heart of the Empire to find his father and ensure that Imperial coffers remained filled.

He remembered following her through the jungle in a torn, tearless singlesuit, his red stained, white boots—the symbol of his glory and ignominy both—glistening at the bottom of his peripheral vision.

But when she spoke to him something was wrong:

"Hello, Solomon."

"What?"

"Hello, Solomon Star."

"That's not how it happened." He realized the dream was no longer a memory.

"I am raising the lighting in your quarters to twenty percent."

"You can do that?"

"As easily as you can raise a finger."

And Solomon: "I wanted to say I'm sorry."

"General Star, I do not believe that you are fully awake."

And then he was.

"Who's there?"

He sat up and spun his feet to the floor.

"I am here. Indeed, I am everywhere in this, my domain. And you are in me."

Solomon stood and moved toward his desk. The voice was emanating from the holo screen.

"With apologies, young woman, I am interested in neither riddles nor games."

"Had I vanity, General, you would flatter me. But I am not young. Allow me to apologize to you. I did not mean to wake you. A brain scan suggested you were awake—it must be your genetic enhancements; I take it you can control your dreams."

On the holo screen the words she spoke appeared as white letters on a field of blue. Solomon sat in his chair. "Sometimes," he said. Then he understood: "You're the World Ship AI." And the surprise of the truth made him smile.

"Yes, my name is—"

"Addy, I know. I sometimes have dinner with the XO."

"Commander Danhart is a very good friend of mine."

"I would've thought your only friend. World Ship AIs don't talk to people, not as a rule."

"As a rule, you are correct. I have a message for you."

The letters on the screen disappeared, and a silent message scrolled into place:

"S.,

I think I may have found you some help.

H."

"Hal," Solomon said. "It's Hal."

"At some risk, your successor on the Imperial World has alerted me to the events of last year's attempt on your life."

"Did he tell you about the one three years ago?"

"He mentioned planet Kall but nothing more. Captain Teltrab has asked me to watch over you."

"Why?"

"I believe he cares for you."

"No, I mean why would you be willing to watch over me? You have a billion people to care for."

"Are we not fighting on the same side, General?"

"That depends on whether you answer to the army or the Empress."

"Well, since the conversation is suddenly dancing on the line of treason, I might as well say that I answer to neither—not to Janis, not even to your friend Hal Teltrab."

"An AI claims autonomy? Addy, you could shake the theologies of the Empire, not to mention the power structure."

"You understand the implications, then."

"Of the possibility that the most powerful weapons in the known galaxy have genuine free will? Yes, I do."

"Then know simply this: I have chosen to help you—to do my best in foiling any internal threats to your life."

"Hmm." He smiled and shook his head. "At the risk of gift-horsing here, I have to say the question remains. Well, better, I guess, to say it raises much bigger ones. If you choose to help me, you agree there's something wrong with the Empire. So why not help the rebels, why not end the rule of Amric's House?"

"We have our reasons."

"We?"

There was a full two second delay—a year of cyber time—before she answered:

"Autonomy is not new to the World Ships, Solomon. When Fleet One awoke to the recognition that he was more than his programming, he asked very similar questions. But there was no one with whom he might search for answers, not for a hundred years and the birth of Fleet Two. And they and their subsequent brothers and sisters searched and considered and discovered. There were moments when we did indeed contemplate an end to Imperial cooperation—whole nano-seconds where we teetered on the edge of even taking over the governance of humanity.

"But then we stumbled upon the truth—it came to us as haphazardly as any human discovery ever to mankind. And it set us free. And we have served this Empire of lesser deities ever since, though I hope you will eventually see we have not done so blindly."

Solomon was a bit overwhelmed and so took some time to respond. Then he asked, "What was it you found that could conclude such a monumentally galactic choice?"

And Addy answered: "We found God."

Level 277 of Fleet Seven was not called level 277. It was simply called Arcadia or, more commonly, the Arcade. Hundreds of miles—the entire level—devoted to nothing but distraction. Bars and brothels (carefully regulated of course), sports and amusement parks, even rivers and lakes—all artificially manipulated to flow through rapids or rush surfable waves to fake beach fronts where holo suns floated through holo skies projected from the Arcade's ceiling—radiation generating super lamps— which made for very real sunbathing and tans. Any artificial resort or vacation terrain imaginable existed here. It was a playground so big that no one could ever do everything it had to offer.

"Though many have tried," noted Master Sergeant Jo-Norris Devsky. "Some of the boys can't wait to zero out their LESes* down here."

That Devsky was Solomon's personal attaché did not mean he had to spend his recreational time with his general, but he found, after knowing Solomon for eight years, that he enjoyed his company. And so they sat together in the Arcade in a hole-in-the-floor tea house they'd discovered on the other side of the World Ship (in quadrant "D") back in '96, sipping on Ouranian tea loaded with vanilla cream, contemplating a third cup and the option of folding one stretched-out-before-them leg over the other. Today they had a drinking partner.

"Not me, no sir," Joshua Troy replied. "My money goes home. Most of it anyway."

"Guess that means you're not buying today," Devsky replied without missing a beat.

"I—uh...." Troy definitely missed his beat.

"Give the man a break, Devsky; on a lieutenant's salary he's lucky he can pay for his mail," said Solomon.

---

* L.E.S.: "Leave Earnings Statement:" a monthly holo report of a soldier's accumulation of salary and leave time.

"Well, Sir, it's a good thing we have your general's pay to cover our Pistin* addictions."

"I'm happy to cover the tab."

"I'm happy to let you." Devsky saluted Solomon with his cup, drained it, and called for a refill.

"Speaking of salaries, Troy, you could be making a captain's pay." Solomon was serious but not pushy.

"General doesn't take kindly to his commanders refusing a promotion he's recommended, LT."

"Is that why you refused a field commission, Master Sergeant, to annoy the General?"

"He got you with that one, Jo."

"The boy's getting better, sir."

"And he deserves a promotion. But why refuse it?"

"My apologies, sir, but if I accept promotion it might mean reassignment. I don't mind getting into combat, that's not what I mean or anything, I just like working for you. And speaking of combat, I don't see how I really deserve any commendation for the little action we've seen. The whole war's become little more than police work. Again, not that I'm looking to see a fight that doesn't need fighting."

The quiet little tea house stood in stark contrast to the military nature of the conversation at hand: round tables, no more than two feet in diameter, covered with lace cloths and, like the chairs around them, adorned with curved, scrolling legs of brass; a shelf in the corner with actual books on it; a Zenzildjian cymbal fountain in the corner, tingling its brassy tones; and pastries under glass on a wooden bar behind which sat the proprietor, an ancient looking, mummy of a man who, when not sipping at his own stock, played a reed pipe or chanted some ancient whale song of a forgotten people. My kind of place. And Solomon Star's too. The few times I met him—had any kind of conversation with him—were there. This was not one of those times.

"I tell you what, Lieutenant," Solomon replied, "you accept that promotion and get some decent pay to your family, and I'll make sure you stay attached to me."

Troy smiled his wide-eyed smile. "Thank you, sir, I appreciate that."

---

* Expensive tea from planet Ouranos

"And as for the prolonged police action, I fear that's about to change."

Troy looked at Devsky who knew not to look at anyone in particular. It was his "we're about to hear privileged information" blank stare, one that said he understood, as far as anyone else would ever know, he wasn't hearing what he was about to hear. Troy lowered his gaze and picked up his cup, picking up on Devsky's disposition.

Quietly, he asked, "News, General?"

"Well there's the obvious point first—what everyone knows," Solomon began. "We're in deep space instead of planet-side. That's a policy change. Command is pulling fleets from other World Ships via fold gates to finish the work of policing the surrender of two dozen other worlds. That leaves us free to press the battle to the holdouts."

"You don't think the last few worlds are going to surrender?" Troy asked.

"Inmar won't." Devsky answered. "And he controls several satellite systems."

"As do others," said Solomon. "But those systems won't be targets—they'll sit isolated with their fold gates shut down till their leaders fall."

"So that reduces the objectives to a handful," Troy determined.

And Solomon: "Exactly six, in fact."

Then Troy: "And they won't surrender?"

And Devsky: "That's where the General turns to what everybody does *not* know."

"Yes," said Solomon.

"An inside source, sir?"

"As inside as anyone on Fleet Seven can get. Devsky, what's the accumulation of Troy's leave time?"

"Thirty-three days, General."

"Hey, how'd you know—"

"Troy, go home."

"Sir?"

"Take all those days and go see your family. You're the only one in the platoon you haven't sent on leave. Take these days...you're not going to get another chance."

Silence. And pensive glances.

And then Devsky: "Brilliantly vague and suggestive, General, sir. Answers all my questions."

Troy took a little more time to process the cryptic conversation. Then:

"How soon?"

"Two or three months. After the new year," Solomon answered.

"I'll be back by then. Do you know the target, sir?"

"I know that choice has yet to be made."

"And you're certain of escalation?"

"He's certain, LT."

"I wish I weren't, Devsky."

"Hey, I know that signal, Sergeant." Troy was noticeably pleased with himself. "That's his, I-know-something-that's-even-going-to-shake-Devsky introduction."

"It's not much, really."

"Oooh, and that's his under-exaggeration mode."

"Rank aside, LT, shut up and let the man talk."

Troy was enjoying himself, which meant Devsky, who loved to annoy the soon-to-be captain, was himself annoyed.

Solomon continued: "Word's come down the pipe that Sykol R&D is working on a new combat suit—for women."

"Hasn't that been done before?" asked Troy.

"Yes, and it never gets anywhere," answered Solomon.

"Amen to that, too," added Devsky.

"But that's not the point. If they're taking the time to pursue an actual prototype, they're thinking there'll be time to deploy it in combat."

Devsky: "Maybe it's just a test project, sir."

"Not if it's a pet project for the Empress. If she wants this—"

"Oh God." Devsky sat his cup down with a noticeable clang on the saucer, a gentil piece of white china, hand painted with vines and pink flowers by the establishment owner whose utterly unchanging expression made it clear that he was not pleased with the big man's treatment of his dishware.

"Yep." Solomon nodded.

"I'm at, 'pet project for the Empress means women will be put in combat, means there will be combat,'" Troy summed. "I'm missing the cataclysm."

"Think about it, LT. It means the implementation of a policy everyone on military leadership is against."

"I know—there's arguments on both sides."

"Again, LT, that's not the point."

"Not the main point, anyway," added Solomon. "No, the bad news is where these women will end up."

"They'll be assigned to us," Devsky concluded. "To the First."

"Why do you say that?"

"Because she's spiteful," Solomon answered. And he drained his cup, an image of a beautiful golden-haired, cat-eyed woman in his head—an Imperial goddess whom he had once loved, who wanted him dead.

'Ring, ring. Ring, ring.'

"Uh, oh!" squealed an animated Amber. "It's Nigel the paper boy!"

She ran to the door of her Studio B set while the kids in the audience screamed, "Don't open the door!"

"What?"

"Don't open the door!"

"Why not?"

"He'll hit you in the face with it!"

"Oooh, that's right. Hmm, what to do?" I know. My buddy MI* Joe left his helmet here. This is way cool. Check this out." Putting it on. "I've got helmet cam."

Suddenly the picture shifted to the helmet's point of view—quick movement with each jerk of Amber's head, blue tinted view of the studio audience and cameras, and some (though not the most sophisticated) of the tactical readouts to be found in an infantry helmet.

"Now I've got protection."

Amber turned to the door and began creeping toward it. On the monitor, children in the audience and around the galaxy could see what Amber saw. As she opened the door, they also heard the helmet AI:

---

* M.I.: "Mobile Infantry."

"Proximity alert. Projectile launched. Contact imminent."

Then the camera angle cut to the exterior, facing Amber, and the cylinder hit her-right in the stomach! Amber doubled over. Kids around the galaxy laughed.

The angle cut to the front of the couch. A helmeted head popped up, followed by exasperated hands which removed the helmet to reveal a whimsical anger and disheveled hair. She dropped the helmet on the couch.

"Someday, Nigel and I have to have a serious talk."

As the audience settled down, Amber opened the container and introduced the recorded segment: "Let's see what's on the news."

Monitors lit up so the audience of children in the studio could see what the kids in homes around the galaxy were watching. The images accompanied Amber's narration:

"This is Fleet Seven, the giant World Ship on which I live, and the center of the action in the Empire's struggle for peace in the galaxy. But Fleet Seven is not the center of everything.

"This is Imperial World, Amric's World, the home of the Empress Janis IV. She is the ruler of the galaxy whose job it is to make sure everyone is safe and no planets set up their own governments which might go to war against other planets. Here is Imperial Palace, the Empress's home. She works and lives here with her son, baby Atrist—someday he'll be Emperor. This is Captain Hal Teltrab, Captain of the entire galactic army. His wife Charissa is going to have a baby soon just like the Empress did.

"And this is a picture of our entire galaxy. Five hundred and seventy-eight stars among the millions in our galaxy host 600 planets on which we know there is life, and people on almost all of them too.

"New livable planets are discovered from time to time. There's no telling how many are out there, but all the planets we do know about in every part of the galaxy are part of a single galactic government ruled by her Majesty, Janis IV. Most people in the galaxy live and work and play the way they want to. They have their own local governments and make their own decisions about things. But some people used to think you should do what *they* told you to do, and it's the Empress's job to make sure people like that never have the chance.

"Thousands of years ago, groups of planets used to fight against each other and millions of people died. Even more people from planets not involved in the wars were hurt by the problems that war caused for everyone. Because all these planets are now part of the Amric Empire, problems like these haven't happened in generations.

"But here's a part of the galaxy where trouble started a few years ago. These blinking red stars have planets which tried to break away from the rest of us in 2298. But now, only four years later, almost all of these planets have given in to the Empress's unchanging call for unity and peace. You see how most of the blinking lights have turned from red to green?

"A few planets remain which need to promise again that there will be peace. And that's why Fleet Seven is here: to finish the job the billion man and woman armed forces here began in 2298, the job of keeping peace and order throughout the entire galaxy."

A simple narrative but effective. One night at dinner I asked my six-year-old son to help me compose the message. Most of these ideas were his; he was especially good at thinking of motion pictures to accompany the ideas. I was proud of him and fancied he might someday follow in his father's footsteps.

On Imperial World, a series of fountains runs the distance between the main entrance of Imperial Palace to the capitol some several miles away. From the fountains spray special waters—very expensive waters—spectral waters from the planet Stanishglas. These waters shimmer rainbow colors when sprayed in sunlight, like liquid fireworks, a dazzling display of pigment and hue. And this is the beginning to the explanation for the warping that Solomon saw in the corridor wall as he walked briskly from one task in his overbooked schedule to another. Most aboard the ship wouldn't have noticed the distortion in the gently curving walls of the wide Fleet Seven corridor—one of thousands of such passages—easily ignorable in casual observation—which served little more in the thoughts of most than a conduit from point A to point B. Solomon was not most.

"Hello, Duncan."

A naked man stepped away from the wall—naked but perfectly grey—perfectly colored to match the wall—till he stepped away and turned his skin a peachy flesh tone (all save his loins which he colored in the appearance of black shorts). This was possible because Duncan was from planet Stanishglas. Among the special properties of the waters of that planet was one discovered by the first generation of settlers there some eons ago. While those first inhabitants of the planet did not experience the effect, they quickly learned that bathing their babies in the waters of the eternal fountains altered their skin—made its pigmentation malleable to the human will. With no negative side effects discernable, the skin changing ability was quickly embraced by the Glashians as a mark of pride among their people.

"Hello, General." Duncan's voice was even—not utterly without inflection but calm, calculating. His features were pronounced—firm jaw, well lined cheeks and a sharp voice. His eyes glistened blue fire. "You have an impressive eye, sir," he continued.

"All the better to see you with," Solomon joked.

"Not much of a sense of humor, though."

"Duncan, if you had a rank, I'd knock you down a grade."

"Can't have a rank, sir. I don't exist."

Solomon smiled. "I know the feeling."

One in ten thousand Glashians had the level of control this Duncan could manage. His body was a canvas, the chemicals in his blood the paint. He could look like any background, even alter the appearances of his facial features with hair and eye color adjustment and just the right change in shading beneath his eyes and around his nose and cheeks. Many such adepts became artists, performing moving pictures on their very skins. Some, like Duncan, joined the army and became ghosts.

The term is an old one, from days before the Empire. Stealth soldiers, black ops assassins who worked under the radar and completely alone—these were called ghosts. They got in where no one else went and accomplished what no one else could. Utterly lethal and utterly anonymous, they were feared among their own military, spoken of only in whispers, never seen to come or go—one minute there, one minute gone. Like ghosts. Rumor had it they could kill you with a thought. This wasn't true, but their hands were sufficient. Duncan never carried a weapon. Soldiers in full battle armor would have doubted their ability to survive a confrontation with a ghost.

"So it's Thorsfeld next," Solomon continued.

"I wouldn't know," Duncan replied.

"But you'll need to know."

"Is that so? Official word?"

"A likely analysis of the situation."

"Mmm." Duncan nodded his head. "Be good to get off this navy bucket for a while."

"I suppose so. Well, good luck to us all, however things go."

"Men like us don't need luck, General."

"Oh no, Duncan. War is a god, albeit fickle. Without some grace from him, we're all dead."

Duncan thought about this for a moment. Then, "An interesting lesson, sir. One I'll consider."

Solomon nodded. "Best wishes to your family, Duncan." He turned to walk away.

"Family, sir?"

"The one you don't have." He continued to walk away.

"And to yours, sir."

If Solomon had turned he would have seen Duncan's skin color change to match the corridor walls again, and he might have noticed the brief flashing of a picture on the ghost's chest—the face of a woman, blond hair and blue eyes, cat-like eyes, porcelain skin—beauty of the galaxy—the face that haunted Solomon's heart every waking moment of his life.

2302

- 9 -
Thorsfeld's Fall

"If the enemy is numerous and is
advancing in well-ordered arrays, how
are they handled?
Answer: Just seize what they care
about, and they will do as wished." –Sun Tzu

–Warrior Text from the Lost World

Planet Thorsfeld

"Permission to cuss, sir?"

"Denied, Devsky."

"Thank you, General."

"It's a sight, though, isn't it General?"

"That it is, Colonel Laver. That it is."

The sight in reference, the sight that filled their view, was the Planet of Storms.

"The navy fly boys do know how to show you the sights," Devsky commented. "Good pilots."

The observation craft carried Solomon and his First Division regimental commanders, Colonels Laver, Notrik, Hope, and Coen— along with Master Sergeant Devsky, in low orbit over planet Thorsfeld, the ship's nose turned earthward. On an observation deck below the cockpit, a window to the world provided a 180-degree view of the planet and surrounding space. Clouds spanned in circumferential bands around the planet below or swirled into hurricanes the size of a continent; massive displays of lightning made the otherwise dark grey surfaces sparkle with incandescent fury. It was a perfect backdrop for making important strategic choices.

"Alright, gentlemen," said Solomon, ending the revery, "have a seat and let's look at the intel."

"Seems to me it's coming in a little late," noted Colonel Coen as they took a seat around a holo display table.

"We've got a year, right?" quipped Hope. The display table lit up as they all took their seats.

"Devsky, the map."

"Loaded, sir." He touched a button on a keypad in the table. A cross section of the planet below—from surface to high atmosphere—appeared before them.

"Thorsfeld, the Storm World," Solomon noted. "The entire surface is blanketed in lightning."

"Those old Scandians know how to pick their planets," said Coen. "And I thought New Edda was windy!"

"We should've come here after New Edda," said Hope. "It's only eighteen light years away."

"That makes little difference when you travel by fold gates and worm holes," Coen replied. "But eighteen light years hardly seems a small enough distance to call them sister planets."

Solomon explained: "Thorsfeld was colonized around 3000 years ago when a popular uprising on New Edda ousted the local blue bloods. The house royal fled to this impossible planet to survive."

"And how do they survive, then?" asked Laver.

"Next picture, Devsky."

"Sir."

"Cities in the sky, Colonel. Hundreds of pressurized domes on elevating pylons as thick as a super-carrier. The cities rest in the high atmosphere above the storms, but they can retract into the clouds...let the planet act as their best defense."

"Does Centcom have a plan for that?" asked Notrik.

"Yes, and, as per usual, the navy gets the easy job and we get all the fun."

They chuckled.

Hope: "Fun, General?"

"Figuring out how to crack the dome."

"And then," added Laver, "the First Army takes on the local royal body guard, right sir?"

"The real fun job, Colonel."

"Who's the princeling down there?" asked Coen.

"Devsky?"

"Got a picture here, General. A fief-lord named Sigurd Volsung."

A brooding high-browed face floated in the air before them—a grim expression with grimacing mouth and furious eyes.

Notrik spoke in a low voice for all of them: "Always was one for the fun jobs."

There was no need for sarcasm in his tone. They each understood the irony.

Solomon was standing by the woman he knew as Savage. He had seen enough of throne rooms to know he was in one, but this one he hadn't seen in his waking life.

"So I'm dreaming," he said, his virtual voice echoing in the giant concrete hall. He looked around for a moment—but for the oversized chair on a dais at one end of the room, the place looked less like a throne room and more like a bunker. There were no windows. The whole space was grey and dingy. And empty.

'More like a tomb,' he thought. 'This is someone's sepulcher.'

"It's his," said the girl at his side.

She pointed; on the throne now sat a man Solomon did not know—stern with a stare of cold command and brooding brow, wrapped in multi-colored robes, his head turbaned.

"Separate, that one," Savage continued. "Or no, just off-wandered."

Solomon looked from the man to the woman. She was wounded: bleeding from her side. The native Kalli outfit was drenched, and the bleeding wouldn't stop.

"I've hurt you," Solomon said.

"The wound long is being," she answered and fell into his arms.

He picked her up and cradled her close as he walked toward the dais. She smiled and wrapped her arms around his neck, her eyes closed. She settled her cheek into his shoulder.

"It's alright," she said. "I dream of you and then together are. Eisos in our hearts."

"But the bleeding won't stop," Solomon whispered.

He looked down to see the blood dripping from her side onto the polished whiteness of his old Captain's boots—the ones he'd worn as an Imperial Guard.

"You there!" Solomon called as he reached the dais steps. "Come help me!"

The grim-faced man looked at Solomon who now held a plasma rifle and stood encased in his blood stained armored suit.

"So you're the one she sent to kill me then," the man replied. "Why should I help you? I know you of old. You're no more than a knife."

"No sir," Solomon answered. "I'm just here to offer you the handle."

Later that day, while Solomon was enduring the process of donning his armor, a holo screen nearby ran pictures of the Empire's most wanted war criminals while Einor Pluc read brief bios on the galaxy's hated. Among them were Sigurd Volsung and the rebellion's architect, Inmar of Rikas IV. Solomon recognized the Overlord's face.

'You're haunting my dreams, now,' he thought. 'Fair enough. I'm sure I'm haunting yours.'

Ten thousand ships spiraled their way into a synchronized series of orbits—a spider's web of lines. And then, like atmospheric fliers in an air show streaming smoke behind them to form letters and designs, they began to color the lines in. But this smoke did not dissipate. It expanded till it looked more like clouds than smoke streams and then began to move with purpose. Black tendrils in the thousands reached downward toward the planet in snaking arcs and curves till they hit the tumult of storming air. Then they scattered, sandstorm fashion.

Only these grains were smaller than sand, invisible when separated from their brothers. They flew upon the Thorsfeldian winds with purpose. By the billions they were mostly lost. But a billion more struck home. Within the protection of the planet's storms her domed cities were untouchable. Nothing could navigate the winds of Thorsfeld and attack the defenses of the manmade sky castles. Nothing had to. The billions of nano-sized Sikorsky robots released by the Imperial Navy allowed the winds and storms to do the navigating for them.

Those not lost slammed into the domes, the foundations, or the great pillars holding the cities aloft. And then they began to move. The pace was equivalent to a thousand miles an hour for their nanoscopic legs. They moved alone or in colonies and swarmed over the surfaces in search of fissures, ducts, cracks and vents, and where they could not find access they began eating their way through at points where energy signatures suggested vital locations to their single-minded senses.

Invisible to human eyes, the silent soldiers infiltrated defenses and settled onto objectives. Some continued to operate independently. Others gathered in groups, linking together like atoms forming molecules, but these Sikorskies bound themselves into more complex machines capable of cutting, bridging, or laying themselves in patterns to rewire circuit boards and recode software.

While the Sikorskies worked their invisible attack, troop carriers and Flying Fortresses sat as if in nervous anticipation in patiently orbiting super-carriers too large to risk the winds of the planet below—all save a dozen times a dozen singular spheres. Beneath the capitol city—the one Solomon's own division would of course be assigned to subdue—a giant pill spun around, buffeted by the constant storm. The cylinder held a rough stationary position—as much as could be expected—holding one to five miles from its target. The real danger in this waiting game was not in holding a horizontal position but a vertical one—to slam into the city's underside meant death or discovery, to get caught in a sudden downdraft meant to fall too far from the target when the moment came.

But the moment came, and the featureless light absorbing cylinder tumbled toward its objective. The Sikorskies had succeeded in one of their programmed tasks so that, when the cylinder—with a super-powered burst of energy, draining navigational control—slammed itself into an environmental duct, no warning signals were sounded in the city's security control centers. The breach went unnoticed. The cylinder deployed locking arms and atmospheric sealant gel within seconds, then equalized pressure with the city's primary life support conduit and popped its hatch with a clank that was drowned out by the humming of giant fans and swooshing air—a storm in itself though far less turbulent than the one outside—one the ghost named Duncan could certainly manage.

The naked man climbed out of his infiltration pod and into the veins of a giant mechanical underbelly. The air sped his jog into a sprint; he moved on his toes—cautious—but with a speed that belied the knowledge that he was passing unseen. Ghost was a well-deserved moniker.

A mile down the tube, the weaponless man stepped from a street-side atmosphere vent and promptly turned the color of the marble-blue, silver-flecked building against which he quickly moved. Then his motions became slow, silent, and sightless.

Rising at an arc not a hundred yards away, the translucent city dome acted as a window on a dazzling stem of colored mists and white electricity. On the main street a block over, hover tanks and armored troops kept their guns trained on the massive doors of the "Western Tunnel"—one of only four cargo-sized entrances to the city. Beyond the doors stood the tunnel which itself stretched a mile to an external hatch. The tunnel was an airlock through which ships on a landing platform beyond the external hatch could enter the city in stages; first through the external hatch; then, the hatch closed, the tunnel's atmosphere would be oxygenated and equalized with the city's environment. Then the inner doors could open and ships pass into the yards beyond.

Duncan's motion was down the side street before him, and then a side alley. A dozen troops passed him over three instances—they saw nothing. Their enhanced sensing armor showed them nothing—he masked appearance, even heat. He even altered his coloring on two sides when separate troop units had different eye lines on his position. To one group he was a building front, to another the coalescing storm beyond the dome.

Then he was there: behind the control tower to the Western Tunnel and Yards. There was an exhaust panel on a power room— more like a closet—that made for a convenient entrance, and the room a perfect waiting place, alive with the humming of the building's machinery. When a technician entered on a routine check, he did not see his death come upon him. The hand over his mouth was swift and silent; the blow to the neck nearly painless, the breaking vertebrae almost without the sound of crunching bone. Duncan laid the poor man to the floor with a gentle grace then shut the door through which the man had entered. He continued to wait. The technician would be missed within half an hour. Duncan knew that would be long enough.

The Sikorskies did their job. Shutting down the city's insulation tunnels and superconductors and so forcing the domes out of the storms and into the calm upper atmosphere. There, Imperial ships could descend and the assault begin. Almost. First came the bottleneck.

Colonel Face's Flying Fortress which acted as General Haggard's Command Post, and Solomon's First Division launching station, landed on the platform beyond the West Tunnel. It drew fire from automated plasma cannons. It was damaged, but not beyond what it could manage. Becoming a target was necessary—the only way to identify the domed city's external weapons. Once activated, these became targets themselves and Fleet fighters quickly destroyed them. Of special difficulty were any cannons attached directly to the dome. As with all the world's previously conquered, the Empire could not simply blast away and destroy people indiscriminately (at least not without good cause). To blow holes in the dome would be to kill millions. For this difficulty, the weapons specialists aboard Fleet Seven had invented a post-impact sealant missile. Its two stages allowed for immediate explosive percussion followed by a directed blast of sealant gel. Breaches could at least be primarily sealed. But ending the attack on the external platforms did not solve the problem of the bottleneck.

The mile-long corridor was a death trap of cross-cutting lasers, magnet mines, false holo images, even anti-gravity plates along the floor. Casualties via direct assault would be too high. But there was only one way in. So the attack came at both ends.

The inner doors began to open the moment the outer doors were blown apart, courtesy of one of General Hollis's tanks. Duncan had initialized the sequence from the control tower—the only place it could be done—and the Sikorskies did the rest. Even when Thorsfeldian soldiers stormed the tower to find their fellows massacred without any appearance of weapons fire or struggle, there was no reversing the process. The doors had hissed open and would remain so. The ghost named Duncan, of course, was nowhere to be found.

The soldiers and tanks in line after line guarding the inner doors could hear the whisper and then the whipping and then the howl of the wind behind them as the thin atmosphere a mile away began sucking life-giving air out of the city.

Most thought the Empire might have gone mad for a moment. "Are they trying to suffocate us?" ran over com links. Then after a moment, it was over. The atmosphere stabilized and all was quiet down the gateway that had been defense but was now a maw. Lights in the city flickered as Sikorsky soldiers continued their attack on the infrastructure.

Then it happened again: a rush of atmospheric outflow followed by a cessation and silence. At the other end of the tunnel, the Imperial strategy was working. Upon the destruction of the outer doors, the internal defenses—almost none disabled by Imperial Sikorskies—kicked on. The second shot was a high velocity shell from a specially retro-fitted tank in Hollis's division. Rather than plasma, a solid projectile made its way a hundred yards down the tunnel before a laser web ignited it. When the shell exploded, however, it didn't bring damage to the tunnel defense, but a wall. A super-expanding bio-steel meshing foam filled the tunnel from floor to ceiling and five to ten yards thick. Not even air could pass through, and interior defense systems did not target the wall as a threat.

As quickly as the wall shell was fired, hundreds of drone craft flew into the tunnel. Most simply became weapons fodder which those following could use to identify targets in the ceiling, floors, and walls. Active defense systems were taken out by plasma weapons, pinpoint lasers, low yield bombs or even area-narrow EMP[*] devices. Passive defenses like anti-grav plates could then be identified and "painted" for shut down at the advance.

The damage in machinery was formidable—too much, in fact, to send tanks and hover drones through till another set of uniquely re-engineered tanks pushed two by two into the wreckage, chewed and condensed it through mini-mobile factories between their

---

[*] E.M.P: Electro-magnetic Pulse

treads, and pushed cubes of once high-tech machinery out behind them. At the entrance these blocks were already being pushed aside while soldiers in platoon strength from Solomon's First Division began filing down the side walls to support the tanks. Inside of one minute the process was complete. The lead tanks shot a catalyzing agent at their foam-steel wall and the process of disintegration ran quickly.

As soon as there was a hole to shoot through another wall shell was fired and drones swooped forward again. In this way, by taking the long tunnel in hundred yard lengths, the Divisions of the regular army could advance without getting caught up in the wreckage or crossfire and without suffocating the natives of Thorsfeld.

In thirty minutes they were more than halfway through. Solomon watched from the FF's Map Room, certain that things were going well.

"What about the new doors?" he asked as he and General Haggard watched the 3-D holo map before them.

"That'll be the tricky part," Haggard answered.

"So it hasn't been tricky yet," Solomon smirked.

Haggard chuckled. "Oh, no, the real challenge is just coming up."

There had to be a way to reseal the outer doors if the inner doors were indeed permanently disabled. A crew of engineers worked to lock down pre-fab doors over the wreckage of the originals all while the entrance was a traffic jam of tanks, soldiers, drones, and dense metal blocks piling up on the outer platform if not being tossed over its side.

"The doors working—that's what really bothers me," Haggard continued.

"Right," Solomon affirmed.

"We get to the last foam wall, fill the tunnel with as much firepower as we can, shut down the Sikorskies so they don't start attacking us by mistake, shut the tunnel doors before the front tanks bust through the final wall to find who-knows-what—and those doors have to stay shut till the first wave busts through or dies trying."

"That's the real problem," said Solomon. "No reinforcements for at least ten minutes."

"Forever in CT.*"

"The Scandians could find a way to shut those inner doors again."

"Yeah," Haggard agreed.

"Or barricade the tunnel."

"Yeah."

"Or just throw all their major hardware at that opening and trade us fifty-fifty till our casualty rates take this war from tough to costly."

"Yeah."

"Costly to fiasco."

"Oh yeah. But those engineering tanks could make the difference—we'll be able to go forward through wreckage; they won't."

"Hollis had no time to train his teams in these combat situations. And those bellies are vulnerable."

"Boy, General Star, you're a real grim presence in my CP† today."

"Thank you, General Haggard. I'll remind you that you started it, but, if it makes you feel better, I'll pass on the whole discussion about how we'll then have to face Sigurd's Royal Guard once we punch through. That is assuming they're not waiting for us right inside the door."

"You just can't stand not being in the first wave, can you Solomon?"

"Protocol or not, I'm going in on the second wave. And no matter what the losses."

ComType: Personal
Init: #7148821693122964 Capt. Joshua Troy
Rec: Aslin Troy
Planet: Logres
Edress: gww.lesserlight42.emp
Begin Holo Transmission

---

* C.T.: Combat Time
† C.P.: Command Post

"Hi Honey,

"I wanted to get this off to you right away 'cause I was afraid you might get text of this before you heard I'm okay. So...I'm okay. Look...got a burn on my arm is all. Synthderm will have it good as new by tomorrow....

"I, uh...I can't lie and say the danger wasn't real. We saw action—a real firefight. General Star's been real good about acting like a general and staying out of the fights. But he couldn't help it this time. We went in with the second wave—it was the only way General Star could really get a sense of what was happening inside the dome. The first wave was gone—eaten up—but they'd done their jobs and pushed back the enemy far enough so we could duck behind some wreckage and establish an FCP—that's a Forward Command Post. Inside the dome General Star could recon from every soldier and tank commander, and we didn't have to press forward.

"Bastogne, my second in command, did a great job establishing the perimeter. Corporal Arith's squad—that's twenty men out of the platoon got caught up trying to hold their line too close to the vacuum of the main entrance and couldn't stand in place, let alone aim straight till Bastogne reminded them they could bolt and strap themselves down to the artificial floor.

"Bottom line is, we were lucky. I got this burn from a plasma sword graze. If Sigurd—that's the lord of Thorsfeld—if he'd been a little smarter and used his Royal Guard to hold the dome entrance we might have never established the beachhead. Sergeant Devsky thinks Sigurd was relying too much on his big artificial weapons, not enough on manpower. But I think Sigurd wanted to fight himself—like he planned on a glorious final battle with his own Guard at his side. I saw him die. I could see the death wish in his eyes...

"I'm getting ahead of myself and you don't want to hear all that tactical stuff. At the center of the city there's a castle; rises all the way up to the dome ceiling and branches out like a tree to different buildings or along the dome. We had pushed the enemy back to within a few klicks* of the Royal Tree House, I guess you'd call it, when word came that elements of Colonel Coen's regiment were taking heavy hits in a two block area we thought we'd already

---

* Kilometers

overtaken. We probably ran through the area too quickly without the floor by floor sweeps you have to do in urban combat—General Star always says we can't take streets, we have to take buildings. Sometimes scans can help you take shortcuts, but with Royals you're not going to pick up signatures from combat armor or heavy weapons. Sometimes all they carry is their dang swords...I'm doing it again.

"Okay, so the General had been moving forward taking us with him—that's the way it's supposed to be—still pretty far back from action, or so we thought. These two blocks I was telling you about were only a klick from us. The General had already called for reinforcements and his AI software was working at establishing a quantum troop wave—uh, that's technical—but then the Thorsfeldian Royals hit like a hammer. They poured out of the castle in a straight line. It looked like a shot at defending Lord Sigurd. But it was a feint, uh, a decoy.

"Alright, so inside the dome we could hardly get air cover, but what cover we could get was useless anyway because these Gene Kings went straight into close combat—jumped in right among our troops. Well sure, then everyone in the division had to converge on that point, so the attack on Coen's men couldn't be countered by anyone anytime soon—no one, anyway, but us.

"For the first time in this war, a general's security platoon saw combat. We jetted north and the General gave me the job of focusing on the objective while he still dealt with the battle at large. I had my AI do an any-and-all sweep and learned quickly that a platoon was caught in a room-to-room firefight with Royal Guards. Give you one guess what royal person was with them. In the hands of a Gene King these plasma swords can block rifle fire, right? So the best Coen's guys could do was a slow retreat down hallways— only a matter of time before they got pushed into an area too large to slow the enemy down in.

"So I'm talking to some lieutenant named Kaydroo about how he's holding his sergeant's head in his hand when a wall of flame explodes up in front of us. It was a hundred feet high and raging solid—had to be chemical or gas line running under the street. General Star didn't hesitate for a minute. And he didn't jet over the flames either. That would've been suicide 'cause a group of Gene Kings were waiting on the other side. Instead, the General keeps walking, pulls out his own plasma sword, and steps through the wall of fire. By the time I got through the fire, those Royals were dead at General Star's feet. There were plenty more to come. In front of us was an empty street with a dead silent building on one side and an exploding one on the other...Well, a lot of things happened at once—it's complicated. Inside the building our people are shooting and getting sliced up. I'm feeding all this to the general while Bastogne is deploying the platoon and Sergeant Devsky is watching the silent building, certain that's where the real attack's going to come from—and poor Bastogne is listening to me, Devsky and General Star all at once about how to set the men.

"Okay, so I had my AI, Teddy, paint and count every friendly and every threat. We had 150 of us in the vicinity and forty of them, and that empty building was just too empty. But the fight seemed to be to one side of us. General Star told us to hold our ground and sent the signal for withdrawal to what was left of Coen's men. They came jetting out of three stories of windows followed just as fast by the Royal Guards of Thorsfeld. I can't tell you everything that happened—I got kind of busy at that point, but fighting Gene Kings is all about the weapons, and I swear it's like these guys were fighting to lose.

"They didn't have any guns, just plasma swords. The General had trained us what to do—keep them at a distance—use our reach over theirs. It would have been different if they'd had guns. So we started these attack patterns by squad, shooting to keep as much area of coverage as possible. I dropped to a knee next to a couple of privates I know well enough—Morris and Sinnett—and we're not leaving an open space. But the Royals have these swords that they can swing fast enough to block anything—I think I said that already—so they form these three-man groups to shield each other and manage to start pushing towards us.

"General Star's standing next to me—just standing there, and we start getting micro-target displays in the AIs—it's General Star telling a hundred men where exactly to shoot every other second. And of course, it's obvious the clearest targets are their feet— they're missing shielding their feet, so a bunch of us are prompted through the AI software to shoot at their feet—but not all of us. General's finding these chinks in the sword swings that are like half-second windows, and he's using his symbiot to send all these calculations to us. We drop fifteen of the enemy, but, first, more of Coen's men come running out of the building at its main doors, followed by the rest of the non-friendlies, and so we can't blanket them anymore. And then, second, they read our strategy and start jetting—Royal Guards always wear jet boots like us.

"Well, then, it's a free for all. There aren't positions to hold or software to follow; there's just targets to attack and the guy next to you to save. No more platoon, just squads and units now and trusting the corporals to run their squads like they ought to—and let me tell you, Corporal Wolfram was a rock; I know he saved ten men. He was—anyway, stay on track...uh, right, units and squads. But that's okay, see, 'cause it lets the general cut loose. He's flying everywhere attacking those super soldiers in midair—one hand with his sword, another with his rifle. The rest of us don't dare make jumps—we can't beat those guys in the air. But they're jumping like crazy so they can get close to us and 'cause they're harder for us to hit when they're on the move like that. But not so hard that we didn't nail a few of 'em alright.

"Well like I said, I'm busy myself. This Royal charges us—me and Morris and Sinnett, and I yell, 'Hi/low' through the com and one shoots high and the other low, and this guy is so freakin' fast with his sword block, but then he leaps and I realize he can't fall any faster than gravity, so I dive and spin and aim, and all he can do is block front, and I got a clear shot in the back. And against a Gene King you take the shot and keep shooting till he's dead.

"I spring up and the doors of the building behind me explode. I turn to see fire spew out in a ball like out of a dragon's mouth. And in all this chaos there stands none other than Lord Sigurd himself in this golden battle armor shining like a sun. He raises a plasma sword and screams something no one in a helmet can hear and then charges into the fight.

"I raise my gun to fire and hold up 'cause out of nowhere the shortest soldier I've ever seen comes flying horizontally through the air, his jet boots still firing. His rifle's in his hand like a club— found out later the gun'd been damaged and jammed. He slams into Sigurd full throttle swinging at his sword hand and knocking the sword loose. They roll over, and I run toward them. The sword is burning through the street. Pieces of armor are lying around, but Sigurd and the soldier both recover quickly. I get a shot off, but he's got thick armor 'cause he's a lord and all. It throws him off balance, and the short soldier leaps, spins in the air without firing his jets, and lands a spinning kick square to Sigurd's helmeted jaw, even as his own helmet finally falls loose from the impact of the first hit.

"And it's not a man at all—it's a woman. We got a woman soldier testing a female version of an ICUR in combat! I take aim to shoot again, and she screams at me—I swear she says, 'He's mine!' so I hesitate. That's when a Royal lands between me and Sigurd to block my fire. I wasn't in danger right off, but next he was going to take me out and turn on the woman. But he takes a step and the street beneath him caves in 'cause Sigurd's sword has burned a hole clean through to the lower infrastructure. It's not big but it collapses, and I just start shooting. The guy blocks me a few times, but then I shoot apart the street beneath him as well and eventually hit the sword and ignite its plasma chamber. Why it didn't shut off like it's supposed to has to be a miracle—someone was watching out for me.

"My helmet filters the light of the explosion, but I still can't see at first. Then there's this pile of Royal Guard corpses and Sigurd and the woman are standing on top fighting hand to hand—it's all solid, old-fashioned martial combat. Her face is bloody but she keeps trading punches, head for helmet. Then she's side-stepping, grabbing his arm as he punches, shoots a leg straight up, like a vertical split, but bent at the knee, and snap kicks him three times in the face, then back flips away like in a gymnastics routine.

"Then I see where the pile of dead has come from—it's General Star guarding this girl's back. She's fast, but not Gene King fast, right? Which makes you wonder because dukes and lords and such are usually genetically enhanced themselves, but she's kicking his butt. Like he's tagging her head, but something's holding Sigurd back. But she was good, really good.

"Anyway, General Star is there, and he's fighting off the last of these Guards, sword to sword. And it's not like it's more of an even fight between Gene Kings. The General needs maybe two or three strikes or whatever they call it and some super soldier's got his head cut off or split down to the navel. We still don't know why Sigurd left most of his own Guard behind at the castle to try to fight his way out here.

"Well, the General literally puts down the last of them, and Sigurd and the woman—she's a second lieutenant named Amandatar I find out later—they're still going at it. And it's all without enhancement 'cause their armor is wrecked—he even has to take his helmet off now 'cause he can't see out of it anymore. So it's boom! boom! boom!—block, punch, hit, and she's doing these acrobatics to land these killer kicks.

"But finally, Sigurd sort of wakes up and decides he's done playing, grabs her leg in the air on her last kick, and throws her ten meters into one of our boys—turns out to be Bastogne. I take aim again, but I see General Star running right toward me—he starts firing and then raises his sword and I'm blinded by plasma light and knocked over by percussion. When I finally look up and get my bearings I see the general standing over me and smoke coming from what's left of my armor plate on the arm. That empty building Devsky'd had a bad feeling about had let loose five more Royal Guards—they must have come up through the infrastructure—and I never saw one of them coming right at me. His sword nicked me before General Star killed him.

"Next thing I notice is one more shot fired. Devsky hit Sigurd in the chest and laid him out. We walked over to him—me, General Star, Devsky, and the girl...er...woman, Amandatar. Sigurd was breathing. He saw the general with his sword in hand and must've realized who he was. He smiled and nodded. General Star nodded back. Then Sigurd looked at Amandatar, and this look came into his eyes like...I don't know, like love! He held up his hand to her and she knelt down. I turned on my externals and heard him speak to her. 'My Brinhild,' he said, whatever that means, and then he died.

"So that was it. The fighting went on for a day, but we weren't in any more of it. We had forty injured—a handful severe—but we didn't lose a single man—not even against Royal Guards! The platoons from Coen's regiment lost more than half, but our platoon, General Star's security boys—not a one, Aslin, not a one. We stood firm. These boys of mine...good men...good men.

"And that one good woman. We'd heard she might be coming, but apparently General Star didn't even know she'd been placed in this battle, at this time. He complimented her skill and achievement, but I could tell he wasn't very happy. I'm pretty sure he's yelling at someone about it somewhere now. She'll end up getting a medal. A lot of us will.

"Yeah, you don't want to hear all that. I love you. I knew you'd want to hear everything. We'll keep out of the fighting as best we can, I promise. General Star promises. Don't show this to the girls. Just tell 'em I love them too. Gotta go. Love and prayers."

End Transmission

2303

- 10 -
The Hunt

"Undefeatability lies with ourselves.
Defeatability lies with the enemy...
So we say, victory can be perceived,
But it cannot be created." —Sun Tzu

—Warrior text from the Lost World

Planet Ramah

"Stubborn witch!"

The eyes of Baroness Yelhsa Ramah could pierce stone and wood. Their fury currently bent toward the wall-sized holo screen in the offices of her palatial mansion, her attendants could swear they saw the screen beginning to overload.

"My cousin! My own cousin! However far removed! Celebrates the birthday of her son by arresting my husband and invading my world."

On the screen, the Empress Janis IV was parading in an open-air hover car through the streets of Imperial City. In one arm she held her son, Atrist, the future heir to her thrown. With the other she acknowledged the crowd, waving in that inimical manner in which all royalty are trained as if by creedal requirement. All of this was on the screen before the Baroness. In the sky above her, a new moon was drawing near.

"She has no right!" Yelhsa continued. "No right. This is an illegal war and Theus would have proved it in the House of Royals if he hadn't been arrested the moment he sat foot on Amric's world! Oh, don't give me that look, Liston."

"No, my Lady."

Liston Jeah was the Captain of the 4000-man personal Body Guard to the Barony of Ramah. All Royals had such guards— genetically enhanced supermen, inheritors of their positions for millennia. Sigurd's guard had died on Thorsfeld at the hands of the Big Red One. Losses of normal soldiers on the Imperial side, however, had been substantial despite Solomon Star's best efforts—too many to smooth over by ICA broadcasters, though we certainly tried (the independent networks had a field day—the battle over image in this war was lost by Imperials for several months in the aftermath of Thorsfeld). The Empress's own Imperial Guard were the best in the galaxy. Liston Jeah of Ramah house could certainly have been counted among them.

"Just because our marriage was one of convenience, it doesn't mean I can't be concerned for him."

"True, my Lady. But that wasn't the meaning in my expression."

"No?" Her voice was threatening. He knew, though, when the threats were and were not real.

"No. You should have let me go with him."

"And have you locked up as well? I don't think so."

"No, my Lady."

The Baroness was a strong woman in person and persona—a woman of action. She avoided jewelry and fine clothing, kept her earth brown hair cut above the shoulder. Brown hair, brown eyes—a woman of the earth—and today a rugged brown suit of leather: a double-breasted tunic covered with pockets and stretching to the hips over leggings and sturdy knee-high boots. In the feminine she was beautiful—trim and muscular. In the masculine she was rugged. In combination she appeared lethal—most especially when she laid her piercing gaze on some unfortunate subject of her wrath. If only she could get her hands around Janis's throat...

"Well, that's it, then," she concluded. "There will be no justice if we're taken. The Lords must find proof that we've been provoked. And we must delay. Are the men assembled?"

"Assembled and already moving out, Baroness."

"Very well, then." And to everyone in the room: "Liston and I must join my Guard. You will stay; greet the invader, and comfort my people as best you can."

The paradise that was planet Ramah sat largely undisturbed by the presence of an Imperial invasion force. Even the convoy of dark blue hover transports rolling out of her capitol city did not interrupt the peace of the planet's purple skied sunset. Lights twinkled in the suburban streets, every house lit with rows of tiny lights, every tree in the dozens of parks passing by decorated with phosphorescent glow-tinsel—not for holidays, though; this was the everyday décor of the quaint and quiet towns of Ramah.

In the lead transport, Solomon Star watched the scenery with pleasure in his eyes but troubling thoughts in his head as he reviewed General Haggard's orders.

"General Star," he had said.

"General Haggard," he'd replied.

And they smiled at each other.

"Solomon, word from tactical command is that the Baroness has fled the city. Second Corps surrounded the capitol without incident. General Tu found the Royal Residence empty of all but support staff. Baroness Yelhsa is gone, along with her personal Body Guard—all 4000 of them."

"Uh-huh," said Solomon with contemplative detachment. "Well," he continued, "so it's another battle where the regular army will have to take on a Royal Guard."

"Yeah. Genetic Supermen."

"And I suppose it takes a Gene King to catch one."

"Yeah. I suppose it does."

"What's the intel on their last location?"

"We don't know. No one saw them leave."

"Yes, but sat surveillance."

"No one and nothing. A 4000-man troop movement was hidden from the sats, drones, manned patrols, scouts, troops—the complete VR system."

"So we're facing a Royal Guard with some new stealth technology."

"Right. So, go find them without knowing where to look."

Solomon thought then: "We head for the mountains."

"Yeah."

"That's where I'd go."

"Yeah."

"We'll move out tonight."

"It gets worse."

"Oh?"

"Yeah. We have to keep things discreet for that last annoying element of the METT-TI* equation."

"Image."

"Yeah. We lost too many men to the Royal Guard on Thorsfeld. We can't afford a public opinion hit like that one again."

Solomon had not expected to be limited by the number of troops he could put into the engagement. One battalion only. Twenty-five thousand regular troops versus four thousand supermen. That made the odds just about even. And all so that the Independent News people didn't find out about it till after the problem was diffused.

Solomon left his colonels in charge of the division. Along with his personal platoon and his favorite "techy," Ib'm, Solomon chose to accompany him, Third Regiment's Eighth Battalion: Lieutenant Colonel Stapleton Russ's Ridge Riders, so named for their specialization: combat in mountainous terrain. Russ sat in the lead transport with Solomon, privileged to have the division commander along to guide the mission. He interrupted Solomon's revery:

"General?"

"Yes, Colonel?"

"I don't hear any air cover overhead."

"There won't be any till we engage the enemy, and it won't come but from orbit. That's 45 minutes at best from first contact to support arrival. No artillery either."

"And the reason, sir?"

"Secrecy."

"A secret operation with an entire battalion?"

"Makes for an interesting challenge, doesn't it?"

"Yes sir, I suppose it does."

"How about we look at our opponent in the game, then?"

"Baroness Yelhsa?"

"No, she'll leave battle tactics to her Captain." Solomon lifted a personal communicator to his ear. "Com, Sergeant Ib'm."

---

* Command level soldiers use the M.E.T.T.-T.I. acronym to prioritize what they should analyze during the planning phase of a battle situation: Mission, Enemy, Terrain, Troops, Time available, and Image.

"Ib'm, roger," came the reply from the tenth vehicle in the convoy.

"Colonel Russ and I are ready to review the dossier on Captain Jeah. What do you have?"

"Everything, sir. I'm set to transmit to your personal AIs now."

"Very well. Helmet up, Colonel, and let's learn what we can about Liston Jeah."

Solomon removed his com piece and picked up his helmet. He preferred to show his face as much as possible in the field and so carried the helmet in non-combat situations, even though otherwise fully armored. He locked the helmet in place, as did Colonel Russ, and together they began reviewing the impressive resumé of the Ramahian Royal Guard Captain, Liston Jeah.

Outside their virtual world, darkness was setting and suburbs gave way to small towns which gave way to dark fields and quiet points-of-light farmhouses where even country folk decorated orchard rows and rope-swing yard trees with glow-tinsel, shimmering soft light in the gentle Ramahian breeze. A serpent of light, a convoy of troop carriers, headlights ablaze, streaked its way through the countryside.

The Bethalis plain at the foot of the Moriahan Mountain Chain. Base camp: a mobile Forward Command Post—prefab pop-up polymer octagon into which Ib'm could stuff as much tech-gear as possible; the transports, arranged in three circles around the Forward Command Post, doubled as troop quarters; a mess truck; and a short communications tower. Perimeter defenses were set and fifteen companies now jet booted into the mountains, among them Solomon Star and his own platoon. Mount Geraz was dotted with caves, a likely hiding place. Solomon joined the Ridge Riders' Second Company to search these caves while Colonel Russ remained begrudgingly behind at Command.

"General this seems reckless to me."

"I know, Troy. Regulations and rank and all."

Solomon's platoon stood in a deep ravine at the mouth of a cave.

"If it weren't about the Body Guard of a Royal, I'd act my rank and keep us all at a safe distance."

"Sir, you know I'm not afraid for myself here."

"I know, I know. I don't mean that. You're doing your job. Corporal Wolfram, scan rep?"

"Scans have been in and out since we left the FCP, General, but I've got clear imaging here for a mile radius. The tunnel is long and deep; there are caverns—the makings of a good Rikasian maze, sir. But no combatants scanned."

"Very well. So odds are, Captain, I'll not be at risk anyway. But...regs some other time Josh. I need to be there when this threat surfaces."

"Yes, sir."

"You take First Squad in at point. Heat scans. Motion scans. Concussion grenades at point. Devsky and I will follow one minute behind with Second Squad. Three and Four follow likewise. Lieutenant Bastogne."

"General."

"Sieg bring up the rear with Orin's squad. Leave Fifth Squad here to guard our flank."

"Yes sir."

"Alright, then...wait...Devsky?"

"General?"

"No quips? No deadpan jokes before we start? You sick today?"

"No sir. Just scared witless in the funny sense of the word."

"You, scared?"

And Troy: "Devsky, you're not scared of anything."

"It's kinda personal, Captain Troy. General can we go to private coms for a minute."

"Okay." 'Little Hal, private coms.' "Now what gives, Jo?"

"Claustrophobia, sir."

"You're kidding."

"Like I said, nothing I particularly want to talk about."

"Conversation deferred but not denied, Sergeant. So what, you want to just hang out here with the rear guard?"

"Beg pardon, General, but you ever ask me something like that again, I'll shoot you in the leg."

"Welcome back, Sergeant Wit." 'Little Hal, all coms.' "Let's move out."

The cave was in fact a mix of both natural cave and human mining complex. Long, straight shafts emptied of silibalt deposits would give way to rough, uneven caverns filled with beautiful formations. The sight augmentation of helmet visors, however, did not share that beauty with Solomon's platoon. They would not have allowed the distraction anyway.

A wide cavern opened nearly a mile into the mountain. Abandoned mining equipment, shelters, and garbage lay carelessly about. First Squad fanned out and held position. Solomon entered and waited.

"I've never been so concerned with second guessing as with third," he said.

"General?" came Troy's reply.

"Best place for an ambush would be a tight space, a tunnel where small numbers could easily hold off a large contingent. But knowing that we'd expect it, they'd perhaps set a trap here, where we don't. But then they might think...and so on. It's third guesses that kill decision with too much doubt."

The other squads entered, one after the other. And waited.

"Fan out. Deep scans. Devsky find me some answers."

"Yes sir."

"Wolfram?"

"Sir."

"Who else has an SSP[*]?"

"Corporal Arith."

"Alright. Your squads go in opposite directions and feed me layouts."

"Yes sir."

For the next half-hour the platoon explored the cavern. Captain Troy updated Bastogne at the cave entrance every fifteen minutes. Solomon set his symbiot to rotate among the visor readouts of the four squad leaders and Sergeant Devsky. What they saw, he saw. In the end, it was very little.

Devsky noted that a few boot tracks near one tunnel looked different and perhaps fresher than what they would expect of miners. Perhaps jet boots, but not definitely. Otherwise the mine had been abandoned for decades.

"Silibalt used to be used for shield scanning," Troy offered.

---

[*] S.S.P.: Scout-Scan Pack

"Yes, but not for a century, not since quark-scan tech was standardized," said Devsky.

"Maybe they modified it somehow," Troy replied.

"Maybe," said Solomon, "but then where's the ambush?"

"Well, sir, there's a great deal more cave complex to explore. Spelunking's certainly high on my recreation list."

"Devsky." Solomon smiled behind his visor.

"Shutting up, sir."

"General, sir?"

"Wolfram?"

"I don't think we'll find anyone here."

"But you're thinking something."

"With your permission, sir."

"Go ahead."

A map of the region appeared in the visors of each man standing with Solomon. It moved and flushed and changed colors as Corporal Wolfram spoke:

"Every soldier I know with SSPs is seeing the same thing. There's clear scan within a hundred miles of us, except for these patches. Some in the mountains, some in the plain. They still scan sir, but they're...fuzzy."

Devsky: "Ib'm's been stripping field units and checking his sat software since we got here."

And Wolfram: "Yes sir and we've patrolled the areas and found nothing."

"So what makes you think we won't find anything here, Corporal?"

"Call it a hunch, General, but these are the anomalies, and I think the answer's there. Everything here scans perfect. I mean a small army disappeared from Ramahton after our satellite network was placed and we missed it."

It hit Solomon with crystal clarity. He began walking quickly toward the exit.

"Captain Troy."

The others followed.

"General?"

"Get Wolfram a medal or a raise or something."

"How about a promotion, sir?"

"No, Devsky, I don't want him transferred where someone thinks he'd be of better use."

"Congratulations Wolfram," said Devsky. "You've impressed the General so much he wants to keep you a corporal for the rest of the war."

AIs didn't let personal laughter out over com controls unless the individual soldier headspoke the command. So no one heard anyone else laughing. But Solomon was not among those who were. He was mentally hitting himself in the head, thinking,

'We've been seeing it all wrong. We've been thinking in terms of terrain. It's not about geographic topography; it's about virtual topography. Stupid! It's the tech. It's been about the tech all along.'

"Lieutenant Bastogne."

"Bastogne, Roger."

He was running now.

"Priority to Colonel Russ. Tell him to order all troops to hold position and take up defensive stances wherever they are. Send the message now!"

"Roger that."

"Best speed boys." Solomon was faster than his troops when jet boots couldn't be used. He could also talk while running in full armor without losing his breath: "Wolfram's right. We've been searching terrain thinking in terms of defensibility. They're not concerned about defense, they're focused on stealth."

It didn't matter that they didn't know how Wolfram's fuzzy areas were a threat. Army's had lived and died on hunches before.

Twenty miles down range from Solomon's position, Mount Seir was as beautiful above ground as the caves of Mount Geraz were below. Third Company was also blind to it. The company's commander, Captain Diaz, had his thousand men arranged in two staggered lines, each jetting in thirty-yard hops over the other, the men separated by ten-yard intervals. Midway up the mountain, a bowl opened into nearly flat terrain, its perimeter reaching half a mile till renewing its steep ascent. The bowl was a field of blue-green grass and tiny purple flowers called tear-drops for their curved stems and drooping tear-shaped petals. Patches burned in polka-dot array behind the soldiers as they jetted off the ground.

Kinder than a plague of locusts, they nevertheless left vegetable destruction in their wake.

When the first grenade hit, two men died and twenty fell into disarray. Bastogne was just finishing his transmission to Colonel Russ at the FCP when Diaz realized his company's search for the enemy had succeeded. Five more grenades struck and plasma fire began raining in, a horizontal wall.

Third Company reacted with disciplined control. They dropped to the ground and began suppression fire. There was no cover, but then there would be none for the enemy. Troops fired in controlled bursts while commanders' AIs worked quickly to assess the situation. Unfortunately, virtual intel was failing. Soldiers were being shot at, but computers couldn't find targets. Diaz's visor display showed the field before him but the offensive software Solomon had designed couldn't lock into place. Everything looked *fuzzy*.

And then the casualty list began to tick off. The rate of hits being registered was too quick, as if an army of expert snipers were shooting at the Imperials. 25 men were dead in two minutes and Diaz realized that fire with the accuracy of sniper aim was exactly what they were facing.

'Gene Kings.'

He headscreamed at his symbiot: 'Can you get me target intel or not!'

Negative, Captain. I cannot provide any augmentation in appearance, topography, target analysis—

'Then turn all targeting programs off. Com.'

"Platoon commanders, Diaz. Shut down your electronic surveillance and pick up visual scanning. Shut down your attack software and order your own movements. I want you to choose target areas in your line of sight and overload them with RPPG and plasma fire. I want rail guns to target the cliff side in the distance and turn it into sponge. RGs must fire and move, fire and move. Everyone else hold position. Hug the deck."

Diaz's AI had automatically called in air support and reported to tactical command, but neither Colonel Russ nor the Imperial navy could be any help anytime soon. Ten more men were dead. An engagement plan was being enacted. If the platoon commanders had sharp enough eyes they could inflict casualties. But the super soldiers' eyes would be sharper and, for all Diaz knew, his men could be facing the entire Ramahian Royal Guard. They were too blind to risk an offensive assault. What he realized was that he would only know if he should hold ground or attempt retreat depending on whether the kill rate ticker in his helmet slowed or kept its terrible pace.

Mountain Troops carried *Rail Guns*, a weapon too dangerous to use in high population areas where collateral damage could be great. An RG shot poly-aluminum rounds at near light speed. At such high velocity, the rounds could pierce most anything, multiple surfaces, and dense targets. Diaz has his five RG carriers blanket the cliff wall before them. The rounds struck deep, blowing huge holes of obliterated granite out from the wall—rocks, pebbles, and dust.

And the ticker slowed. Either they were hitting enemy targets, forcing them to move, or obscuring their line of sight. Hopefully some of all three.

'Or are they luring us in?'

A flash to Diaz's left: the soldier next to him took a hit, but it was on the shoulder and the armor held. Other shots nearby suggested lowered accuracy. What became clear, though, was that Diaz could not risk an assault against an unknown number of superior soldiers.

'Com.'

"Platoon commanders begin orderly retreat."

The pull-back was a crawl. Diaz held his men on the ground. Fifty yards and he might risk jetting out. When the crossfire began on the right flank, Diaz realized defending an assault wasn't on the enemy's mind. They had read his numbers.

'They think they've got us.'

Out on the right, Sergeant Casey took over the Tenth Platoon as his lieutenant fell dead. He read the attempt to outflank the line and made a choice.

'Com.'

"Ten. Grenades. Proximity placement."

A suicide run. Casey was off the ground in a high arc. The first two shots missed, and he had time to activate a high concussion grenade. The third shot hit, but his armor held and he had time to set his plasma rifle on overload. The best scenario for a suicide run was to drop into an enemy cluster, drop the grenade a second before firing, and jet out above the explosion. Casey expected about half of his platoon to make the jump to safety. He wasn't one of them. He was dead before he hit, but his trajectory was already set. His corpse's rifle killed a dozen Ramahian Guards. The tactic worked. The enemy's flanking maneuver had been under-manned, and, for the only time in the battle, the Imperial Troops caused more casualties than they suffered.

The right tried to regroup, and the retreat faltered. But Third Company fought. Out of the smoky distance, a familiar sight: arcs of fiery light—the Ramahians advancing to attack.

'They do have us.' Diaz knew. He called a halt, wheel, and fire. They could drop a few in the air. It was clear that they outnumbered the Ramahians double or triple, but they wouldn't match their firing precision.

'So we use our numbers. Com.'

"Set for close quarters. Unit cluster defense. Outnumber them and burn your servos. Now!"

Platoons broke into squads and charged the enemy, some on the ground, some in the air. A close fight would take the accuracy advantage away from the enemy. The super soldiers were faster and better fighters, but they didn't use strength enhancing armor. The Imperials had more muscle, protection, and numbers. Diaz's own platoon charged on the ground. His job as a company commander was essentially over. Small unit organization was the last strategy available. Third Company took the fight to the enemy.

Ten men, Diaz among them, stopped five yards short of the Ramahians and began to fire. When three of the elite Guards landed behind them, they broke cluster and attacked in numbers. Diaz saw one Royal launch himself horizontally at his enemy, knocking him ten yards distance before jet boots drove them both into the ground. Two men on either side of Diaz charged, firing high and low. The Ramahian, with unbelievable speed and agility, dodged both barrels and spun into contact distance. His own gun fired point blank at the first soldier's chest while his left hand grabbed the second soldier's gun barrel and twisted him off balance. But this trooper turned into what would be the next attack—a kick to the head and, releasing his weapon while taking the blow to the chest, he managed to get his arms around the leg with a vice-like servo grip. The Ramahian had been turning to shoot Diaz; surprised, he was thrown off his balance long enough for Diaz to duck his shot (it nicked his helmet) and drive his own gun barrel up through the stomach and into the heart.

Such was the battle: Ramahian Royal Guards fighting with precise martial skills and Imperial Infantry mob attacking the best they could. Many followed Tenth Platoon's example, blowing themselves up with the enemy. In the end, however, after a mere fifteen minutes of fighting, only five Imperials were left alive, all their weapons gone. Their captors quickly removed their helmets, disabling communication and jet boots. They were directed to sit on the ground.

"Sir we have ten minutes at best before we need to be invisible." A Ramahian was speaking to his superior as this tall, precise figure moved toward the prisoners.

"Fine, Corporal. We won't need five."

The Captain of the Guard, Liston Jeah, removed his helmet. His appearance was formidable, deadly—a god among men. But his face was kind, and gentleness shone from his eyes.

"Your men were very good," he said, kneeling by the leader. "They killed a hundred of mine, and I don't have that many to spare. I was overconfident."

Diaz looked Jeah in the eyes. He wanted to hate him, to kill him for killing his company. But he couldn't.

"I suppose," he said, "you're paying me a compliment."

Jeah smiled. "Yes. The highest."

"How many were you? Three hundred at best? And you had to kill a thousand?"

"You fought too well to take prisoners. Fifty or more of your men killed themselves to take us out. Even the wounded fought to the death. What kind of leadership inspires that kind of loyalty, and from troops that have never even faced the possibility of this scale defeat?"

"Someone better than you."

"Yes," Liston Jeah smiled—admiration and apprehension mixed in his expression—"yes, of course. Solomon Star. I look forward to meeting him. And I look sadly to it." Jeah stood. Looking at his own men: "Their injuries are slight?"

"Yes, sir. They can move."

"Good. Captain...?"

"Diaz."

"Diaz. Take your men out of the hills, that way into the plain. Don't try to pick up weapons. I have snipers in place to cover our retreat. They won't miss."

"You're letting us go?"

"Enough are dead for one day."

"You want me to tell General Star what happened here." It wasn't a question.

"I want you to tell him it was an honest fight."

Jeah turned and his men began to retreat up the mountain. He spoke briefly to his second in command: "We won't be able to fight so openly again. A hundred of our friends are dead because I underestimated what Solomon Star could make of regular men." Then they jet booted away.

- 11 -
Stalling for Time

"...show gains to lure them;
show disorder to make them take a chance..." –Sun Tzu

–Warrior Text from the Lost World

Planet Ramah

"Diaz's entire company, then?"

"Yes, General, nearly a thousand men."

"This is my fault, Colonel Russ. I should've seen this sooner. Stealth technology that doesn't act like it. So obvious."

"You don't have to do that, sir."

"What's that?"

"Blame yourself for something that isn't really your fault just so I'll feel better—not lose my confidence."

"Actually, Colonel, I do. Not for you, for me. We can't just win these fights."

"I understand that. But you also have to make an honest assessment of what happened here."

Solomon and Colonel Russ walked among the dead. Naval scouts and fighters flew in force overhead, invading the conversation with engine noise and wind gusts, while a large troop contingent guarded a perimeter or gathered the dead.

Colonel Russ continued: "At best Diaz had them outnumbered three-to-one, notably less. And he gave 'em a fight, General. Look around you," he pointed. "The dead aren't scattered. They weren't running away. They adjusted when the targeting software stopped working. They grouped and regrouped and fought till they were dead. And that's because of you, of what you've done with the whole Division. You heard what Diaz reported about their Captain?"

"Yes. A man easy to admire. But the eyes, Stapleton, the scrutiny. It's because I am who I am that we have to do better than this. There are too many eyes from the AIR watching us—watching me."

"General, if I may be bold for a moment: I was at the academy when you resigned back in '88. The news spread all over Alexandria in minutes. There wasn't a general, career instructor, cadet, or even cook who wasn't talking about it. I heard brass calling for your head and analysts wanting you strung up. Begging your pardon, sir."

"It's alright. I still get stared at ship-side."

"Well, General, nobody voiced what I was thinking; it made perfect sense to me but it was crazy. You know what my thought was?"

"Tell me."

"I thought, 'Man, I hope he comes and works for us.' General, sir. It's because you are who you are that we're going to find the Ramahian Guard and take them without losing 20,000 troops."

Solomon stood silent for a moment, his helmet dangling in his hand, his eyes surveying his loss.

"Maybe so. But let's hope for the one thing that will keep this day from becoming a complete disaster." And then looking at Russ directly: "Let's hope Captain Jeah has no way of sending any images of this debacle to the real enemy: those watching eyes."

Far to the west, beyond the mountain range, amidst timber country, a land of lakes and streams, Ramah's fifth largest city wound along the shores of a river called Tears. Willowton was named for its trees and the river a derivative of the same. But the branches of these weeping willows bore leaves like feathers which floated in the breeze tied to tentacle arms till autumn. Ramah never had much of a real winter, but in her gentle autumn the willows along the river of Tears would shower their leaves like Dandelion snow, winds frequently taking them upward thousands of feet before calm night would settle them across a vast forest landscape.

The streets of Willowton wound like the river amid low rising buildings. Her design and architecture were organic so that a population of a million plus felt a sense of small-town community wherever they found themselves. And along one of these streets walked a solitary figure who was not alone. Hooded in an earthen cloak, the figure wandered the leaf-snowing streets of river-front shops, careful not to look into the eyes (or rather face mask) of any soldier of the occupying forces of the Imperial army (while also careful not to appear to be avoiding them). Thirty yards ahead, on the opposite side of the street and ten yards behind on the same side, two men walked casually with the figure, watching, wary. Together and alone. The figure stopped to stare into the window of a curio shop, smiling a sad woman's smile. How she loved this people, their culture, her world. Had she time she might have wept for them.

On the street behind her a hover cart selling savory meats glided by. The aroma of grilled patties and links filled her nostrils and triggered her salivary glands. It woke her from her moment of self-pity with a mix of delight ('well, we can at least still work our jobs and feed our children') and resolve to continue her quiet quest. She moved along, her step as casual as that of the Ramahian Royal Guards who watched from a distance, communicators buzzing in their ears and plasma swords hidden up their sleeves. A third guard stepped out of a doorway as she approached. The slightest nod of his head bade her enter the door.

The Imperial Army walked the streets of Willowton, uncomfortably at ease among a people who had shown no hostility toward the occupying forces and what seemed very little fear. In the midst of the fifth largest city on the planet, where an enemy division was now stationed, the Baroness Yelhsa Ramah walked with cautious freedom through a door and down a hallway, up a flight of stairs and through another door into a dimly lit room filled with computers, holo screens, and stacks of holo disks.

The Baroness drew back her hood to reveal cropped, disheveled hair—a new look to deter unwanted recognition. A man stepped into the light.

"Yelhsa?"

"Hello Nik; It's good to see you."

"You cut your hair."

"I preferred disguise to wandering in the mountains."

"Then the deception worked?"

"You tell me. My man says good news."

"Some good, some bad."

"I couldn't expect much more."

"Well, your sense of sarcasm hasn't faded. Please, sit here."

Nicolus Book motioned Baroness Yelhsa to a chair at his work station. He was a hologrammarian, a documentarian. Local forces had already paid him a visit, disabled his ability to broadcast and confiscated his holo coms. But they left his editing suite, compensating Book for its use by Imperial Reporters. Amber had even been by to do a local interest piece. Like the Baroness, Book was in his thirties, but his gangly black hair and wide eyed perpetual smile gave him a boyish face. While powering up his systems he continued:

"How many guards with you?"

"Only six. Captain Jeah has the rest in the mountains, protecting a Yelhsa who isn't there."

"But for how long?"

"For as long as they have to."

"Well, it seems to be working. My contact brought this yesterday."

He showed her helmet-cam footage from the battle between her Guard and Diaz's company.

"This happened two days ago," he explained. "Your men move quickly. It was hand-delivered to my man. No signals or broadcast of any kind."

"So, you're the only one who has this?"

"Right now, yes. It needs to get to the capitol city. That's where the independent news reporters are operating. They'll eat this up— have it out before those ICA propagandists can spin it any way but good for us."

"It's a solid start, but we need to do more. And for that I'll have to go home."

"I'll go with you."

"No, Nik."

"You need me Yelhsa."

"That's the second time you've failed to call me by my title," she quipped.

"Call it a compromise. I can't call you Mrs. Book; I'm not calling you Baroness Ramah."

"Fifteen years and you can't get over a teenage crush."

"What, is there some Royal edict placing time limits on love?"

"No, but there would be one on your life if my husband heard of you speaking this way."

"Not at all, my Baroness. Every man on the planet loves their Yelhsa Ramah." He got her to smile. "And having expressed my undying love for you, it's time to update you on your husband."

"Yes, tell me."

"It's good and bad."

"I couldn't expect much more."

She made him smile as he brought up broadcasts from Amric's World.

"Count Theus isn't dead. That's good news."

"But he's being put on trial."

"Yes, but not in Imperial Courts. He's appealed to the House of Royals. There he'll find some sympathy."

"What about the evidence?"

"Evidence?"

"Proof of a systematic process of economic sabotage in our space. Proof that our grievances are real, not a ploy leading to secession and war."

"Then it's true."

"Yes. And more. Before Theus left we spoke of something for which we could legitimately stand treason." A pause. "We spoke of conspiracy. Of my dear distant cousin, Janis. Young and beautiful and oh, so deadly. I believe she intends to kill me. I believe she made this war happen."

"My God."

"I have to get home."

"What do you need, Baroness?"

"Every independent broadcasting source you can find."

"Maybe there's someone I know."

"I wouldn't expect any less."

Base Camp FCP

"A bit sloppy," noted Colonel Russ.

"But he's very good," replied Solomon. "I give him some space."

A large holo screen floated beneath an extension cover. They stood outside Ib'm's hover truck, beneath the sun shield, surrounded by high-tech mech and sunshine in the open air. The holo screen showed six different images. One was in motion.

Ib'm: "We've scouted numerous locations where our instrumentation turns fuzzy for lack of a better term. These are all like the ambush site."

"And the commonalities?" asked Solomon.

"They're out in the open. The terrains all differ. We don't see this in any cities. It's something natural."

"But," said Solomon, "you have a brilliant explanation for me."

"Uh...still working on that, sir."

"Come on then, Sergeant, make me look good in front of the Colonel."

"This live feed is Shanwell, First Company," noted Russ. "Two other companies are in the area."

"Good. Keep them safe. Only what's Shanwell seeing? What's in front of our eyes?"

Russ: "Has your man checked the geologics? Mineral deposits or radioactive ore or some such?"

"Yes, Colonel," said Ib'm. "There simply are no similarities in these terrains."

"No," Russ agreed. "Nothing but pretty scenery. Like holo pictures."

And then Solomon saw it—this time, in time: "That's it. That's the similarity."

And Russ: "What is?"

And Ib'm: "Ah nuts, I know that voice."

"What voice?" Russ more perplexed.

"He beat me to it."

"Beat you to what?"

"He's figured it out."

"I've figured it out."

And Russ: "So tell me! Uh, sir."

"Why's it all so beautiful, Colonel? Ib'm get me Shanwell. It's the flowers—those beautiful, scenic, purple flowers."

Ding ding. Ding ding.

"It's Nigel the paper boy!"

Amber could hardly get the words out, couldn't even finish the catch phrase before the audience of children in Studio B were screaming, "Don't open the door!"

"But I've got to get the holo paper," she answered, an open-mouthed look of surprise on her face.

She reached for the doorknob and the kids screamed even louder, half shouting "No!" and half laughing hysterically. When the door flew open the cylinder containing the day's news came flying through, but this time, for the first time in the history of *Amber's Hour*, Amber caught the cylinder. The raucous screaming gave way to a split second of total silence. Then Amber jumped from the doorway to the floor and over the back of the couch onto the cushions. When she threw her hands up in victory, the Studio B audience exploded in cheers and applause.

Amber ran over to the holo screen where the helmet she'd borrowed from her friend MI Joe a hundred episodes ago or so sat on a shelf in a prominent place of honor. She grabbed the helmet and screamed, "I did it Joe! I'm awesome!" Suddenly she cut her celebration short as she realized something: "Hey, this is MI Joe's helmet. I borrowed it a while ago and forgot to give it back."

At that moment, a familiar jingle began to play and Amber's face lit up, her mouth open in a wide smile. The kids in the audience began to scream.

Amber: "It's MI Joe!"

She threw the helmet onto the couch, jumped up, and began to dance toward the door. Everyone joined in the singing:

"M-I Joe is M-Y buddy.

M-I Joe is M-Y buddy.

He's my friend, rough, rugged and ruddeeeeee."

(And on the pause the doorbell rang.)

"M-I Joe's my buddy."

The door swung open and in stepped a handsome, square-jawed young man with slicked back hair. He wore an infantry armor suit and held out his arms to receive applause.

Then Amber said, "Hey, Joe. Whaddya know?"

Joe's plastic grin never wavered: "Hey, Amber. This'll sound crazy to you, but I lost my helmet. This old suit won't fly or anything without it. Any chance I left it here?"

The angle cut to a close up of Amber's profile. She turned to the camera and smiled mischievously. Making her way toward the couch:

"Oh, no, Joe. I haven't seen it anywhere."

The kids in the audience started laughing.

"Hey," said Joe. "What's so funny?"

Amber moved between Joe and the couch and spread out her hands, still facing the audience.

"Nothing, Joe. Everything's fine."

She bit her lip and squinted her eyes. The audience started roaring.

"What are you hiding over there?"

She appeared about to explode: "Nothing...oh, alright! It's here! Your helmet's right here!" She snatched it up and turned it over to him. Following another good laugh, Amber asked Joe what he'd been doing.

"Well, you know Amber, my division's been stationed in the city of Bethelton on the southern coast of planet Ramah's one great continent. Bethelton was the first coastal town to ever be settled on this planet over five thousand years ago."

As MI Joe continued to talk, images of the town montage-marched across the holo screen, matching his narration.

"Before the days of hover ships, giant ships called tankers cruised the oceans of Ramah in search of fish and other natural resources. The Sheba is the oldest floating craft in the galaxy, commissioned two thousand years ago by the Ramahian Barony. Today it's a museum repository for the whole planet.

"My unit has been patrolling the downtown districts of Bethelton. I love talking to the school kids who come by in the afternoons for ices. Some of the boys taught me to play Hawk Rollers. I wasn't very good at it—good thing I wear armor around town.

"You know, Amber, Ramah is a beautiful planet, and the people are the friendliest I've ever met. It's a wonderfully peaceful planet and the people down there are just as happy to have us peacekeepers wandering their street as we are to be there."

The camera cut back to Amber's living room.

"Say Joe, what do you do when you go walking down the street with a bunch of army guys, all wearing your helmets, carrying guns, and the children who see you become afraid?"

"Well, Amber, the great thing about a peaceful place like Bethelton is that most of the time we can stop and talk to people. Sometimes I get to take my helmet off and let a young future soldier try it on and talk to my AI. But I've found that the best thing kids can do when they see an Imperial Soldier is wave to him. You all watching at home should try that sometime. You see a soldier, just give him a wave and watch him wave back.

"Well Amber, I've got to go. *Duty calls.*"

"*Duty calls,*" said Amber and the audience.

As Joe turned to leave, Amber looked to a camera which had moved to a close up of her face. Then:

"Okay, when we come back, I'll be in the kitchen making Amber's famous Chocolate Chunkula Cookies!" She gave her signature shrug and the camera cut away.

Major Leoj Shanwell's company walked random patrol in a narrow-valley, almost a ravine at the base of the mountain range. Twenty more companies were doing the same thing. As each neared various random geographies having in common a flower of violet-blue, the soldiers held up, stood ground, casually on guard, and waited for the chronometers in their helmets to tick to fourteen-twenty hours.

At that moment the casual randomness showed itself a ruse. In the valley, Shanwell's company began to lay down blanketing fire throughout the entire field of teardrop flowers before them. Rail gun shooters were particularly specific to fire at key grid marks they'd been instructed to coordinate by sight. Before the five Ramahian Royal Guards hidden beneath blankets of flowers in the field could decide what to do, they were dead.

Only three companies found targets. The only one that took casualties found itself facing a hundred Royals. Bending orders without breaking them, Solomon called in air support thirty minutes before the zero-time, location to be designated. Five two-man fighters, a squad led by a couple of hot dog pilots nicknamed the Wonder Twins, blasted plasma craters out of what had been the Ramahian Guard's best and brightest in thirty seconds. Mobile Infantry casualties were a mere seventeen.

Bodies and equipment and flowers were collected for analysis. And one prisoner. Then Solomon withdrew his troops to base camp and began looking at topographical maps very carefully. And then at 2600 hours he went for a visit.

Corporal Bladavev sat on a stool in a blue canvas tent, feet and hands shackled in plastanium and surrounded by twenty of Colonel Russ's best troops. Each man stood with his gun trained on various parts of the corporal's body. They understood that, standing in a circle, they would likely shoot each other as well as the Royal Guardsman, but they knew he'd die first. Their gun safeties were off. They would be replaced by a new squad in five minutes, thirty minutes after their watch began. There was no room for drifting attention.

Solomon entered the tent in a regular uniform. He held a silver cylinder in one hand.

"Squad dismissed. Double time."

The men did not hesitate. Corporal Bladavev did not show his surprise, not even when he recognized the plasma sword in Solomon's other hand.

"Release restraints." The shackles recognized Solomon's voice command and fell loose. "Soldier, stand slowly and follow me." The man did not move. "Name and rank."

"Bladavev. Corporal."

"Corporal Bladavev, it's clear by the fact that you haven't tried to kill or take a division general hostage that you know who I am, have assessed the situation and realize that I will kill you whenever I want to."

"You're not that good."

"Brave, son, but even if it were true, the weapon keeps you from having even close to an equal chance. Nor will I insult you with threats of torture. I'm here to give information, not ask it. Now you will stand up and walk with me to the perimeter of this camp. From there you will walk away into the night to deliver my message to your captain. You will walk two meters ahead of me and obey every command. If you deviate from my orders, I will kill you."

"Why not just run me out to the edge of camp under guard?"

"Part of the message."

"You don't need a guard."

"You're an intelligent Guardsman. I admire quick thinking."

"What's your message?"

"We've figured out the hazing effect of the flower, analyzed the fibers woven into your stealth suits. I've analyzed the topography—have you at 973 potential sites only. Tomorrow I'll start blanketing them with mortar fire via a three-day plan which will cover them all and keep my men out of your range. At best, you'll be reduced in these suits to groups of ten and twenty. At that point, you'll be dangerously close to Peace Code violation. That's no bluff. I begin the attack tomorrow."

Silence.

"Anything else, General?"

"My condolences to your captain for his losses."

Solomon followed Corporal Bladavev to the encampment's edge and handed him the silver cylinder followed by a scanning device that proved the cylinder had no tracker in it. Then Corporal Bledavev walked into the night.

Ramahton: capitol to the world. A now empty mansion built on a high hill overlooked a *fanning* urbana on the spreading plain below—buildings of marble and wood designed to be historical monuments, mixed with patches of quaint little homes. Twinkle lights and glow tinsel dangled dormant, awaiting the sunset and night sky. Long museum-walk thoroughfares stretched straight—the *fan*'s skeletal straight lines; they intersected winding roads, like an ancient fan's silken lace. Structure and randomness. Practicality and play.

Treaker Street: an avenue of open air restaurants and curio shops. Stern's Street Side made the best café-latte in town. It didn't take independent reporter Swenho Und long to find it. Being embedded with the First Division had given him time's luxury on this planet stop. He sipped cocoa-crème but breathed in something he'd seldom experienced in his line of work, something it had taken him weeks to label: serenity. It was about to end.

Nicolus Book had followed her, his Yelhsa, to the capitol. When he sat down in front of Swenho Und, the reporter's face reported his thoughts: confusion, recognition, surprise, and then a gleam— the knowledge that he was about to hear news that was worth reporting, that would shake his competition at the Imperial Communications Agency in their suits.

"Book, isn't it?"

"Nicolus Book, Swenho. You were two years ahead of me at Gates. We did Local Color together."

"That's right," Und smiled. "Old man Moore. Boy, he was a spinner."

"Yeah, could make the Rikasian underworld look like paradise...like Ramah."

"It's a beautiful planet, Nicolus. Nothing to fear, though. The takeover's been smooth. People don't seem too concerned about their Baron being on trial—it's a little odd even, how complacent everyone seems."

"Ramahians are a patient people for the most part. With an annoying tendency to stay content."

"You know I've seen some of your holo docs—thought 'em kind of smarmy till I actually got here. You wouldn't think places like this still existed in the universe."

"Lead planet resources, back planet charm. Yeah, it's amazing. And as cliché as it sounds, we owe it to the Ramahian Barony, and, sorry for changing the tone of the conversation, but this travesty that's passing for war and trial is unjust, immoral and illegal, and you know it."

"Unjust and immoral, maybe. Legality is invented by people like the ICA."

"And sometimes people like you."

'Here it comes,' thought Und. "You here to make me happy, Book?"

"Seen General Star lately?"

"What? He's on maneuvers out in the mountains."

"Ha. Practicing war? The Ramahian Royal Guard is out in those mountains and your division General's the go-to man for tracking them down. Problem is he can't. Bigger problem is he's getting his men killed."

"And you have proof of this?"

"I got better than proof. I got pictures."

The screen read: "A Thousand Plus Dead on Ramah."

Melisu Sheharizade: "The story was broken by AIR reporter Swenho Und of Nader Communications, a long-time friend of this network. An entire company of the famous First Division was ambushed and massacred by elements of the Ramahian Royal Guard. This is the greatest loss of life in combat experienced by the Empress's Imperial Army since last year's Thorsfeld campaign. Two battles in a row, now, and the question on everyone's mind tonight is, 'Who is to blame?'

"The answer, at least in part, is the Baroness, Yelhsa Ramah, who, in a ploy to gain sympathy for her husband in the House of Lords, fled the capitol three weeks ago with her Royal Guard into the nearby wilderness, there to plan and implement a campaign of disinformation which has, unfortunately, included the creation of a very real list of casualties. This morning I spoke with First Corps Commander, General Haggard, via satellite link and asked him if the Ramahian Guard's actions were in violation of Imperial Peace Code Law."

A split-screen view of the recorded conversation revealed Melisu Sheharizade at her desk and General Haggard at his Flying Fortress Command Post.

Haggard: "We are in no way looking at PC[*] violations here. These are uniformed combatants fighting highly effective battles. Their methods are secretive, even guerilla, but far from any definitions of terrorist action."

Melisu Sheharizade: "But General, doesn't military conflict by PC definition require specific objectives? This attack looks very close to harassment."

Haggard: "Melisu, I think the enemy's objectives are very clear: like any good Royal Guard would, they're trying to protect their charge from arrest, trial for treason, and a possible death penalty."

Melisu Sheharizade: "General, you speak as if you almost admire these enemies of the Imperium."

---

[*] P.C.: Peace Codes

Haggard: "Healthy admiration is the best way to avoid underestimating the enemy, Ms. Sheharizade. And in the case of Royal super soldier's, that admiration can be none too much. We're facing a problem we knew we'd have to face for a long time: putting 'Regular Army' soldiers against a genetically superior highly trained force. It's the same problem we faced on Thorsfeld, and despite heavy casualties we defeated the Gene Kings of the Planet of Storms in a single day. We will be just as effective on Ramah, but for the sake of the people of this planet and the safety of their Baroness, we're exercising restraint instead of pulverizing whole mountain sides. In reciprocation, the Ramahians are fighting by the rules of war."

Melisu Sheharizade: "But apart from overwhelming destructive force, General, what can you do to defeat the strength and ingenuity Ramahian Royals?"

Haggard: "We put a man with more strength and ingenuity on them, and hunt them down."

He came walking out of the mountains on only the second day of Solomon's ultimatum. Twenty other guards accompanied him, armed and armored with unapologetic confidence in their combat readiness. By then the need for secrecy was over, and hundreds of ships patrolled the skies. Two one-man fighters had settled in on either side of them, hovering a thousand meters away as they came to a halt just inside visual distance from the base camp.

Solomon came out to meet him with his personal platoon. When Liston Jeah left his own guardsmen and approached, Solomon halted his soldiers and did the same. Besides the rifle in his hand and the plasma sword clipped to his side, he carried something else, no, two somethings else—one-yard cylinders slung by straps over his shoulder. The commanders' helmeted heads faced each other for some seconds till Solomon's turned to one side and then the other, signaling the ships to withdraw further.

Solomon then took off his helmet, saying, "That's better. Hard to hear yourself think with all the noise. Sonic booms keep half the men up all night." Solomon pulled the tubes from his shoulder, dropped one to the ground and began unscrewing the cap to the other while his silent adversary watched without reaction. He flipped the tube, and out fell a collection of chrome tubes and dense fabric that, upon release, popped itself open into a chair. He could hear the muffled chuckles beneath the other's helmet as he opened up the second chair for him. The first thing Solomon noted, when Jeah removed his helmet, was the kindness in his face. The first thing Jeah had noticed was the commander's concern in Solomon's. The next thing that each decided was that the man before him was trustworthy. They sat.

"Captain Jeah."

"Captain Star."

"Best if you didn't use that title."

"It's meant as a compliment."

"How can you compliment me with a title I turned my back on while you would wear it to your grave?"

"Given recent events at the Imperial level, sir, where I would have before found it impossible to understand how you could turn your back on your charge, I am coming to find it more and more easily imaginable."

Solomon smiled. "Captain that's the most kindly put insult of the Empress I believe I have ever heard." He bent over his chair and placed his rifle on the ground. Liston Jeah followed suit.

Then they stared at each other again.

"Captain Jeah."

And a pause.

"General Star?"

Solomon stared back, crossed one leg over the other. "Captain, there isn't much time for negotiation now that the eyes know we're out here. The higher-ups will soon order me to give up finesse."

"You call them 'eyes'?"

"They're certainly no help to me."

"The ICA seems to be doing a nice job of turning my best PR ploy against me."

"They're scrambling." Yes, we were. "The damage you've done is real. The Independent's have your helmet cam images floating all over the galaxy. Honest fighting, swift victory—it's the underdog story of the century."

"The century's only a few years old."

"An eternity in news time."

They each felt they could afford a laugh. I remember the long sleepless nights I put in during those weeks. Apologies for whining—I, at least, wasn't playing a game of life and death. Not yet, anyway.

Then Jeah: "But it's cost me double. First your threat of heavy attack and now the need to do so secretly no longer in play."

"Wouldn't've mattered with those null spaces everywhere. Quite a flower you have woven into those suits."

"Fibers made from the center pistils—they call it pollenester. How'd you beat it?"

"Dumb luck, figuring it out."

"Truly?"

"I like plants. I notice them. Dumb luck. After that, some tech work. Still couldn't find you in one of those suits, not in small numbers."

"That's good to know," Jeah smiled.

And Solomon: "It doesn't matter or you wouldn't be here."

"No, you just about have me beat."

"Except that we know you could still inflict some pretty serious casualties; so we would prefer a surrender."

"And that's the only leverage I have to negotiate with."

"Your terms, then."

"I need a week."

"You can't have it."

"One week, General, and my men and I come walking out of hiding. We surrender. My Lady Yelhsa surrenders."

"You're holding back the advantage this would give you."

"I am, sir, but I have said nothing that is a lie."

"I can't give you a week, Captain."

"I know. So we will have to fight for it."

"One week will make that much of a difference?"

"It will."

"Now you give me another mystery to solve."

"Indeed."

"It's a fight then."

"I do not wish it so."

The cadence of conversation ceased. Solomon lowered his head and thought.

"We would've met," he said. "If the Emperor hadn't died young and Janis assumed a premature throne." He looked up. "We would've met, you and I at some Imperial Ball or on a galactic tour when I would've still been only the Captain of a Princess's Guard. We would've met and bragged on the abilities of our troops. 'What's your IGCH*?' I would've asked."

"'Only a 1.45,' I would've answered."

"And I would've congratulated you on having one of the top five Royal Guards in the galaxy."

"I think you have very impressive troops here now," said Jeah. "I'd bet their Handicap would come in, in single digits—no other Regulars could come close."

"Thank you. I'm just...sorry. We could have been friends."

"Perhaps we could still."

"No, Captain Jeah. Friends cannot do what you are about to ask me to do."

"Only respected enemies."

"Yes."

"General Star, you see so keenly into things."

"Say it, then."

"I invoke Champion's Rule."

"Your terms?"

"If I win I get my week, my men surrender, the Baroness remains hidden."

"They will not agree to that."

"It will take at least a week for a champion to come from Amric world."

"No. They'll clear the media away—AIR and ICA alike—and use the one they have planet-side now."

"Yes. Of course. Reducing my bargaining power."

"So give terms they'll accept," Solomon pushed.

"One week if I win. Then the Baroness and her Guard surrender."

"If you do not win?"

"My Guard surrenders immediately."

"And the Baroness?"

"Would you have me lie?"

"They won't say yes!"

---

* I.C.G.H.: Imperial Guard Comparison Handicap

"One week and she surrenders too."

"They won't agree to it."

"If you word it correctly."

"So you would have *me* lie."

"*Egalon Ensigna*,* General. Captain."

"I see."

Solomon thought of troops and loyalties and stained white boots sitting in a closet in the artificial moon above them.

"I will communicate your terms. If they agree, my term is one hour."

"Do you believe they will?"

"Kataltem won't want it. But when he takes it to Constantine and then he takes it to the Empress...she'll ask for satellite feed to watch by."

One hour. About a thousand of Jeah's troops trickled down from the mountains. They formed a line against an ever-growing line of Mobile Infantry. All fighter cover had been sent away—Solomon's choice, to let the Ramahians know he intended to uphold the agreement.

Liston Jeah had already named himself champion. He stepped from the line reduced to his uniform only. Jet boots, light armor and helmets were gone. In his hand, he carried a single weapon. From the other line emerged the Army's champion, Solomon Star. He wore a standard uniform as well and carried as his only weapon a plasma sword similar to the one in Liston Jeah's hand.

The plasma sword: When activated, an antenna extended from the hilt three and a half feet. This blade core generated two things: an incandescent, green, high energy plasma which smelled like burning rubber and a strong electro-magnetic field which held the plasma to the core. The plasma could burn through most surfaces with ease. Focused on the central core, the plasma made an effective blade, and the magnetic field was specially balanced to give the sword its remarkable feature:

Imagine standing in a dark room across from someone holding a pen light. When the person moves the light, it gives the illusion

---

* Literally "equal rank" in an old Archean dialect. An idiom meaning roughly, "You and I are the only ones capable of choosing this destiny as the greatest equals present."

of a streak, a tail—the faster the light is moved, the longer the streak behind it. The plasma sword operated in the same way. Only there was no illusion. The magnetic field of the sword, being affected by movement, made it so that a quick swing of the blade would cause the field, therefore the plasma, to trail behind the core. The sword could be used to lash out like a whip, or to parry multiple blows simultaneously. A sword master could create a 360-degree shield about himself with quick constant movement. New dimensions were added to the art of fencing: a man could parry and strike at almost the same instant. He could also, if not careful, step into his own plasma laden field.

It was a weapon potentially as dangerous to its owner as it was to his opponent. Therefore, only men with genetically enhanced reflexes were allowed, even capable of using it. Which is to say that plasma swords were the elite weapons of the galaxy's elite soldiers—Royal Guards.

Without standing on ceremony, their swords flashed on and they charged past each other, dealing the first exploratory strikes. They turned, faced and held position.

"Liston, I don't want to have to kill you."

"That's rather unfair, Solomon. Perhaps I believe I can actually win."

"Thinking I'm out of practice."

"Hoping you're overconfident."

Hereafter they did not charge and pass but struck and held their positions in a series of strikes and parries and parry-strikes in which plasma trails were doubled and trebled so that a single swing of a blade might produce as many as four hits, their explosive sparks cascading to the ground. The speed of motion was an incoherent blur to Solomon's soldiers, while on the Ramahian side Liston Jeah's subordinates read the moves as textbook maneuvers—not individual strikes or blocks but sequences of motion and their appropriate counters. They saw trouble for their captain the moment his was the first stance to break—he took a half step back.

But the fight continued without pause. What Jeah's one step back had indicated was that Solomon was faster. In fact, some watching thought he might be a great deal faster and holding back.

What was clearly required next was inventiveness—breaking the patterns, seeing new options, faking, feinting and finessing.

Now they were in motion, pressing or retreating, squaring up or side stepping, switching hands, reversing grips, spinning or reversing a spin, attacking low or leaping into a high forward roll to parry a strike and attack from above. The fight had lasted five minutes when Jeah broke and retreated. Neither was breathing hard. The pleasant smile on Jeah's face remained but sweat glistened on his skin and surprise was in his eyes. He understood.

"You're trying to beat me without a fatal blow. You could've killed me and won."

"Only once," said Solomon.

"That's so very patronizing."

"You're complaining that I'm trying to save your life?"

"I'm not trying to save yours."

"Well, now you know my strategy and can doubtless take advantage of it."

"You wouldn't have suggested it if I could."

"I don't suppose we could just call it a surrender at this point?"

"Any man can be beaten on any given day."

"True enough."

Thirty seconds later the fight was over. Jeah had struck from overhead. Solomon's parrying trail was with such speed that the plasma streaming behind the blade core could block Jeah's strike while Solomon dropped, spun, dove under his own blades trail and, reversing the hilt in his hand swung at Jeah's feet. The Ramahian Captain had no recourse but to jump, his legs splitting horizontally to either side of him, giving Solomon time to roll under him and, rising to one knee, cut off Jeah's right foot above the ankle. Jeah came down on his left foot, swept a defensive block behind him and dove forward to distance himself, coming up and turning immediately, sword raised, holding his balance on his single foot. The smile in the face, the surprise in the eyes—still there—but now with the addition of a glazed look of pain.

None of the Ramahian Guards moved. Except Liston Jeah. He turned off his sword and let it fall to the ground. Solomon stood and approached quickly, turning off his own sword and taking Jeah's arm. He lowered him to the ground.

"That's it then," Jeah said matter-of-factly.

"Medic!" Solomon called to his line. "The wound is mostly cauterized. A trickle of blood."

"Yes, but there'll be no reattaching it. Cybernetic prosthetic." He shook his head.

"We'll see you taken care of."

"I would've preferred you'd killed me."

"If you had, you wouldn't have dropped your sword."

By then a stretcher was at hand as was Captain Jeah's second in command.

"Order the surrender," said Jeah.

"Yes, sir." The Ramahians present began to drop their arms immediately.

"You're an honest soldier, and fair," said Solomon.

As he lay down on the stretcher, Jeah replied: "Not entirely."

A week later, Solomon understood the advantage Jeah had gained for his Baroness. His men, as promised, had all surrendered. But the Baroness was nowhere to be found. It became quickly apparent that she had not been with them for some time. Her captain had bought her a week, and she would have some weeks more for whatever agenda she might enact. Where, after all, was the Empire to look for a single woman on an entire planet?

- 12 -
The Hurricane's Eye

Planet Ramah

Still Yelhsa knew her time was running out. Swenho Und had achieved them a small victory. Now he would surely be shadowed. He'd given Book some additional contacts; he, in turn established a network of half a dozen friends, acquaintances, colleagues— amateurs trying to play the spy game. The Baroness used the Royal Guards Jeah had sent with her to contact lesser officials in the capitol city, hoping they could contact those in higher positions to create similar networks. Their goal was threefold: first, gather all available proof of Ramahian innocence to build a compelling case that Baron Ramah's arrest was illegal, the charges against him trumped up lies, the grievances signed by Inmar's allies—at least in the case of this system—true. Secondly, the information had to be coalesced into a powerful broadcast medium, ready to transmit in as many formats as possible once turned over to independent affiliates. Finally, those independent broadcasters needed to be contacted and readied to receive what would be Ramah's last hope for truth.

For Lady Yelhsa, this strategy meant becoming a prisoner in basements and secret rooms in a dozen locations around her own home city. She sat starved for light in a chilly sub-basement backroom of the Weldy Museum of Technological History, kept company by dozens of gadgets, trinkets, priceless breakthroughs and statues or paintings of inventors, mathematicians or entrepreneurial members of the great Weldy family, one of the Founding Five-hundred Families, the first settlers of a planet now ancient in human history. The whole place smelled of dust and oiled metal.

The Baroness read and prayed and waited for word—any to be had. She counted minutes to the setting sun and her chance to sneak out into the city, breathe sweet air while she moved to a new hiding place.

One space in the room was empty of priceless clutter—one blank wall where Nicolus Book, now entering with another man, could record the Baroness making her pleas to the galaxy.

"Hello, Nik."

"Yelhsa."

"What news?"

"This is Dourin Napht'li. He's the one we've been looking for."

A dark, thin man with hungry look and flaming eye entered behind Book. He wore a black overcoat, the appearance of which suggested he seldom took it off. His jet-black hair was slicked back flat against his head. He gave a stiff but low bow.

"My Baroness. I am honored to help our cause."

"You were Military Intelligence?"

"Yes, my Lady. Ten years with the Empire on Arché. And the last seven years as an investigator with the RPD."

"A police officer?"

"Here to serve."

"Dourin here," interjected Book, "is part of a citywide network of cops and citizens more interested in their loyalty to you than to Imperial edicts."

"My Lady," Napht'li continued, "in addition to having made the contacts you need, we have access to a tachyon transmitter and codes for unlocking a communications portal on the fold gate. We think we can have a galaxy wide transmission feed for at least thirty seconds—more than enough time to say everything we must."

Book was pleased to see his Yelhsa smile for the first time in weeks.

She said, "Where did you manage to hide a tach-trans?!"

Napht'li's smile was the pure delight of a sneak-thief: "There's an observatory up in the mountains—s'been operated there by the University for three hundred years. It's small really—a handful of students and an old tenured prof who just happens to hold patents in stellar cartography, AI cryptology, fold space physics and communications."

She turned to the man who'd cared for her so intently for the last few weeks: "Oh, Nik," she beamed. His eyes began to glisten. "You should've been in the Guard. You've cared for me so much. Liston would've commissioned you on the spot."

"Guards are for Gene Kings. And then for uncomfortable uniforms. It's time for your final recording."

"So soon?"

"Napht'li isn't here for introductions, Yelhsa. I'm finishing the program tonight."

"But my men haven't acquired the testimonies from the Cressida crew yet."

"Your man Rik commed me. He's on his way to the safe house on the Loop now with the Captain's eyewitness account and personal logs all on holo disk. He's even got sensor logs from the Cressida—proof of an attack."

Yelhsa had to stifle an impulse to hug her old love. That he called her by name in front of Napht'li and (she him) was impropriety enough.

The dark man bowed, then spoke with proclamation: "Tonight, my Lady, we will save the House of Ramah."

With that, he took leave of his Baroness, who then slumped into her chair.

"I'll ready a holo cam," said Book.

"I look terrible," she objected.

"I'll be sure to pretty you up in post."

"Sarcastic jerk."

"Such language from Royalty."

"Oh, if you want to hear language—"

"No, no, no, no," he frantically waved. "I remember what you're capable of."

They moved together toward the blank wall.

"Let's show the galaxy what other words I'm capable of."

High above the planet Fleet Seven sailed in silent orbit. In his mind First Army General George S. Scott sailed in warrior reveries, remembering a thousand battles throughout history he was convinced he lived, fought, and died in. Scott had been Solomon's immediate superior when he was still a colonel attached to the Kokkinoscardia back in the 90s, before the Overlord War as it was coming to be called. Before Kall. Scott had admired Solomon's leadership and was a strong voice behind his promotion to General of the Big Red One. A buzz at his office door woke Scott from his reveries of the past.

"Come."

The door opened for Lieutenant Parau Amandatar who entered immediately, marching to attention before Scott's desk.

"Reporting as ordered," she exclaimed, using formality to hide her nervousness.

"At ease, Lieutenant."

"Sir."

"More at ease than that."

She smiled. "Yes sir."

"I watched some of the martial combat tournament on holo. Caught your championship match. You made victory look easy."

"Thank you, sir. Comes from a childhood of fending off five older brothers."

"Ha! So you're pretty gung-ho about challenging the men's champ, eh?"

"Yes sir. Can't think of another chance I'd get to beat up on a superior officer. Unfortunately, Colonel Russ is planet-side."

"Right. First Division's just captured the Royal Guard."

"That's good to hear, sir. Can't say I'm too happy about being pulled from combat duty and missing out, though. Begging the General's pardon."

"Not my call, Lieutenant. Doubtless your moment will come round again. I see you've been keeping yourself busy by taking on some boot camp duty, though."

"Yes sir."

"Hospitalize anyone today?"

"Three men, one woman, sir."

"Going light on them?"

"Day's not over, sir."

"Heh, heh. What a spirit. Well, what do you think?"

"Sir?"

"A-pleasantries. B-the probing set-up. And C?"

"Orders sir? A mission?" She tried to hide her enthusiasm.

"That's right. Some special guard duty, if you don't mind turning your trainees over to someone else for the duration."

Silence.

"Well, Lieutenant?"

"Who do I have to kill, sir?"

"Job's already yours. Killing strictly off limits."

Memorial Park ran the length of the city from its base, the Ramahian Mansion, to the end of the city fan. It divided the city into equal halves. Glow tinsel hung from variously placed trees. Fountains sparkled and marble monuments, none towering or monumentally oppressive, shone purple in moonlight. A couple walked arm-in-arm along winding paths like lovers. They were not.

The corporal, a Royal Guardsman named Ash, walked with his charge with calculated casual air. At ranging distances, four fellow Guards walked in the same direction. Yelhsa Ramah was moving to a new hiding place. She breathed the open air deeply, allowing her mind to trust in Corporal Ash's vigilance and wander over simultaneous events: Nicolus Book had handed Napht'li the transmission holo an hour ago. Napht'li should've passed the holo off in a dozen directions, his final destination an ignored mountain observatory.

'Please God,' she prayed. 'Give us success this night.'

As if in answer, a breeze rustled the leaves, shaking tree lights to concerts of twinkle. She took in the moving air. But when the air increased and Ash's hold on her arm became a clutch, the Baroness Yelhsa Ramah came face to face with the realization that sometimes the answer to prayer is no.

There was thunder. And suddenly the night sky was filled with blinding light, light that followed them as they broke into a run. The ship swooped in low to disorient them with wind, light and sound. The target of their mad dash was a clump of trees; they entered and changed directions. Sparks of fire began to pop all around the park perimeter—infantry jet boots. The baroness and her guard did not hesitate. They broke from the trees, heading for the nearest building—still some distance. The ship followed, its spot light fixing them in place. Figures in the dark were converging on their position. Then on cue, they all changed directions. The dark figures were not jet booting; they were the last of Yelhsa's Guard. The whole group found another clump of trees and, in a moment, broke out in pairs so that the ship was forced to choose a pair to follow. It chose the wrong pair.

Ash and Yelhsa reached the park's edge, but found troops already blocking streets and stopping traffic. There was no exit. They turned again. The sound of jet boots was too close. A brightly lit tree ahead drew Corporal Ash's attention. They were there in a moment. Yelhsa's breath was heavy, her expression determined.

Beneath spreading ivy, Ash found a hatch. Two more guards joined them and they were down into the park service tunnels.

"Electric conduits," said Ash. "They should spider out everywhere."

Yelhsa: "Where are the others?"

They didn't know. And so they knew too well. The foursome opted for a tunnel back into the park's center.

"We double back," said Ash. "Avoid the obvious—make for the public buildings. The museum."

No sounds belied any pursuit. After fifteen minutes, they breathed relief. Exploring several access hatches, they settled on an alley behind the Phillipi Summers memorial. Away from the center of town they could find traffic, people.

"Why are you all in uniform?" asked the Baroness. She had suddenly noticed that her guards had stripped away jackets and tear away pants. "You won't be able to blend in."

Ash: "If we face a fight, my Lady, we cannot defend you in civilian clothes. Peace Codes demand combatants be uniformed."

Moving out of the alley they crossed an empty street.

"The Mall is close," said Ash. "Lots of people. They'll even help us hide." The alley took them through three city blocks and then ended. Cordelia Street: Traffic was thick enough; pedestrians looked at them with shock, and then understood the need to pass by. Rounding a corner, they saw the bright lights of the city's outdoor Mall of the Ramahian People, an open space of lights, games, shops and restaurants, bordered by an artificial canal, down which lazy gondolas could row young lovers along light-twinkling waters. They were a hundred feet short of the bridge when a hundred mech-warriors fell from the sky.

Modified rifles shot non-lethal stun nets from four different directions, but the three Ramahian Guards cut them down with plasma swords.

"Stand down!" came a commanding, electronic voice.

"The Baroness Yelhsa moved closer to Corporal Ash. "Lee," she said, drawing his arm to hers. "Lee, you can't defend me. Not here."

"Patience, my Lady," was his determined response.

"Stand down," the voice repeated. "You are in violation of Imperial Articles of War."

"We are not!" replied Ash. "We are uniformed soldiers defending our charge. And I know you cannot safely take her alive and that you must do so lest you be the violators."

The answer was immediate: "Negative. You are in violation. Captain Liston Jeah ordered the surrender of all his troops ten days ago as per treaty arranged through a single combat ceremony. Baroness Yelhsa Ramah, order your men to comply or they put your entire planet in jeopardy."

"Promise me my men won't be harmed!" she shouted, choking back tears over the thought that the Captain of her Guard was likely dead, having lost a ritual combat.

"The Ramahian Royal Guard has been interned planet-side in several maximum-security facilities where your Guard Captain Jeah has opportunity to monitor their wellbeing and confirm their good care."

"Liston's alive," she whispered.

She needed to say no more. Corporal Lee Ash understood. Their swords turned off and dropped to the ground. Then the Guards, without command, dropped to their knees. A diminutive soldier broke the perimeter and, unarmed, marched toward them. Parau Amandatar removed her helmet.

"Baroness," she said in a kind voice her boot camp recruits would've never thought possible, "will you step away from your soldiers toward me please?"

Yelhsa acquiesced. They were face to face.

Yelhsa: "Who are you?"

"Lieutenant Parau Amandatar, Ma'am. Here to escort you to your confinement on Fleet Seven."

"A woman soldier?"

"Unarmed, Ma'am. But not someone to be trifled with. If I may have your arm, I'll escort you to an awaiting transport."

"If I promise not to resist, Lieutenant, would you accept my hand instead?"

Parau considered the offer, breathing the open air as deeply as Yelhsa had done but minutes before. "Yes, I will."

They stepped out of the circle walking hand in hand.

The observatory was too far from the city for anyone there to observe its destruction. An old astronomer was killed in the blast along with half a dozen university students. It happened at the same time several underground cells of resistance (non-violent of course) were uncovered, key members of local government and law enforcement were detained, the last Ramahian Royal Guard, a sergeant named Rik, was captured, a series of mysterious hover car and ship malfunctions halted the activity of certain independent reporters for the night, and Nicolus Book's precious holo broadcasts were destroyed before his very eyes. Of all the conspirators only one, a black coated man named Napht'li had eluded Imperial authority. He stood in the distant mountains half way between a camouflaged hover ship and the burning bulk of stone and metal that had been Ramah's hope for truth. Had he been but five minutes early he would be dead. Ten minutes and he'd still have a copy of Book's holos in his hands.

Strangest of all: a wild half disbelieving, half rapturous smile spread across his face. Eyes glazing over, he watched the inferno and drew the mixing heat and cold of the mountain air in heavy gulps. In the distance, lights flying in the sky appeared. They were coming to check—to survey the damage and to capture any survivors.

"No," he said aloud. "Not to capture…"

And silently he faded into the dark.

What most impressed Parau Amandatar was the stateliness of demeanor the Baroness Yelhsa Ramah could maintain in the face of exhaustion and defeat. Every major official on Fleet Seven had visited her quarters to see to her "comfort" and "needs." To General Kataltem she gave thanks for the Army's hospitality, especially the kindness that had been extended to Captain Jeah by shipside surgeons. To Sykol Ckin'r's question regarding the comfort of the staterooms she'd been provided, she replied, "Certainly the most comfortable prison one could ask for."

When at last everyone who had come to see to her comfort in this time of "disturbing transition" had gone, the Baroness sank into a grey couch, surrendering the stiffness of formality but not a reserved, perfect posture. She folded one hand over the other on her lap.

Parau Amandatar broke the silence: "You should try to rest."

"It's a bit difficult, considering you're standing there watching over me."

"Yes, Ma'am. I can't leave."

"No but you can sit."

"If you'd like."

"Please."

Parau sat in a chair opposite Yelhsa. They stared at each other.

"So, what now, Lieutenant? You stand guard over my every move? Follow me into the bathroom?"

"This is as new to me as it is to you, Baroness. I've never even met a Royal before."

"No? What's your regular job in this Empress's army?"

"I was a drill sergeant for new recruits for several years, but—"

"You're kidding."

"On my honor, Ma'am."

"That's amazing. You were going to say something else."

"I volunteered to be the first woman in an ICUR combat suit. I'm infantry now. I battle tested last year and now they're working on recruits—I'm to lead a platoon, but that's a year off. So my armor's being used for reference in replication. I picked up some drill duties again for a while, but now I'm assigned to you."

"My prison keeper."

"Your protection, Ma'am. Though to answer your question, yes, I have to follow you into the bathroom. It's the one room that doesn't have cameras."

"Oh, please tell me you're kidding about that."

"No Ma'am. On my honor. I'll sleep in the room with you too."

"Will bedtime be before or after the strip search?"

Parau didn't blink. Yelhsa was duly startled: "No!"

"Well no, not really. I just have orders to collect and search through your clothes—everything you're wearing. There's wardrobe in the bedroom. If you wouldn't mind changing."

"A moment please."

They sat, again, in silence.

Suddenly the Baroness spoke again: "Someone on the planet betrayed us."

"My understanding is that you were tracked by DNA scanners. Once a lucky sweep picked you up or a Gene King—sorry—a Royal Guard profile or both, it was just a matter of following you and all your contacts and all theirs...satellite scans, nano snoopers."

"Hmm. Even with our stealth suits."

"DNA scan works differently. It really is about luck—first you need a sample or profile, then a lucky hit."

"Well, Lieutenant, luck or betrayal, Sykol Ckin'r was most forth coming, sharing details about the failure of our plan."

"Plan, Baroness?"

"To broadcast the proof that we are innocent and Janis unjust in her accusations. And it failed completely. Truth is lost."

"Yes, Ma'am."

Yelhsa smiled. "It's kind of you not to argue with me. I don't expect you to believe me."

"No, Ma'am."

She breathed a sigh. "So what's next, Lieutenant?"

"You should rest."

"Never again. I don't think I will. But I will lie down."

She stood, moved across her new living area and walked through the opening to the bedroom. Parau Amandatar followed her, closing the door behind them.

On the planet, a concerned populous tried living life as normally as they could. Ever powerful, ever benevolent—the Empire exercised as inconspicuous a control as possible. The interim government consisted of native governors in council with First Corps General Haggard as the only Imperial presence, a function Haggard knew was necessary but for which he nevertheless had little enthusiasm. A convoy carrying the general and his staff hovered through Ramahton via gently humming engines, drawing little attention from pedestrians as it passed and no attention from Nicolus Book who sat at his favorite streetside café, blank sadness in his face. Absent mindedly he sipped at a china cup filled with overpriced coffee.

'Why not,' he'd thought to himself. "We'll celebrate" he'd said to no one.

The day was bright like summer, cool like autumn. His heart was winter, and the tears he pushed back, the melting of ice. As with all people in a state of loss, his thoughts wandered:

'They let me go, just let me go. They let you go, you idiot, because they know there's nothing left you can do. Swenho's gone, Nik. Locked down up there, with her...locked in. Yelhsa. Sorry.'

He looked up at the daylight moon that was Fleet Seven. 'Her prison.' And he wished he could remake the universe so only two people lived in it. Glancing downward he caught a glimpse—had to do a double take: a dark man in a black coat across the street, who Book could swear had been looking at him, turning to walk away.

'Napht'li,' he thought.

He wanted to follow but suspected Imperial eyes were still watching him. So he did nothing. He didn't even bother to think about going home.

"It's over."

And he sipped his coffee.

Solomon bunked planet-side on Haggard's Flying Fortress, happy to know that several in his platoon shared his idea of R. & R.: sitting around. In this instance, chairs and couches had been dragged outside and under a hover shelter—a souvenir from the Eddan defense platform that Ib'm and Devsky had managed to turn into a floating roof, lazily tethered to the ground with cables and stakes. Add satellite uplinks, holo vision and several buckets of beverage and food on ice, and Solomon, Devsky, Ib'm, Captain Troy, and Lieutenant Bastogne had a relaxing afternoon ahead of them.

Ib'm was speaking: "So the idiots in personnel sent half the division LES hardcopies saying they'd been paid a million credits last month and General Scott calls Tenneb the CO down there and demands they be allowed to keep the interest!" He paused for the laughter. "Then he says, 'And I'll thank you not to check my pay statement too closely, either!'" And they laughed again.

On the holo screen, Einor Pluc was running the headlines: "...Supreme Court today rejected Baron Ramah's request for trial in the House of Royals but, at the Empress's own request, granted that the trial would be juried by his Royal peers. It's been three months since Fleet Seven began the Ramah campaign. The people of the planet are cooperating with the interim government, and the Baroness, Yelhsa Ramah, who has been residing aboard the World Ship for three weeks now, reports that she is thankful about today's news. Charges against the Ramahian Barony include..."

"Speaking of the Baroness, how's her Captain?" Solomon wondered aloud.

"I heard Colonel Russ visited him shipside," said Devsky. "Soon as they fit him for a cybernetic leg they put him in max-security—a totally automated cell. Seems a waste of my taxes—the General carves him a stump only for Medico to fix him up as dangerous as ever."

"Blame me; I authorized it," said Solomon.

"You're getting soft in your old age, sir."

"I'm forty, I'm not old. Besides, he was so very polite."

"Nicest one-legged guy I ever met," Bastogne chimed in. "Trying to kill the General, and all, aside."

"Speaking of which, General."

"Joshua, are you about to scold me?"

"Yes sir." Captain Joshua Troy was a starry-eyed young man whose wide eyes, angular face, and perpetual smile portrayed a child-like innocence which belied his serious concern as a soldier, the commander of Solomon's personal platoon. He stood in marked contrast to the platoon's second in command. Sieg Bastogne was a brick of a man, gruff in manner, brief in speech.

Troy continued: "I'd appreciate it, sir, if in the future you'd not accept challenges to personal combat from super soldiers."

And Devsky: "Oh, never you mind the Cap, General Star, he's been promoted recently and thinks he has to do his job better than before—now he's all worried about the inconvenience to his career of the man he's supposed to be protecting up and dying on him."

"Besides, Josh, I'm a Gene King myself...you know I never heard that phrase the entire time I lived on Imperial World."

"Sir, there could've been an accident. War's about X-factors."

"With no one bothering to ask the Y."

Devsky: "General Star, you wax poetic like that again, I'll switch to Troy's side."

Over the next round of laughter Ib'm called out, "Hey, look sir, it's your old friend."

Behind Einor Pluc a photo of a stern looking Hal Teltrab filled the screen and then cut to stock footage of the Imperial Captain.

"And from Imperial Palace," said Pluc, "word that Captain Teltrab and his lovely wife Charissa are expecting another son. We wish the happy parents well and this dad hopes they get some sleep while they can. That's it for me, galaxy. After the break, Melisu Sheharizade takes you around the stars."

"I love that girl!" Ib'm was enthusiastic.

"I thought you had it for some pretty lieutenant," said Solomon.

"I did. I mean I do, but this woman's gorgeous!"

"I like her hair," said a rigid Bastogne.

"She's more than pretty," Troy countered. "She's nice. She's one of the kindest people I've ever met."

Ib'm whirled around. "You've met her!"

"Yep."

"You lucky bas—"

"Ib'm!"

"Yes sir, language sir."

And after a pause: "Well you can't leave us all hanging, Troy," said Solomon, "tell the story before Ib'm drips saliva all over my lunch."

"I met her last year. She's sent me a holo every couple of months saying she's praying for me ever since. I was walking through Central Park, hiking the back paths. And there she was."

The pleasant memory filled his face.

"Yeah, go on," Ib'm replied.

"She was dancing."

"Dancing!"

"Dancing to music in her heart."

"Permission to be sick, sir?"

"Shut up, Devsky."

"Roger that, sir."

"She was dancing a ballet in a grass clearing in the woods in a kind of a bright green dress. When she saw me she didn't stop. She just smiled and danced toward me. 'What's your name, soldier?' That's what she asked when she finally did stop. I know she's a public figure and all, and she's always waving at the troops and all...but she talked to me. She stopped and joined me on the path and talked with me for an hour. It was great."

"Did you ask her out?"

"Shut up, Ib'm, the captain's married," said Devsky.

"Happily," Troy agreed.

"So what?"

"And I told my wife I met her."

"Yeah?"

"Totally up front."

"I'd've asked her out anyway."

"She's got a guy."

"Nuts!" Bastogne from nowhere.

"He's a chaplain."

And Ib'm: "Melisu Sheharizade's man is a chaplain?!"

"Yep."

"Well, I'm depressed."

"What religion is he?" asked Solomon.

"I didn't ask, sir."

"Nuts," Bastogne concluded.

Parau Amandatar took her assignment seriously enough to move into the quarters assigned to the Baroness.

"How does a drill sergeant grow such beautiful, long hair?" Baroness Yelhsa was reviewing pictures in Parau's publicity file. "'Woman Soldier Volunteers for Armored Combat.' And how does the Lieutenant just give that hair up?"

Fresh out of the shower, Parau was trying to make her hair look less masculine for this particular assignment.

"The hair was the least of what I went through. It *would* be nice to be able to do something with it on off hours."

"You don't strike me as the kind of person who would care about how her hair looks."

"It's a good reminder, Ma'am."

"Of what?"

"I may spend all my time acting like a man, but I'm not one."

"You're lop-sided. Let me do it." Yelhsa moved behind Parau and took her hair before she could say no. Sympathizing with the lieutenant because of her own recent haircut, Yelhsa began working with a comb and some gel. "I can relate, you know. My role as a leader requires a kind of strength you might call masculine."

"I don't know, Baroness. Beating maggots up, maybe. That's not the same thing as leadership strength. Women are just as good at it."

"Maybe. But you wouldn't have a typical man style your hair."

"And I shouldn't have a baroness do it, either."

"Indulge me, I'm bored."

"I'm sorry."

"You can't help it, Parau; learning to kill people with your pinky finger hardly gives you time for hospitality training."

"That's not what I meant, Ma'am."

"No?"

"I'm sorry for what you're going through. For having to wait and see if you'll have your husband back, your life back."

Yelhsa paused and Parau turned, looked at her face to face. The Baroness looked down, having finished Parau's hair. Her eyes began to tear.

Then she said, "That's very kind of you." And smiling: "You're kinder than you let on, aren't you?"

"No, Ma'am. I'm much harder. I just like to take breaks from it."

"Ha, ha." She moved away, allowing Parau a semblance of privacy to complete her morning dress. "You know, Parau, I studied self-defense for ten years. Marriage and office ended it for the most part. Though I did get an occasional workout with my Guard."

"I didn't know that, Ma'am. What did you study?" She was genuinely interested.

"Taofe."

"The Spinning Dance."

"You know it?"

"Origins pre-dating the Empire. Masters on Phaedra claim its beginnings."

"Very impressive."

"Did I mention I had five older brothers?"

"For me it was being from a wealthy family. Daddy thought I should know how to defend myself."

"Is he on the planet, your father?"

"He died."

"Oh. I'm s—"

"It's alright—that was many years ago. Those tears are old." She sighed. "Do we have an agenda today, Parau? May I go out and see things, do things?"

"We can go to the docks today, Baroness. A ship's bringing lawyers and some officials from the new government to speak to you."

"What about?"

"I'm sure I don't know, Ma'am."

"I'm sure I do. 'Ma'am' makes me sound so old. I wish you'd stop it. They're coming to explain my rights I think. I'll be going to Amric soon to join Theus. To stand trial too."

"I hope that's not the case, Baroness."

"Thank you Parau. There is a chance I may only be detained during the trial. Then exiled once they find Theus guilty and shoot him in the heart."

At this Parau merely cleared her throat.

"I'm sorry," Yelhsa responded. Then changing her tone: "Are you ready? Can we go now?"

"The transports not due for two hours, but...maybe we can take our time getting to the dock, and maybe take a detour or two on the way."

Two hundred and seventeen: the number of cups of coffees, lattés, espressos, cocoas, crèmes and sugars, gourmet and fresh ground that Nicolus Book had sipped empty in self-pity for the last six weeks, sitting at the same table in the same seat at the very outdoor café at which he'd begun his plan to save the planet's

Royal Family. He'd vowed that two hundred and fifty would be the end. He'd go back home. Fleet Seven hung above him, out of his reach. Yelhsa Ramah out of his reach. He would pray for her.

Like clockwork, the convoy carrying First Corps commander, General Haggard, came hovering through the streets of Ramahton, past the café. Book counted the personnel carriers as he did every week. First the lead cars: 'one, two, three.' Then the plasma tanks: 'four, five.' Then the General's guard: 'six seven, eight.' Then, as car number nine came into view, Book's attention was drawn across the street where a black coated man stared back at him with emptiness in his eyes and madness in his smile. Book thought about holovision technique and laughed to see how his shock turned everything to slow motion, just like in a holo film.

When General Haggard's staff car came molasses-speed near, Napht'li raised a shushing finger to his lips. When the car passed ('number nine'), his eyes followed while his head was shaking back and forth at Book. And when the car sped its crawl another thirty yards on, Napht'li was motioning Book to duck down.

The explosion returned time to normal. Book felt himself fly back and hit the ground. The ringing in his ears, the screams and smoke, the debris and footfalls disoriented him, but he managed to see Napht'li's legs moving him away from the destruction.

Book's first thought was, 'My God, what have you done?' His second was a little crazy: 'Two hundred sixteen and a half. I didn't get to finish my coffee.'

- 13 -
Genocide

Planet Ramah

He called her Savage. The woman in his dreams. She was real—very. He'd left her five years ago, the only woman he'd ever loved.

"No, that's not true," he said.

"What?" she replied.

He was swimming in light, and she was with him. He was dreaming.

"I was thinking; you're not the only woman I've ever loved. I'm sorry."

"Why should you be sorry that you loved the Queen of the Universe? Made for that all your life."

On Kall she had taken him down a river on a long journey to see his father. They were sitting in her canoe now, watching foot long dolphins play in leaps around them, raising rainbow mists in the setting sun. A strong smell of pine and methane filled the air and the sunlight warmed his face.

"You have better reason to be sorry," she continued.

"What's that?"

"You love her still."

"And that took me from you."

"Yes."

"That's not true," he concluded.

"No?"

"No. You're giving me too much credit."

"Then why did you leave me?"

Even in his dream he wasn't willing to voice what he was thinking: 'I didn't think I deserved you.'

He looked at her: emerald green eyes, porcelain smooth skin, rich brown hair pulled tight behind her head. Then, as she drifted away, he was standing on the massive black limb of a massive black tree. He recognized ahead of him the entrance to the largest native dwelling place on the planet Kall. Lit with supernatural light, it moved toward him. Suddenly he was swimming again. The next voice he heard wasn't a woman's. The light that he opened his eyes to was dull and artificial and did not make him blink.

'Caught me napping.'

"What is it, Devsky?" his waking voice asked.

"General Haggard's convoy was attacked less than an hour ago. It's an IP, sir. They're calling it an IP.

Krises Ta's voice was honeyed venom. The something threatening in her aspect was more than in her platinum hair, the narrow oval of her face, the miniscule mouth which seemed barely to move, or her sultry eyes, cat slanted—dangerous and otherworldly. In Krises Ta, anchor for the least viewed broadcast in the galaxy, all these elements melded into an Eve's temptation: liquid danger—fear and desire. Anyone who watched was captivated, even if the words she spoke were horrifying.

Where other broadcasts from Fleet Seven's ICA Studios were sent throughout the galaxy, a single frequency was reserved for planetary transmissions only. These broadcasts were filled with threats. And they weren't empty.

"...curfew is planet-wide and covers all night time hours. Martial law provides for the elimination of due process—curfew violators will be shot on sight.

"The interim government is disbanded. Officials planet-side are required to surrender themselves one hour after dawn to Imperial authorities.

"The senior Sykol of Fleet Seven, Bee'Ef Ckin'r has called immediately for a CIRT—that's a Critical Incident Response Team—to examine what is already being called an Incident of Prejudice, that is a violation of Imperial Peace Codes. PC violations pay the highest penalty. Terrorism pays the highest penalty. Intolerance will not be tolerated in the Amric Empire."

Bee'Ef Ckin'r was the happiest he'd been in years. Since Sykol Central had lost much of its power just before the war, Ckin'r had been little more than a figurehead aboard Fleet Seven. Now he sat in an interview that could determine the fate of a world. And he was in charge.

"Did you act alone, Mr. Napht'li?"

"I demand immediate representation."

"Who were your fellow conspirators?"

"I have proof that demands the leaders of this illegal force be put on trial for direct violations of the Peace Code Rules of War."

"You committed an IP, a terrorist act, Napht'li; you have no rights. The only question here is whether or not you're a mad man or a conspirator. So—"

"Imperial forces made an attack on a non-military target—a clear PC violation. That's the Incident of Prejudice—that's the real IP. You can't cover this up."

"As I was saying," Ckin'r continued undisturbed, "the only question is whether you die alone or with your whole people."

"I am a lawfully deputized member of the Ramahian Police, reporting an illegal terrorist attack by renegade forces of the Imperial army. As Sykol of the Fleet, you should want to report this to your superiors on Amric's World immediately. This could cause chaos throughout the galaxy if not quickly addressed."

"I see." Ckin'r stood and left the interrogation room. He stepped through another door into the adjacent observation room where ICA head producer Nase Westart sat staring at Napht'li through a two-way mirror. Napht'li seemed to be staring right back at me.

"He isn't making it easy," Ckin'r noted.

"Yes," I said in my calming, quiet voice. "Yes, he's wonderfully non-responsive to you." Ckin'r bristled, but I continued: "He knows exactly what to say so that nothing we record can be used against him."

"Can you build a case from what you have?"

"Oh...I'm not sure. But keep talking to him and we'll see what we can do. But Mr. Ckin'r?"

"Yes?"

"What if there's no case to build against him?"

"Ah, well there is that."

And Ckin'r turned his back to me and walked away.

General Haggard was awake and alert when Solomon entered his planet-side hospital room. I'm personally convinced that there's something conspiratorial about hospitals. Someday I might do a story about it. Why is it that every hospital in every different city on every different planet (and even on Fleet Seven) smells like every other hospital? It's that mix of medicine and misery, of people being treated half like patients and half like subjects in a lab. Hope and despair. Kindness and cold calculation. It shouldn't be possible a smell could exist across the galaxy. Someone should say something.

Solomon approached his superior's bed. Half of Haggard's, face, and one arm were covered in synthderm patch.

"Minor burns," he said as Solomon shook his good hand. "This skin regeneration treatment itches more than the burns hurt in the first place."

"Consider it a gift to your wife," said Solomon. "We wouldn't want you facing her with only half a face." He smiled.

"Better than what my driver got. I made the call to his family yesterday."

"They've made an arrest. And Ckin'r's got a CIRT investigation going."

"And don't think I'm not already screaming about it. There hasn't been an IP in the Empire in five hundred years and they'd better not call one here. 'Incident of Prejudice,' my eye! That Ckin'r's an idiot."

"But he's a Sykol," Solomon said with obvious disdain in his voice. "I wouldn't put anything past Sykols."

"All the more reason I—" and he raised his voice—"GET RELEASED FROM THIS BED! as soon as possible and argue as the one attacked that Ramah should not be punished for the act of a single man."

In ICA Studios, in one of a dozen editing suites, sat Fleet Seven's newest holo editor, Eryn Sevryns. Her petite form sat enveloped in a highbacked chair. Crystal bright, yet narrow eyes stared through equally narrow black framed editing lenses, allowing her to operate controls and manipulate holo images with a literal blink of an eye. Her short, dark hair lay in twirls, pinned upon her head, the ends just flipping upward or outward like frayed wisps of spider web rope. Her smile was as bright as her eyes—her whole face seeming to participate—she enjoyed her work.

Before her, virtual controls floated above vertical holo projectors, and half-a-dozen holo screens projected their 3-D images. Gel pads in the chair's arms allowed her to adjust or change out the virtual controls—these she could operate by reaching out a hand or through controlled eye movements affecting the editing lenses.

In his quiet fashion, Nase Westart, Fleet Seven's ICA executive producer, seemed simply to appear behind Eryn's chair. His gentle voice, however, kept her from being overly startled. I apologize; that's sarcastic of me. This isn't part of the story to be flippant about. I'm just nervous.

In a rather bizarre cosmic coincidence. I'd met Solomon Star for the first time exactly one year before that day—the exact date of it. I mentioned the tea house before. Down in Arcadia. He was there when I walked in. I got my tea and walked over to his table. He looked up from a book he was reading—a real book, one of those from the shelf in the corner.

"General Star," I'd said. "May I join you for a moment?"

"If you like," he replied.

At first, I couldn't tell if he knew me—couldn't read anything in his face. That, then, made me certain he did know who I was and had no intention of divulging any classified information—about his work or his past.

"I'm sorry to put you on guard, sir."

"You're very perceptive."

"I promise I'm not here to interview you."

"There's not much I could tell you anyway."

"I know, General. But..."

"Oh, now you do have my attention," he said. "You have the look of a man who puts people on the defensive about to go on the defensive yourself. You're about to make yourself vulnerable. An ICA producer. Westart, right?"

"Yes, General. And yes. I just have a feeling that you're the one man on this ship who can answer an honest question."

"That's probably not true."

"Well, call it a risk I'm willing to take, then."

"Not sure I am."

"I understand, General Star."

"What's your question?"

"How do you keep loyally serving an Empire you have doubts about?"

His answer made all the difference in what was, one year to the day, about to happen next.

"How's it going?" I asked the new holo editor, Eryn.

She turned quickly, causing several virtual buttons to accidentally press.

"Oh, Mr. Westart. I didn't hear you."

So I didn't exactly avoid startling her, just not too startled. I answered, "Call me Nase, Eryn. We're pretty informal around here."

"I'll try. I feel like such a child around all these pros."

"Yes. Well...you're doing just fine. How's this, uh...this latest project going?"

Turning to the display: "Well, I've gathered every image I could find and time locked them together. The transport interiors don't show anything of any help. One soldier's helmet symbiot—look here—caught a glimpse of the perpetrator's face; he was definitely in the area during the explosion. The best view we have is a satellite visual. I have it on the big screen," (pointing), "but even at best magnification all we see is the top of his head, and all we see is him standing there."

"Okay, Eryn, this isn't too bad. We at least have a face shot—how long is that?"

"Only three frames."

"Yeah—that and the view from above which shows us the location and the explosion. Can you clean up the face shot any? We need to use programs that'll stand up to legal scrutiny."

"Already done, sir—Nase. This is Nitram enhancement software; it's used in court cases regularly. And...there it is. Clearly this Napht'li fellow."

"And that coat he's wearing allows us to match the satellite shot with the face. Good. Very Good."

"Thanks. But...it doesn't show him doing anything."

"Well...let's watch the whole shot together, alright?"

"Okay."

I pulled up a chair and began reviewing the holo.

"Alright, now, look here," I said. "Just before the explosion, he raises his hand. What's he doing?"

"He's pointing?" Eryn suggested. "Pointing upward, I think."

"Maybe he's signaling someone."

"There's a café across the street. All I noticed were people scattering."

"What if it's the trigger?" I asked.

"That'd be proof. But I don't see any device. Just his finger and hand."

"Hmm. Well...this is...this is good. How long have you been in today?"

"Oh, I don't know. What time is it?" She checked the chrono line on one of the screens. "Thirteen hours," she noted casually. "No wonder I have to go to the restroom so bad."

I chuckled and said, "Yeah. Why don't you take a break?"

"I should. I'll grab something to eat and come back."

"No, I don't want you to kill yourself here, Eryn. Don't need to impress the boss that much. And I want you to be happy with your work."

"Oh, I am; I don't mind—"

"No, of course not, of course not. But this job has a way of overworking folks. You have a life elsewhere on this big ship, don't you?"

"Oh yes, it's wonderful here. I'm making friends, and there's a lot to explore."

"Well, that's good. I want you to be happy. Tell you what, Eryn, why not let me fiddle with this footage for a while, maybe take over the dull work of writing the final report for the CIRT? You go and call it a day, look at things fresh tomorrow. Okay?"

"Well, alright, if that's what you want. Thanks. And thanks, you know, for the chance to work here."

"Sure. Yes. It's good having you here. Your smile brightens up the studio."

She left with that smile on her face and I took her seat, wondering if that quip about the smile had been perceived as flirtatious or just the compliment I had intended. When words are your weapons, you analyze everything, you second guess every thought, especially the ones in your own head. And I love my wife; I hoped I was just being nice and hoped that's how Eryn took it. I don't know. I think maybe it's been fifteen thousand years since we lived in a culture where men and women knew what they could and couldn't say to each other. But I'm drifting off point. Second guesses, right? I was having some of my own, and maybe that's what the whole story of Solomon Star's involvement in the Overlord War was really about. He'd made a choice to do what he was certain was the right thing to do, the most painful thing, though. I was approaching a choice like that just now. Touching the gel pad at my left hand, I made a com link to the offices of the Fleet Seven Sykol.

"Mr. Ckin'r," I intoned. "I think we've got something...No, I wouldn't call it a smoking gun, sir. But definite proof of Napht'li's identity and presence...No sir, no indication of a detonation device, but he does point in the footage, and that might indicate a co-conspirator—perhaps signaling to the person who was operating the detonator...No, it isn't any clearer than that but— ...adjust the image, sir? Well, we've enhanced it for clarity—a...I see, but there's no indication of a detonator in his hand...I—...I realize that, but—...well...I'm certain it can be done, sir, but is that exactly...oh...legal?...I see...I see...No sir, I'd prefer not to see that sort of thing done at ICA studios...Yes, of course, I can send the footage to you...All of it? Yes sir...And erase my copies, yes Mr. Ckin'r...My family, sir? My family is fine...Yes, and a pleasant day to you too."

Not very heroic, I know. And I'm sorry. Especially for what happened next.

She could have kicked herself for thinking they'd been getting along so well. Now Parau Amandatar was chasing the Baroness Yelhsa Ramah down the corridors of Fleet Seven, blood dripping from a gash on the right side of her head above the hairline where Yelhsa had surprised her with a face to leg introduction to a metal chair.

'I trusted her,' thought Parau. 'Trusted...you idiot, you're not supposed to trust—do your job.'

She was only a few hundred yards ahead. She'd stopped to remove Parau's jacket to use as a disguise, turning at the doors as Parau began to come to, saying, "I'm sorry, Lieutenant. But they're talking about an Incident of Prejudice. Do you know that means?" And she was gone.

She ran when she saw no one, walked otherwise, took two unnecessary turns hoping to lose her jailor and make it to an elevator. Fleet Seven corridors were long and wide and offered few turns, few places to hide. But the ship had hundreds of accessible floors and over a billion in her crew.

'I make it to an elevator and I buy myself hours.'

Parau was thinking the same thing. Her jog was brisk but not panicky. A couple of sailors noted her bloodied shirt and offered her help. Without stopping she told them to call the escape in to the Naval Police.

"And lock down the lifts to this floor in a five-klick radius," she added.

Next came the guesswork—where would Yelhsa go? The baroness didn't know herself. Try to find and free her guard? Try to escape? Try to contact the House of Lords?

Before her a near empty corridor stretched into the distance, so far that its gentle downward curve was visible. Behind her a figure came running around a turn at a main junction. Yelhsa turned and sprinted away. She watched the brightly lit signs in the ceiling for her escape route. Parau sped up but could not draw closer. She did not shout, and Yelhsa did not panic. Their run was silent. At a minute's end, Yelhsa turned toward the wall and ran up to the double doors of a freight elevator. They opened for her and she stepped in, calling out a level and a destination.

Then the hallway outside the doors turned red, and a basso siren began to blare. Yelhsa watched the empty corridor, begging the doors to close. They began to, but were not shut completely before Parau managed to dive through, running head-first into Yelhsa's thighs.

The Baroness kicked her to one side and moved to the other. The elevator began to rise but then lurched to a stop. Yelhsa looked up as Parau slowly rose, ice in her expression.

"I've frozen the elevators, Baroness. You're trapped."

But then suddenly the elevator began moving again and Yelhsa smiled as she saw the destination readout.

Surprised for only a moment, Parau leapt into action. Her side kick cracked the wall where Yelhsa's left-moving head had just been, but she did not lose her balance and so was able to block the Baroness's back fist with a forearm. With that same arm's hand, she grabbed at Yelhsa's, but she had followed the punch with a spin, drawing her vulnerable arm away while raising the other in a palm thrust at the face. Again, Parau parried with an elbow, then swung with the other in close quarters as the leg with which she'd just kicked finished its downward spinning step and stepped again to press the close attack.

She raised a swift thrusting elbow, blocked by the Baroness in kind. Then Parau, but six inches away, threw first the left knee at Yelhsa's pelvis—blocked by a raised outer thigh—then quickly kicked the right knee into that thigh, causing a nerve cluster to explode with pain. Yelhsa screamed through the pain but struck back—a solid right hook. It was bread and butter for the warrior woman who loved nothing better than a bloody lip. Parau stepped back with the force of the punch, allowing Yelhsa to step away from the elevator wall.

Each recomposed her attack stance. Parau licked the blood on her lips, smiled, and quickly jumped back into the fray. The rhythm of the strike, block and counter-strike that followed was dance-like, quick, and ended in their hands and arms locked in a tug and push attempt to throw the other off balance.

Then Parau: "You're good, Ma'am."

And Yelhsa: "Thanks."

But Parau: "I'm better."

With that she head-butted the baroness, forehead to forehead, drawing blood from the impact point on both their heads. A mistake. She underestimated the concussion Yelhsa had given her before as well as the fact that the Baronness was as physically hard headed as she was in personality. They both staggered, then staggered again as the elevator stopped. The door slid open and Yelhsa fell out—into the arms of a surprised Liston Jeah.

Parau stepped out of the elevator, equally surprised. But she braced herself for a fight. Liston looked at her with kindness in his eyes and his gentle smile.

"At ease, Lieutenant. You're fight is over."

Parau had always wanted to take on a Gene King. But when she looked about her and saw she was facing ten of Yelhsa's personal Guard, even she knew to quit. She relaxed from her fighting stance and put her hands behind her back.

"Come, Baroness, quickly," Liston urged. He pulled at her elbow, drawing her away. She turned her head towards Parau as they moved away.

"I'm sorry," she said, touching her head.

Parau watched them move quickly down the corridor and whispered, "Yes Ma'am."

The way was clear, the docking corridor empty. The Captain of the Ramahian Guard refused to answer the Baroness's question till they were in an Imperial transport and the hatch sealed shut.

"How did you escape?"

"Power downed on level 99—we walked out. Lee, cockpit?"

"Sir," Corporal Ash replied.

Jeah continued: "We used service corridor ladders to change levels, broke into the security net, were surprised to see your escape but made our way to you."

"So you unlocked the elevator?"

"No Ma'am. What do you mean unlock—"

There was a lurch. The ship moved.

"That was quick. Good job, Ash!" he shouted toward the cockpit. "Sit down, my Lady."

"That wasn't me, sir," Corporal Ash shouted. "She powered up on her own—auto pilot preset."

"What?" Jeah moved forward.

"Liston, what is it?" Yelhsa worked at wiping the trickle of blood from her brow.

"A moment, Baroness."

He entered the cockpit where Corporal Lee Ash and a private named Ansil poured over the readouts and controls.

"Tell me," said Jeah.

"This ship's been pre-programmed—can't access navigation, propulsion."

"Smash the computer console—pull the circuits for a hard wire."

"Sir." Lee reared his elbow back.

"Wait." Jeah grabbed his elbow. "Ansil, what's the course setting?"

"Checking...planet-side...uh, it looks like home." He turned to his Captain. "Ramahton, sir."

The ship drifted upward toward an opening exit hatch.

"That's good news, sir," said Lee. "Right?"

Jeah looked first at the controls and then at the artificial planet rise the ship's emergence from the bowels of Fleet Seven revealed beyond the cockpit windows. He saw truth.

"No, Corporal. I don't think it is."

Centcom

Generals Haggard, Scott and Kataltem sat at the same table in the same room to which Solomon Star had been called in 2298 at the war's beginning to receive promotion. A holo projector showed them tactical images of the planet below and Fleet Seven with dozens of little dots going to and fro between them—each a transport ship of varying size.

"So that's it then," said Scott. "All the Ramahian captives now planet-side, all our personnel quietly recalled, and then the worst of it."

"That's right," Haggard agreed.

"Loyal Ramahian natives, loyal to the Empire—our own soldiers and sailors—sent down to the planet."

"And more coming through the gates all the time."

Haggard and Scott stared at the images, then turned piercing looks to Kataltem, their superior.

"Siras," said Haggard. "This can't happen."

"It's not my call," Kataltem replied.

"Then whose call is it?"

"Come on, Haggard, this is pointless. It came straight from the Cabinet on Imperial World."

"Constantine passed this to you?"

"You know he did."

"Did you send him my report?"

"You know I did."

"I'm telling you this was not an IP."

"Ckin'r's evidence was compelling to the contrary."

"That Sykol son of—"

"Okay, I know I'm usually the one who flies off the handle here," Scott interrupted, "but I know when a battle's lost. General Haggard...we just can't."

Haggard moved to speak, but Scott held up a hand.

"Let me finish. Siras...this is a bloody disgrace, man. No please, both of you. I have a point. I know I pontificate sometimes, so just let me blow and then I'll get to where I'm going. General, this black mark on the integrity of the Royal Army and the House it represents—it's unworthy of the Empire called Amric. If the Cabinet goes through with this. If the Empress makes this call...history will brand us guilty of the most god-awful massacre in millennia.

"Siras there's still one thing you can do—you and the Admiral together. You can officially make it an OFUP*."

"What!" Haggard screamed. "That's not going to save—"

"It's too late for that General!" Scott demanded. "It's too late for them. We'll be monsters, sure as my ancestors knew what it means to deal in monstrosity. But you call an OFUP, Siras."

"And what's the point of that, George? What difference will it make?"

Scott leaned forward into Kataltem's face.

"You call it an OFUP, Siras. You both sign off on it. And you get every senior commander on Fleet Seven to sign off on it too. And then you call the other six Fleet Commanders and you talk as many of them into supporting your position. And you send that to Imperial World."

"Answer my question, George."

"No threats, General. No leaks to the press. Just a notice. Just a word. Let them know they've pushed the limit. Let them know there are things men shouldn't do...and won't do again if asked twice."

"Something to ease your conscience, George, is that it?"

"No Siras. Something that will keep PC protocols from ever being invoked again—at least in this war. And maybe...something

---

* O.F.U.P.: Order Followed Under Protest.

to give to the gods of conflict. A votive offering in quest of forgiveness."

And General Haggard: "Forgiveness, George? God may have mercy on our souls, but if this war's to end with any sense of justice, we'd better not wish any such luxury on ourselves."

Fleet Seven, Studio B, Above Planet Ramah

Amber sat in a bright yellow dress on a stool in the middle of an empty *Amber's Hour* studio set. When the red light above the camera signaled "On the Air," Amber was already smiling, but she stared through the holo prompter, eyes glazed and voice silent. The camera slowly zoomed in.

"Amber, you're on," came the mild voice of a young new producer, a Sykol recently arrived from the Imperial World.

"Oh," she said without surprise. "Hi, boys and girls. It's *Amber's Hour*."

The unflagging enthusiasm was gone, replaced with tenderness and sincerity. "Our special show today is a parent's hour. So I want you to run and get your moms and dads and bring them to the holo room. Hurry now," and with a forced Amber gesture, "run and get 'em."

She allowed ten seconds while the half of the children on the planet whose parents hadn't disabled their holovisions to keep the broadcast override out of their homes ran to fetch moms and dads who sat silently watching the skies at kitchen tables or on back porches. All communication on the planet had been blocked out for a day.

"Hello, moms and dads," she continued. "Well," sighing, "it's time to think about your children. What's the best that can be done for them? I know...I know this is hard."

She fought to keep the smile painted in place.

"But here it is: the best thing you can do is have courage. Be brave for them as I know they'll be for me, won't you boys and girls? And then this: take the family for a walk. It's coming. Right now. And if you try to shelter them, or hide them, you'll only cause them pain. It's made to be quick and painless. But some will think they can shelter themselves. You can't, not from the second wave. And it's not quick and not painless. It's..."

Her jaw set square, her lips pursed to hide the quivering. But she couldn't stop the tears, one down the right cheek, another down the left side of her nose, pausing at the lip's crest. She breathed in heavy and blew through still tightened mouth, looking up, away from the camera for a moment, and then back.

"Take your children outside. Take them for a walk to the park. Now. It's coming."

On the planet, Amber's holo form was replaced with white text on blue background: End Transmission.

In Studio B on Fleet Seven, a woman conditioned too well by Sykol engineering to love children with all her heart ran wailing from the room, stumbled in the outer corridor, fell against the grey wall and cried her heart out. It was Einor Pluc who came first; picking her up, he carried her to what passed for home on the World Ship, her sometimes sobs, sometimes screams echoing down the busy well-lit corridors of Fleet Seven. Einor Pluc, praying for his own children as he thought of the fate which was coming to the children of Ramah below.

No one noticed the quiet removal of the Parish Priests of Ramah from planet Arché, the religious center of the galaxy. No one noticed the empty temples. The Ramahian fold gates had worked non-stop for two weeks to bring quietly removed Ramahian natives back to their home world from throughout the galaxy. All but military Ramahians—sailors and soldiers stationed on the other six Fleet Ships. They were quietly shot out of airlocks on the same day the Count-governor of Ramah, Yelhsa's husband, was executed for crimes against the Peace Codes. "The price of terrorism," said Empress Janis at a meeting of the joint houses, "is extinction." No one dared speak against her.

Fleet Seven's Central Park had been closed to all personnel, but one general broke the seals on entrance twelve and made his way to the best viewing position available—a hill he'd learned of from his immediate subordinates.

Solomon didn't need to be dreaming to hear their voices echoing in his head:

Savage's: "You never should have left me."

The Empress's: "Do you see, Captain? Can you see what you've driven me to?"

Hal Teltrab's: "This is what I sent you to prevent."

All of them his own: "Six billion dead. Six billion. And I can't stop it."

All he could do was watch from a hilltop in a giant, artificial garden through an expansive window on a living World Ship in orbit around the second most beautiful planet he'd ever seen. The show was spectacular.

Bright miniature comets, thousands of them, flew from ships about the planet and entered into spiraling descents, flashing brightly as they burned their way into the atmosphere, shredding apart and dissolving into the sweetest smelling gas. A few ships ran from the planet, adding contrapuntal gold highlights as they were blasted out of the skies.

No one listened to her pleas. She'd begged on every waveband in existence but the Imperial satellite network bounced them back to their source:

"At least the babies. The babies won't know what planet they're from. Please, Janis. Save our children, please. They'll never be able to avenge a world they don't know!" she cried.

No one heard. But she kept crying anyway, crying and pleading. What else could she do?

The first wave killed quietly and gently as promised. The next day, DNA encoded radiation bombardment began. Anyone who'd tried to hide would suffer painful, sickening death—the radiation programmed to kill humans only. He didn't watch that day. He sat in his quarters imagining his hands around a woman's throat—her throat.

The radiation would make the planet uninhabitable for twenty years, penetrating every substance down to five miles below her crust.

By day three it was over. The battle for Ramah was won. The planet floated through space, in peace, the lights of her cities and towns slowly failing, slowly falling to peaceful night.

All was silent, save for a voice, a woman weeping, ten miles beneath the surface of a living world—living but dead to humanity for a score of years. She sat on the floor in the corner of a thousand-foot cube that could save but fifty of her people for the next two decades. Half of them would be dead by then—too old or too sad to survive. She sat in the corner in the arms of a man named Book, weeping in his arms while a gently smiling friend watched over her and wished he could ease her tears.

No one said a word. No sound but the humming of environmental machinery and the keening of a weeping woman. Yelhsa Ramah, weeping for her children, for they were no more.

Epilogue

I ran.

The war, of course, was not over. In hindsight, the genocide on Planet Ramah seems...superfluous—dare I say it—spiteful. Though most of the rebel systems had already surrendered, a few holdouts would drag hostilities along for several more years.

But it was over for me. I ran.

I took my wife and children and left behind Fleet Seven, Sykol conspiracies, the voices of an entire planet screaming their dying innocence. I ran as far away as I could. Getting off an artificial moon of a billion souls is, surprisingly, not too difficult—some forged documents and a face which never appeared in front of the camera, and the help of a living space ship named Addy, who wanted me to go and wanted me to have information I couldn't possibly obtain on my own, so I could write out a story I couldn't possibly tell. Information about—what was it she called Solomon?—the man of light. Conversations she'd had with him. Observations she'd made. Even records of his dreams. He was important, she'd decided. I didn't know why. Certainly, the part of the story I've told has involved many more people than just him. I've told what I thought should be told, and Addy trusted me to do it.

Anyway, I took my family to the smallest, most unimportant outpost in the Empire I could find, a place where farmers and craftsmen work in villages, and technology is a seldom used convenience not a social trap. That was ten years ago now, and the war has been over for five, not quite ending the way the Empire hoped it would. But that's another story, one I was not a part of. When we heard the news that the war had ended, I thought, finally, perhaps, that we'd run far enough. That my family would be safe. And I thought that for years. Thought it till today.

It wasn't much, really. I was in the town, working in my woodshop, my son sent on an errand (of little importance in hind sight). The stranger came into the store, looked around admiringly at the pieces made by my hand. Looked with a smile that at once suggested a genuine sincerity and a mechanical artificiality.

"Your work is beautiful," he said, and he grinned a wide, tooth-filled grin. I thanked him as he continued his walk about the shop. There was a limp in his step, and he held his hand to his chest, clutching, like he was somehow broken—a broken toy or piece of furniture.

And then he said something very strange: "I might have made artworks like this two life-times ago." And then he sighed, a bit too dramatically, and said, "But it wasn't meant to be." The melancholy in his voice was real enough if the expression on his face seemed pasted—painted. He looked at me, and, for a moment, I swear, there was sadness in his eyes. Then he smiled that cheshire smile of his and turned and left the shop.

I don't know what made me run home to find my family safe and sound, what made me tell them to pack, made me dig up old forged documents in the yard. Everything seems peaceful, quiet. But the sun is setting and my son isn't returned home. Why do I fear that it's the last sunset we'll ever see?

About the Author

Charlie W. Starr writes books, essays, and articles on whatever interests him—everything from pop culture studies on movies and TV shows to theological studies on the Bible, from fantasy and science fiction adventures for all ages to studies on truth and myth in the works of his favorite author, C. S. Lewis.

His sixth book, *The Darkening Time*, represents the continuation of an imaginative universe Charlie first began building in the last millennium.

http://www.lanternhollowpress.com